The Rt Hon Lord Hurd .... at Eton and Cambridge, where he obtained a first-class degree in history. Following terms as Minister of State, he became Secretary of State for Northern Ireland (1984–85) and Home Secretary (1985–89) before his appointment as Foreign Secretary in 1989. He was MP for Mid-Oxfordshire (later Witney) from 1974 to 1997. Upon his retirement as Foreign Secretary in 1995, Lord Hurd joined the Nat West Group and is now Deputy Chairman of Coutts Bank. He is also Chairman of British Invisibles and Chairman of the Prison Reform Trust charity.

Lord Hurd is the author of twelve books and lives in Oxfordshire with his wife Judy and their son and daughter. He has three grown-up sons from his first marriage.

Andrew Osmond was a full-time writer and journalist and one of the founder members of *Private Eye*. Prior to that he had been an officer with the Gurkhas and a diplomat. He wrote four books with Douglas Hurd. Andrew Osmond died in 1999.

SCOTCH ON THE ROCKS

Douglas Hurd
AND
Andrew Osmond

WARNER BOOKS

A *Warner* Book

First published in Great Britain in 1968
by William Collins, Sons & Co. Ltd
Published in 1980 by Coronet Books
This edition published in 2001 by Warner Books

A CIP catalogue record for this book
is available from the British Library.

ISBN 0 7515 3081 6

Printed and bound in Great Britain by
Mackays of Chatham plc

Warner Books
A Division of
Little, Brown and Company (UK)
Brettenham House
Lancaster Place
London WC2E 7EN

www.littlebrown.co.uk

This concludes the series which began with *Send Him Victorious* and continued with *The Smile on the Face of the Tiger*.

D.H.   A.O

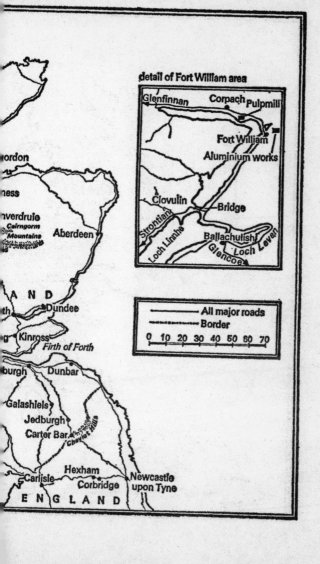

detail of Fort William area

Glenfinnan   Corpach   Pulpmill

Fort William

Aluminium works

Clovulin

Bridge

Strontian

Loch Linnhe

Ballachulish

Glencoe

Loch Leven

All major roads

Border

0 10 20 30 40 50 60 70

ordon

ness

nverdruie

Cairngorm
Mountains

Aberdeen

A N D

th

Dundee

g Kinross

Firth of Forth

burgh   Dunbar

Galashiels

Jedburgh

Carter Bar   *Cheviot Hills*

Carlisle   Hexham

Corbridge

Newcastle
upon Tyne

E N G L A N D

PLOTS IN MAY

I

The Gorbals had gone now, buried under new grass and determinedly bright cubes of flats. But South Side still had a thing or two to titillate the conscience. Here in west Kingston for instance, the money had run out, the developers had stopped at the overpass. The sandstone tenements, blackened by a century of smog, still stood—though some barely, their façades slipping and crumbling into asymmetry, and others not at all, demolished before they collapsed, leaving the impression of a recent bombing raid: patches of exposed wallpaper, fireplaces hanging four floors up, jettisoned furniture and piles of rubble in the empty spaces. Above the chimney-stacks the blue cranes of Prince's Dock reached into a bluer sky, but below them a sulphurous haze clung to the landscape, tinging it with the sad sepia of an old photograph. All but a few of the shops were boarded up, their clients evacuated to the suburbs.

But people still lived here, pensioners and Pakistanis, huddled together in the half-empty buildings. Here and there a touch of paint or a lace curtain was evidence of human survival. Some of these curtains twitched aside as the car drew up and shadowy faces watched the two men go into an abandoned laundry. It was assumed they came from the Housing Department.

Hart stopped in the centre of the room and inhaled, analysing the components of the smell: woodrot, damp stone, soot, frying fat and urine. He emptied his lungs with a rush.

'I tell you, Rennie,' he said, 'if I'd been born here I'd

have been a Red.'

That remark had been heard before in Glasgow, but coming from an officer of the Security Service it had some force. Like most of his profession Hart lived his life in the faith that the English upper class was the finest instrument for rule to emerge from the mind of God.

'Or a crook,' Rennie said without looking round.

'I can understand these Nationalists too. You Scots have had a pretty raw deal in some respects.'

Rennie turned from the window to face his diminutive companion, spruce as a tailor's dummy among the fallen plaster. It amused him to watch the Englishman's discomfiture. But he himself was against change. For him, who had been born here, Glasgow's poverty was part of the natural order, not a cause for anger or pity, but for satisfaction that he had escaped it.

'Those bastards don't care about Scotland,' he said, 'they're out for themselves.'

Hart advanced to the window. Every pane had been smashed; the bricks still littered the floor. 'Is this gang territory?'

'No, there's nothing here. Just wee lads. They have to break a window to get in the team.'

Hart remembered the shops they had passed in Paisley Road, barricaded with wire mesh, and the groups of hard-faced boys on the pavement watching the car in silence, and on every wall in every street the aerosol-painted graffiti of the junior gangs: YY COWBOY, MINI CONG, COSSACKS, ZULU, TINY HAWKS. Territorial claim and counter-claim. Nothing better to do.

For a moment he pictured himself trapped in this room by those little monsters, blades and spikes coming out of trouser pockets, cutting at his fine clothes and soft skin like a shoal of piranha . . .

But Rennie was reassuring: 'It doesn't matter who sees us here, and if your friend is as easy to follow as I think he'll be, we want him to come across an open space.' He nodded at the window and they both looked out again.

10

The laundry backed on to a hollow square of tenements, but two sides of the square had gone. For a hundred yards there was nothing but mud and clinker. 'I told him to come that way,' Rennie said.

Hart wondered if MacNair would turn up. They had travelled from London separately, MacNair hitching lifts in transport cafés and moving into a doss-house, Hart taking a night flight and booking into the Central Hotel. It was agreed to make no contact until there was a definite lead. After three days MacNair had telephoned Rennie on the direct line and asked for a meeting.

That was quick work, but hardly quick enough. Hart's instructions were to find the leader of the Scottish extremists before the election, and the election was only two weeks away.

They stood without speaking for another five minutes. Rennie was straining to catch the roar from Ibrox which would mean a goal for Rangers. Hart's eyes followed a girl across the clinker, unshaven legs lurching in ill-fitting shoes, face pop-eyed and knobby with deprivation. Oxfam would have thrown her clothes away.

'That'll be him,' Rennie said.

The man had appeared from behind a line of washing. He shambled slowly towards them, kicking a tin can. He wore a peaked cap and a brown mac tied at the waist with string.

'Not bad,' said Hart. 'For an amateur.'

'Why the racket?'

'Nothing on his tail anyway.'

'Let's get out of sight.'

MacNair positioned himself for a third kick at the can, then stepped over it as he saw them pull back from the window. At the bottom of the steps he stopped to scavenge in a dustbin and glanced back across the waste ground. The girl had gone. He climbed the steps and turned into the close-mouth next to the laundry.

He came into the room cautiously, eyes flicking to left and right, which was a new habit for him. Hart was

11

exactly as he had been a week ago: stiff white collar, Artillery tie, polished brogues tiptoeing through the muck. If this was Africa he would look the same. Overgrown public schoolboy. Beside him a tall heavy fellow, big pink shiny hands, ditto face. No doubt about him.

'Well done, MacNair,' Hart said. 'Allow me to introduce Chief Inspector Rennie of Special Branch.'

'Pleased to meet you.' MacNair held out a grubby hand.

Rennie shook it without hesitation. 'Still in one piece?'

'Aye, so far.'

Hart offered MacNair a cigarette from a silver case and lit it with a silver lighter. Minimal courtesies observed, he became brisk. 'Now, let's hear what you've been up to.'

MacNair sucked deliberately at the cigarette, pulling up into his nostrils the smoke which escaped from his mouth. The expensive brand looked odd in his unshaven jaw. 'Hanging round the pubs in the Calton mostly.'

'What've you found?'

'It's just the neds. The Cong, the Hawks and the Zulus. They've called a truce, they're in it together.'

'We could have told you that,' said Rennie.

MacNair stopped and stared at him coldly. The Chief Inspector produced a small but apologetic gesture, and a current of mutual respect passed between them, Scot acknowledging Scot. Some day they would share a laugh at Hart's expense.

MacNair went on: 'At first it was just paint jobs—you've seen those—UDI, Nats OK, that sort of thing. But now they're getting braver. Labour people are being warned away from the polls, and they're threatening to cut up the Derry.' Hart looked baffled. 'The Derry, rival gang—Protestant Irish, usually vote Tory. Then they'll go for the party offices, you'd better put a guard on those. And you can count on trouble at all the rallies.'

'They sound well organised,' Hart said.

'Well informed too,' said Rennie. 'That Labour committee they broke up in Govan was called at an hour's notice.'

'Are they getting paid?'

'No,' MacNair was definite. 'It's not money these laddies want, it's excitement.' Rennie agreed. He wondered what MacNair was saving.

Hart was getting restless. 'All right, but you didn't drag us out here to tell us this. Who's running them, that's what we need to know.'

'I was coming to that.'

'Well?'

'It's Brodie.'

Hart shot a triumphant glance at Rennie. 'So we were right.'

Rennie was dismayed. 'Brodie? Are you sure?'

MacNair looked almost tenderly at the Chief Inspector; Hart had no idea what the police were up against. 'He's been here all along, like Skinner said.'

Rennie nodded. 'We should have thought of it. The one man who could bring those gangs together. He's the only hero they've got, outside the Celtic forward line.'

'They never use his name. Just Chibber. Chibber says stir it up, Chibber says lay off. All the orders come from him.'

'Chibber?' Hart was mystified again.

'Chib, transitive verb to slash,' said Rennie, and to MacNair: 'You're sure it's him?'

'Just hints at first, then last night a couple of them got bevied and came out with it.'

'Know where he is?'

'Blackhill.'

'Tell us some more good news.'

'The Zulus are taking care of him, I can't get near.'

'Don't try.'

'But you must,' Hart protested excitedly. 'Brodie would never take this on alone. Someone's promised him something. It's all too well timed, too well judged. There's a political brain behind it.'

'So you said.' MacNair was no longer bothering to look at Hart.

Rennie's mind was on the practical problem. 'It won't be easy,' he said.

'That's why I called you,' said MacNair. 'There's only one way.'

Ten minutes later MacNair went back the way he had come. Hart and Rennie returned to the car, squinting against the hard sunlight. The discussion had reversed their moods. Hart was now full of bustle, oblivious of his surroundings; Rennie seemed gloomy, oppressed suddenly by his native city. Hand on the car door, he stared for a moment at the tall black slums and thought about a case he had seen here last week, two Pakistani children sprawled in a roomful of blood, killed by their despairing father.

'It looks worse in this weather,' he said.

II

Spring had touched Aberdeen then disappeared. A raw fog had rolled in from the sea, and the two cloakrooms of the Medina Ballroom were packed tight with service-able coats and sober umbrellas. Down the steps in the ballroom the management had installed the system of decoration which they reserved for occasions of special festivity; skeins of blue and red bulbs, white and yellow tinsel, fragments of synthetic evergreen, coexisting with the paraphernalia of a political meeting.

Lunch was almost over, and the audience was drinking coffee expectantly from solid white cups. The speeches would soon begin. Some of the ladies had already slipped into their handbags the big souvenir menus which carried on the outside cover Henderson's face above the stylised thistle of the Scottish National Party. Above the top table between the flags of Saint Andrew and the Lion of Scotland hung Henderson's poster portrait. It was a faithful like-ness: thin sandy hair brushed back, pale eyes behind the round-lensed spectacles, bumpy freckled skin, mouth shut firm, scraggy neck rising from the orthodox white collar and tie. Underneath in glaring red letters: AT LAST—A LEADER FOR SCOTLAND.

Henderson had finished looking through his notes, stacked neatly beside his coffee cup. He had made the basic speech twenty times already in the campaign and knew it by heart; but there had to be a new passage slotted in each time for the press to take, and this needed careful study.

Looking out over his audience he was content. Things were going well. These were the folk he was at home with, the street-corner chemist, the fifty-acre farmer from west Aberdeenshire, the trawler skipper in his best suit, the small local builder. These were Henderson's people and the muscle of the SNP: men of a little substance, with bulky wives, men worried about the future, jealous of the growing wealth south of the border, suddenly conscious and proud of being Scots. Before polling day Henderson would be back in Aberdeen for the inevitable mass rally, but he had insisted on having this meeting first. He wanted a calm atmosphere for explaining his calm policies, and he wanted to touch their pockets. They would listen the more attentively for having paid £10 for their lunch. A clear profit of £8. Eight hundred people, at least £6,000 for the Treasurer.

Henderson's mind was always most relaxed when making little accountant's calculations. The party was as short of hard cash as it was of hard heads. He glanced down the table to where Mrs Merrilies sat arguing with the Lord Provost. A fortress of a woman, high-coloured face streaked with powder for the occasion, thick yellow-white hair checked by a comb. She was a veteran of the movement, and her battered Morris Minor was a feared and frequent sight on the Highland roads. She made long eloquent speeches at the end of which her audience said to one another, 'Well, she certainly knows her mind.' In Henderson's experience her mind was a confection of outdated fantasies; but he needed her support, as he needed the support of John Mackie, the socialist firebrand from Clydeside. In the last two years the SNP had grown fast, embracing all sorts of mutually hostile elements. They were held together only by the common goal of independence. Failure, or success, would blow the party apart.

The candidate for Aberdeen South was on his feet, a garage proprietor with something of a stutter, but well liked, and a hard worker on the Council. He might well tip the Tories out, the way things were going.

'. . . great honour as well as a great privilege . . . this momentous campaign . . . inspired by our leader . . . needs no introduction . . . and so I introduce to you the man who will before long be the first Prime Minister of Scotland . . . James Henderson.'

On his feet, looking across the top table to the hundreds of faces turned away from their coffee cups to watch him, Henderson gauged the reaction from these closing and opening hands. Not bad for a lunchtime audience with little liquor in them; but cautious, reserving the final accolade. He preferred it that way. It was the tumultuous rallies in great crowded halls, the kilts, the marches and laments of the pipers, the weeping of excited women which he feared. He knew he could not satisfy demands so openly emotional. Tonight at Inverness he would have to play the exaggerated patriot; here in Aberdeen he could deal sensibly with the things that mattered.

Investment grants, the upward curve of emigration, tolls on the Forth Bridge, shipbuilding on the Clyde, the failure of the Common Market Development Fund to help Scotland . . . The faces below him slowly glazed. Here and there a chin dropped, a wife was nudged awake, a watch secretly consulted. Henderson flowed on in his thin Edinburgh voice, unnoticing, uncaring, continuing the task which he most enjoyed: the education of his fellow-Scots.

A red arrow on the page in front of him showed that he had reached the extract which Grampian TV would take for their news bulletin. The sudden glare of the camera lights showed the Medina Ballroom in all its splendour. Henderson speeded up his delivery so that it would be as fast as the newscaster. The attention of the audience quickened.

'And to-day I have learned some grave news which bears out my argument. I have been informed that the Shell Oil Company are about to cease exploration off the east coast of Scotland. They do not allege that there are insufficient reserves of oil to justify continued exploration —on the contrary, reserves already proved would supply all the needs of Scotland for at least twenty-five years. But the company estimate that the return on their capital would now be only six per cent, and this reduction in profitability is to them a sufficient reason for abandoning the whole enterprise. I must state plainly that this decision is unacceptable to the Scottish National Party.' (A mild ripple of applause.) 'I have constantly emphasised that we welcome outside investment; but we shall have to consider carefully whether the exploitation of our essential natural resources can safely be left to companies whose first loyalty is not to Scotland but to shareholders in London and on the Continent.'

The camera lights faded, and Henderson hurried into his peroration. An abrupt exhortation with a couple of stiff gestures, and he was done.

The applause came slowly, then swelled. The top table straggled to their feet, and the others followed, with a grinding of chairs and groping for handbags. Henderson raised his arms above his head in ungainly salute, and everyone sat down again.

'Call that an election speech? More like a bloody university lecture,' said the *Aberdeen Free Press*, scribbling 'standing ovation' in his notebook.

'Hold it, boy,' said the *Daily Record*, who was following Henderson round from speech to speech, 'we've got the questions to come.'

'You don't mean there's more?'

'He won't let them go till they're sure they've had their

money's worth.'

'And when for Christ's sake will that be?' The *Free Press* was English and easily bored.

'When he's shown he knows all the answers. '

And so it proved. The fee-paying schools, the monarchy, the boatyard at Buckie threatened with closure, summer time, the new US duty on whisky in cask, the legal status of the Church of Scotland, the civil war in Zambia, they rose in turn like sluggish trout, and Henderson deftly hooked them all. Long courteous answers, never cutting a corner or scoring an unfair point. Mrs Merrilies sat purple with enforced silence. The *Daily Record* was filled with admiration. The *Free Press* slept.

A mutter of consultation, and the chairman said that this would be the last question. A young man in a dark suit at the back, a precise Edinburgh voice like Henderson's. Did Henderson's statement about Shell mean that the SNP would denounce the present agreements with the oil companies, and what effect would this have on future exploration?

Henderson paused for a moment. His statement had been carefully calculated, he could not afford to make it more precise. He found the right form of words, but before he could speak the booming voice of Margaret Merrilies filled the room .

'D'ye work for the company, laddie?'

She had assumed the ferocious accent which was part of her stock in trade. The young questioner shook his head, but it made no difference.

'Why d'ye come here to an honest gathering with all that Charlotte Square blather about investment and exploration? That kind of talk stinks in the ears of decent folk. Whose *is* that oil out there in the ocean?' Her great arm with its bracelet of worked silver swept forward and only Henderson noticed that it was pointing firmly inland. 'I'll tell ye, laddie, it belongs to the people of Scotland, and we'll not be robbed of it by the likes of you. So away and tell that to the Dutch and English gentry that hired you. Our bairns will have the comfort of that oil, if we have to dive for it ourselves.'

From the audience a titter, a scattered clap or two. The top table shifted and murmured in embarrassment. Henderson rose, and for the first time there was real edge to his voice. He answered the question as if Mrs Merrilies had said nothing.

'We think that the present agreement with the companies offers too generous a return on capital, particularly in the later years of the concession when the risks have all been taken. Our proposals . . .'

'I see what you mean,' said the *Aberdeen Free Press*. 'Perhaps he is a bit of a leader after all.'

III

'I wonder if you realise the danger of what you are suggesting, Mr Hart.' Sir Alan Blair, Chief Constable of Glasgow, examined Hart and Rennie over the top of his glasses, as if his Saturday afternoon had been spoilt by a pair of troublesome schoolboys. 'James Brodie is the worst young thug we've had in this city for many years.'

'A hard man,' echoed Rennie nervously.

'He's done two stretches for assault, and we believe that on more than one occasion his services have been hired by a London protection racket.'

'I've seen the file,' Hart said crisply.

The eyes above the glasses did not blink. Considering that Hart held all the cards, it was a fair performance. 'A few weeks ago he was set on by three boys from Castlemilk, and he did them more damage than you would believe possible. When we tried to pull him in for questioning he disappeared, and since that time our local press, of whom the less said the better, have elevated him into something of a cult figure.'

'I'm aware of this.'

'Then you understand my position. Our information was that Brodie had gone to ground in London, now the Security Service tell us he's here. If that is the case, we must find him. It's my job to protect the people of this city.'

'And ours to protect the nation.'

Blair's mouth opened then shut. 'Which nation?' he wanted to say. Instead he pushed his glasses back up his nose and strode round the room, which was full of heavy mahogany and brown velvet, all scrupulously polished and dusted, to be preserved until its usefulness was utterly exhausted. Like the furniture Blair was solid and well-preserved, a chip of the granite on which Scotland is built, raw material for generations of policemen, soldiers, surgeons and bank managers.

A brass clock, correct to the second, ticked in the silence. Hart prepared to speak but Rennie held up his hand.

Framed in the bay window the Chief Constable turned to face them again. Behind him the new foliage in Kelvingrove Park was vivid in the evening sun. 'Very well, a threat to national security is not my business. But I think I'm entitled to ask what exactly you conceive that threat to be.'

Tread softly, Rennie's eyes said to Hart.

Hart cleared his throat. Again that uncomfortable feeling of being too far from base. 'As you know, several of the gangs seem to have become politically minded. There's been trouble in the Central and Govan constituencies. We believe that Brodie has been recruited by the Nationalists to organise it.'

'But I know the SNP candidates in those constituencies. They are sincere, respectable men.'

'Mackie has said some dangerous things.'

'Mackie has denounced the gangs, he's always been opposed to violence.'

'Except in the last resort. We've read his speeches carefully.'

20

'And what about the opinion polls? Do you read them? What possible motive could the Scottish National Party have for using these methods now? They are winning anyway.'

'You're jumping to conclusions. I'm not accusing the SNP.'

'I'm relieved to hear that.'

'But the movement has always had a fringe of wild men. We've had some ugly incidents.'

'Ah yes, the famous Scottish Liberation Army. I wondered when we'd come to that. We Scots hear very little of that organisation except from the English press.'

'You've seen the reports from Special Branch—increased recruiting, coded messages, arms caches. It's more than a bunch of cranks. Right, Rennie?'

Rennie glanced miserably from one to the other. 'The last six months, yes. Someone's put a lot of steam into it.'

Hart punched home. 'And we want to know who that someone is.'

Confident steps approached across the hall. A portly face topped by a shapeless hat bobbed round the door, observed the silent tableau, bobbed back again. Hart raised a smile for what he assumed to be the lady of the house but failed to earn an offer of tea.

Blair took up a new position in front of the fireplace, an ugly affair of shiny red tiles. 'Tell me more about this MacNair,' he said. Hart held out a sheet of paper. 'No, you tell me.'

Hart shrugged and slipped the paper back to his briefcase. 'Mid-forties, born in Paisley. No dependants, no surviving relatives. Spent most of his life abroad. We put him into Lumleys', a demolition contractor, on a slum clearance job in Islington. After two weeks he raided the stores and took off. They won't trace him back beyond that.'

'What makes you think this man will be admitted to the higher councils of the so-called SLA?'

'He's an explosives expert, used to be in the Sappers.'

Rennie listened helplessly; coming from Hart it sounded like a pep-talk for the second fifteen. 'Bridges, tunnels, roads—you name it, he can blow it. He was on the Alaskan Highway for years, quite a name up there. He's carrying some of Lumleys' stuff. He may have to play along with them for a while.'

Blair's expression did not alter, but a subtle change came over his face, something like a cloud passing over a bare hillside.

Hart saw it and fumbled for reverse. 'Of course, he'll report back first. He knows how to keep it to a few harmless bangs . . .'

'He's a good man, sir,' Rennie pleaded.

The reply, when it came, was no more than a whisper. 'May the Good Lord preserve us.'

'Just until we get the names,' Hart began, but Blair was tired of listening.

'All right. I agree. I have no alternative. When is it to be?'

'To-night, sir,' Rennie said.

'I'll speak to Northern Division. Rennie, you'd better stay with it. I don't want anyone hurt. And let me know the minute there's anything on Brodie. I want that sadistic little maniac back in Barlinnie.'

'As soon as my man's clear,' Hart said and stood up.

But Rennie knew there was more to come.

'Mr Hart, have you seen Blackhill?' The tone was conversational; Blair filled a pipe, taking his time.

'On the map, yes.'

'On the map. Then let me tell you what the map doesn't show. It was one of the first resettlement schemes. It is now the worst ghetto in Glasgow. Nothing grows there, there is nothing new or pretty or clean in the place. It smells from top to bottom like a public lavatory, which indeed it is. The old slums were bad, but they had something—a sense of community, a common political ambition, call it what you will. At least in those days it was no disgrace to be poor. But the people in Blackhill

22

have nothing—no money, no jobs most of them, no dignity and no hope. Anything which reminds them of a better life is an insult. Their first instinct, and only satisfaction, is to destroy it. Before you moralise about him remember James Brodie is the product of such a place.'

'We'll watch our step.'

'It's not you I'm worried about!' It was the first time Rennie had heard his master shout, and there was something deeply shocking about the loss of control in such a man.

Hart fidgeted. 'Yes, well we'd better be going.'

'Sit down. While you're in my house you'll hear me out.' Hart sat down. 'It may not have occurred to you to wonder why in these times you have to come to Glasgow to see such a place. But we wonder. Did you know that this was once the Second City of the Empire? People still come to look at our streets and buildings—look at them yourself as you go down the hill.' The pipe, still unlit, jerked at the terraces across the park. 'The Industrial Revolution began here, did you know that? Planes, cars, locomotives, ships, we made them all. But one by one they have been taken away from us. Birmingham and Manchester flourish while Glasgow is allowed to decline, like some abandoned slagheap. You can do what you like to undermine the Nationalist movement, Mr Hart—and nothing you have said persuades me that that is not your true purpose—but you can't get rid of these facts. The English have often been afraid that a revolution would begin in this city, and with good reason. If you stay with us the next two weeks you'll see some surprising things, and perhaps learn something. And now good day to you.'

Mutely obedient, Hart gazed from the car window as they headed back to the centre. University, Art Gallery, Sauchiehall Street, City Chambers . . . To look at it you'd never have guessed you were abroad. Like Delhi, for Christ's sake. They were all the same—MacNair, the Chief Constable, Rennie—touchy as hell, biting the hand that fed them. Wogs begin at the Tweed.

He felt a desperate urge to break the silence.

'Rum fellow, your chief.'

Rennie's pink cheeks creased in a slow smile. 'They're everywhere now. Come on, I'll buy you a filthy English beer.'

IV

The train began to slow down for its stop at Aviemore, and Lord Thorganby pressed the button marked Tea by the side of his plate. His cup filled automatically from the bottom, supplied by a pipe which led back to the kitchen at the end of the dining compartment. The mixture was too milky and not very hot. Colonel Douglas Cameron, eating toast in the seat opposite, noticed his grimace and smiled sympathetically.

Lord Thorganby thought briefly about trains. The exciting gloom of King's Cross, the landmarks leading swiftly from Eton to home, the hulk of Durham Cathedral above its ravine, the thrill of rattling points and huge locomotives, the frontier bridge over the Tweed, the self-conscious half-bottle of claret, the worry about the tip, the dramatic swing of the train under the protecting shadow of Edinburgh Castle. Steam, diesel, electric, and now it was gas turbines, and they would be in Inverness six hours after leaving London; air-conditioning, reclining seats, no vibration, no waiters, enormous expense, not much good to anyone so far as he could see.

Colonel Cameron emerged again from behind *The Scotsman*; a bulky, restless man with close-cropped grey hair and the eyes of a hawk. 'Doing much speaking this time?'

'No, I'm almost out of it now, you know. I said I'd speak at Perth next week, but that's about all. Henderson was through there the other day, and the Nationalists are putting on the pressure.'

'Can't imagine anything except a Tory at Perth. Are

the SNP really going to do that well?'

'I had a word with the PM at the Goldsmiths' dinner last week, and he wasn't at all happy about Scotland.'

Cameron wanted to ask how Thorganby got on now with Harvey, whom he had replaced for a few days as Prime Minister during the crisis over Rhodesia three years before; but Cameron was twenty years Thorganby's junior, and he held back.

They watched the tourists pile in and out of the train at Aviemore. Through the birches they could see the cluster of hotels round the central dome which held the skating rink and the new swimming pool. Across the valley the lines of the deserted ski-lifts were just visible, tacking this way and that across the bare hillsides. Farther still, on the highest of the Cairngorms, there were still messy patches of snow.

'Dunmayne's forest starts somewhere up there, doesn't it?' asked Cameron.

'Yes, at Inverdruie. I've stalked there once or twice.'

'They say that good-looking girl of his has taken up with the SNP.'

'I've heard the same from Dunmayne. As a matter of fact, she's my god-daughter. Impulsive girl, but she's got a head on her shoulders.'

'Extraordinary, isn't it,' Cameron said, 'the way this nationalism has blown up? What's behind it, do you think?'

Lord Thorganby had no doubt. 'Boredom,' he said, and found himself rehearsing the speech he would make at Perth. 'Of course the Scots have always had their own institutions to remind them they're different, and geographically they're more remote than the Welsh . . .'

'The economy's gone through a bad time.'

'Yes, and that's felt more up here—old industries dying faster than the new ones start up . . . But the SNP's strength is not in the slums, it's in the suburbs and the New Towns, and there the enemy is boredom. People want to feel important, you know, they want to get excited about something. So they go for nationalism—rather like bingo.'

'Bingo! That's good.' Cameron laughed: a loud whinny, exposing strong white teeth. He was an aggressively good-looking man.

'It's the sort of political epidemic you get in quiet times—a sudden collective release of energy. It always burns itself out.'

'Or ends in a war.'

'Indeed. But not this time, I think.'

They sat comfortably, two upper-class Anglo-Scots, watching the last tourist stagger with his tartan suitcase up the platform, musing on the strange course of human nature. Cameron showed signs of returning to the cross-word. Aimless music began to dribble out of holes along the side of the compartment. Thorganby detested this inane bombardment of sound and as a distraction felt bound to talk.

'What brings you up to Inverness? You're still stationed at Perth, aren't you?'

'Until yesterday, yes.' There was a pause, then Cameron asked a question with surprising force, as if he had been bottling it up.

'What sort of man is Scullard?'

Scullard was the Conservative Secretary of State for Scotland.

Thorganby thought for a second; he had never had occasion to think much about Scullard before. Scullard had been around for years, a man to be nodded at in corridors, not much more. Thorganby had left the Cabinet just about the time that Harvey had brought Scullard in.

'An Edinburgh draper, as you know. A bit rough, but a decent enough fellow I should say. Why do you ask?'

'Well, I shouldn't tell even you, I suppose, but it's on my mind. Several of us were called to a meeting in London with Scullard yesterday, and that's why I'm on my way to Inverness.'

26

Thorganby did not follow, and said so.

'It's these extremists we've been hearing about. The police have had all kinds of vague reports. They've got the wind up, and want the Army to help.'

'The Army? But surely . . .'

'If half the reports are true, there are arms coming in from somewhere, quite a well-organised set-up. They've even mobilised the gangs in Glasgow.'

'But that's absurd,' said Thorganby. Some things did not change. Scotland was Scotland, and Scottish regiments were meant for service in desert and jungle, at a pinch on the Continent. The only soldiers in Scottish towns were carved in granite and stood at market crosses with many names written beneath.

'Of course it's absurd. Nothing to do with Henderson, goes without saying. But Scullard spoke as if some of the more extreme SNP chaps might be involved.'

Thorganby thought immediately of John Mackie, the revolutionary Clydesider whose hair looked dirty on television. It was difficult to imagine what his god-daughter, daughter of an Earl, could have in common with such a man.

'Anyway,' Cameron went on, 'Scullard's asked me to co-ordinate operations on the military side. I'm on my way to Fort George to brief the Black Watch on defence of the Invergordon smelter.'

At the next table two young Englishmen were finishing breakfast. They were pale and wore spectacles. The flesh under spotless white shirts was beginning to strain a little against grey flannel waistlines. One was reading a glossy magazine called *Alumina*. They represented the new Scotland: lines of neat bungalows running up the glen, bright schools, supermarkets and trim municipal lawns, a cafeteria in place of the old inn by the burn, jobs for a few Scots and dividends for shareholders all over the world. They were the future, whether one liked it or not. So were they not invincible?

Thorganby snorted. 'But that's ridiculous. This isn't the Forty-Five.'

'Do you think Scullard would invent it to raise a scare for the elections?'

'No, he wouldn't.' Thorganby held no brief for modern Conservatives like Harvey or even Scullard, but he knew that the Tory Party, like the Foreign Service, was a good deal less capable of unscrupulous tactics than outsiders supposed.

'It would be sad work if it came to anything,' said Cameron.

'Orders,' said Thorganby elliptically. 'And anyway it won't.'

'I hope you're right.' The train began its approach to Inverness, and the two men parted to find their cases.

'Bloody thing, politics,' said Cameron. But Lord Thorganby had heard that remark before, and he did not reply.

V

It had been a good day for the Zulus. Celtic had won away, British Rail had lost some upholstery, and now there was the promise of a punch-up. They came out of the pub in a rush, twenty-handed, high on Bacardi and Coke, whooping their warcry into the night.

'Zooloooo!'

A paddy had come in just before closing time to say that the Derry were waiting by the canal.

'Zap the Proddies!'

'Zooloo, ya bass!'

All they needed was an audience, but that they would never have. As they fanned out into open formation, pelting the shuttered shops with stones and bottles, the street emptied before them. Doors closed, locks turned, lights went out, blinds came down. Blackhill cringed under a gibbous moon, obedient to the three first rules of existence: hear nothing, see nothing, say nothing.

'*Zooloooo!*'

Voices squeaky with booze and fright; but numbers, and a blade, bring courage. Under cheap suits just out of fashion fingers groped for the touch of steel. Chapman in front, they started down to the canal.

Rennie's eyes were on the pub, which looked like a strong-room, with thick glass blocks for windows. The door banged open again and a three-cornered wigwam of songsters lurched out. One was sick where he stood. They were joined by a fourth, who dropped his hat and stooped unsteadily to pick it up.

'That's our man,' Rennie said. 'They've got the message.'

'Shall I get after them?' the driver said.

'Not yet. How many, would you say?'

'About twenty.'

Rennie had asked for ten men, and got eight: a driver for himself and Hart, two constables for bait, a rescue party of four and an undercover man in the pub, an Irish detective-sergeant from Marine Division, who now picked up his hat and drifted off into the night.

Rennie reached for the microphone under the dashboard and called up the Land-Rovers.

'Car to Lima Bravo five. They're on their way, approaching down Nith Street. We estimate twenty. Move to Eden Lane. You can pick MacNair up now. Lima Bravo four, come in please.'

'Lima Bravo four.'

'Move to Dinart Street and wait there. Lights off. contact Lima Bravo five on personal radio, then report back.'

Rennie rehooked the microphone and blew his nose, twisting and dusting his nostrils, which were totally without catarrh, in a big clean white handkerchief. When other men smoked or drummed their fingers Rennie blew his nose.

'We're off then,' said Hart from the back, wanting to be helpful.

At a nod from Rennie the driver took the car across Cumbernauld Road and into the estate, heading slowly in the direction the gang had taken.

Blackhill spreads down from the Cumbernauld Road to the Monkland Canal in an optimistic planner's pattern of terraces, blocks and crescents. Between the bottom street and the canal is a stretch of waste land, littered with dismembered bicycles and abandoned cars, which reminded MacNair of the wreckage left by a retreating army. He was sitting in what was left of a Jowett Javelin, smoking carefully behind a cupped hand. Behind him the water of the canal shone between islands of flotsam and the shells of more cars, half-immersed. A steady hum of machinery was coming from the gasworks on the opposite bank. Beyond the gasworks the Red Road flats thrust slabs of light above the orange glow of the city. There was plenty of light, he thought. Too much. We should have waited for a darker night than this.

He looked at his watch, then up again, sharply, to a gap in the houses where the lights of the Land-Rover flared, flashed once, then died. He stubbed his cigarette and put the butt in his pocket. The beam of a torch bobbed towards him. Behind it he could just make out the diced caps of the constables. A brave pair, they should be getting danger money.

They expected him to walk towards them but that was impossible with all this light around and the houses only fifty yards away. It had to look like a genuine arrest. He decided to wait where he was, even if it spoilt the timing, then run for the canal, let them catch him.

'Easy now.' Rennie waved a hand at the driver. 'Not too close.'

You can say that again, Hart thought. Never in his life had he seen anything so bleak as these squat barrack-like buildings, perched on their hillside of black grit. The headlights missed nothing: blistered pavements, chalked obscenities, the sagging remnants of a wooden fence where someone had tried to make a garden—and that odd glitter on the streets, which looked like frost, until you saw that the road was paved from kerb to kerb with shattered glass. For the second time that day a vague embarrassment at prying on human misery had turned to a sharp fear for his own skin, and he wanted only to be back in his warm hotel, between clean sheets with a nightcap and this week's *Punch*. Perhaps he was getting too old for field work. Funny, the less you had left to lose, the less you were prepared to lose it . . .

A voice rasped from the radio.

'Lima Bravo four to car.'

Rennie scooped up the microphone, abandoned signals procedure. 'Yes?'

'They've got him, sir. Coming back up to the jeep now.'

'Tell them to hurry it up. I want them back on the road before anything starts.'

The Zulus stopped when they saw the police Land-Rover in Eden Lane. Like all predators who move in packs they could be triggered into flight or attack by the slightest thing, and it was always a toss-up which they would choose. It depended on the mood of the leaders. While the others hesitated Chapman and Micky Duncan, who was fresh out of Borstal and needing to re-establish his position, sauntered forward and saw that the vehicle was empty. Instinctively they both reached for a brick.

MacNair felt the constables' hands twitch on his arm as they heard the glass go.

'Bastards,' hissed one and pulled out his truncheon. He was shaking all over.

The other was firmer. Keeping a tight hold of MacNair with one hand he held a walkie-talkie close to his mouth with the other. 'They've found the jeep. We're going on up. Give us thirty seconds from now.'

'Lima Bravo four. Thirty seconds.'

They moved on up the slope towards the gap in the houses. Suddenly the night was full of whispered exclamations and running feet. Between the houses there was no light, a patch of utter blackness twenty yards wide, untouched by the moon or the street lamps. They were half-way across it when a stone flew over their heads, then another, then a bottle, which struck MacNair on the knee. He staggered, cursing, his leg numbed.

Both constables bent to support him, muttering desperately through their teeth.

'Keep going, man.'

'Just to the street.'

'They'll not show their faces there.'

But when they straightened up two of the gang were in front of them, anonymous in the dark.

'Ye've broke yer windies, copper. Careless.'

'Whu's that ye got theer then?'

Other voices came close, behind and to their right.

'Let the feller go.'

'Chase us, copper.'

'Zap the bogies.'

The constables stood still. The one with the truncheon was turning his head this way and that, not to be taken by surprise. The other looked straight at the two figures in front. They would be the leaders. All he had to do was keep them talking; to move now would be fatal. 'Beat it. We don't want trouble. You've had the windscreen, that's enough.'

'That's right, no trouble. Let the feller go.'

'An' get on hame tae yer mammy.'

Yells of laughter from the invisible chorus, braver now, and a new chant:

'*Zooloo si, bogee no!*'

'Catch us, copper.'

A shifting of feet as the ring closed.

MacNair watched the two in front, saw their hands move and heard the snick of a knife opening. He started to pee in his trousers.

32

Several things happened at once. From up the hill came the blare of a siren and screech of tyres as Lima Brown four accelerated down towards them. On the signal Mac-Nair broke free of the constables, as arranged with Rennie, and ran back towards the canal. Micky Duncan lunged forward and got the truncheon across the side of his face. Chapman, a cannier fighter, went for the constable with the radio, who fell before he could defend himself. Mac-Nair heard him scream but kept on running, favouring his numb leg.

Hands reached out of the darkness to help him.

'This way, Dad.'

As the crew of the second Land-Rover charged across the waste ground in pursuit the Zulus scattered expertly. The two who were helping MacNair abandoned him and ran ahead, veering right along the canal bank, but he knew they were safe. Gasping, stumbling, limping, he followed them round the base of the hill and up again into the estate; and when they saw he was clear they waited to let him catch up.

Hart and Rennie ran from the car to where the constable was lying, one hand still clutching his radio, the other pressed to the side of his face.

'Come on, lad. Let's see the damage.'

'No! No! Jesus, no!'

As the hand came away Hart saw the cheek come with it, revealing the teeth. The left ear was hanging by a thread.

Rennie shouted for a first-aid box and they bound him up and lifted him into the car. He was semi-conscious by then, so they laid him across their knees on the back seat, Hart holding his feet and Rennie cradling his head, dabbing at his neck and talking to him all the time. At the hospital it was a routine Saturday night: he was lifted on to a trolley and wheeled away at the trot, through swing doors which opened and shut like a busy kitchen. Relieved of their charge, Hart and Rennie became aware of each other. But Rennie, who was on the edge of a bitter rage, could not bring himself even to look at Hart, and Hart, sensing this, could think of nothing appropriate to say.

They were rescued by the nurse on Casualty Reception. 'I expect you gentlemen would like a wash,' she said.

VI

MacNair was the sort of Scottish expatriate who can still be found wherever the map was pink, often the only white man for miles around, but needed still for his technical skill—without him the mine and the dam would stop, the secondhand Comets never take off, the gunboat run aground—and accepted more easily than before, because now the natives see that like them he is just a hired hand, a victim rather than a legate of the old metropolis. Often they even like him: he is so discreet, self-contained, demanding almost no human contact, amusing them with his funny ways (after twenty years in the bush he will still be ludicrously Scottish) but respecting their customs, laying their pipeline or railway but never their women, or hardly ever, and then discreetly.

A marvellous person to employ, this Scot; a man of iron morale and iron bowels, who needs no comforts beyond a good supply of drink and tobacco, who is careful with his money, but not avaricious. Pride in the job is the ruling force of his life. The London Office will know him as 'the man who is holding up our end in Gambia', but will have to look up the file to tell you more.

MacNair was like that. No one who had met him could remember much about him. If he had been a mass murderer he would have driven the identikit artist to tears. A man of blunt indeterminate features, without noticeable enthusiasms—until you asked him how to blow the side off a mountain.

'And what am I doing here? MacNair thought. Why am I sitting in this cruddy little room, half-crippled, waiting to be finished off by a pack of ignorant neds? For the money, that's why. Two hundred a week plus expenses, five hundred bonus if I find the top man. Worth taking a few knocks for that. And it makes a change. If I take it carefully I'll be all right, and if they want me to use the plastic I'll show them a thing or two. They'd never manage it without me, probably blow their bloody arms off. What do they want to do it for, anyway? Scottish Liberation Army—it's crazy if you ask me. Trouble is, they will ask . . .

He thought back to the questioning which had just finished. Had he convinced them? Of course this lot were easy, fresh out of school, too thick to get a decent job. They'd believe anything. The one they called Chappie and that wee fellow with the black eye who brought him to the house, they thought they were big shots, but they were nothing. For two pins he'd have given them both a good skelp. Brodie was a different matter. Older, and no fool. They were all scared of him . . .

And so am I, let's face it. What's the matter with my bladder? Haven't touched a drop all night, must be psychological. It's thinking about Brodie brings it on. That scar running up to his ear—they say the doctors never bother to do a decent job on these boys—those fish eyes watching you all the time, and those hands hanging loose, always fidgeting. Very quiet he is, very relaxed, but you feel the violence underneath.

Brodie had asked some dodgy ones. All that stuff about meeting Skinner in the club, that was all right:

'Yes, Skinner—he did a stretch with you in Barlinnie . . . Yes, he said if I felt that way I should get in touch with you, said you were working for some secret outfit . . . No, I don't know how he knew . . .'

That was all right, that was true. Hart had set it up. But what about getting run out of Kenya, going on the dole, taking that lousy job at Lumleys' then doing a bunk up here to fight for the flaming cause? Had Brodie swallowed that? It didn't seem to interest him much. All he wanted to know was how I had found him.

'Whu telt ye Ah was here?' he had said. His accent was as thick as porridge, all back in his throat, as if the words had a fight to get past his lips and teeth.

'What, here in Blackhill?'

'Aye, here in Blackhill.'

'I got talking to a couple of fellows in a pub.'

'D'ye see them here?'

Brodie had jerked his head at the half-dozen Zulus standing round the room and MacNair had searched their faces under the naked bulb. Micky Duncan's eye was leaking under a vicious bruise which had spread across his temple. Chapman was rubbing blood from the cuff of his jacket with a wet rag, but stopped when he heard the question. Brodie had this way of creating a stillness round himself.

'No, they're not here.'

'Where was the boozer?'

'Down by the Barrows.'

Grins of relief in the Zulu high command. 'The Barras!' said Chapman, and spat. 'Ah warned ye the Cong widny keep their traps shut. Ye canny trust they Calton bastards.'

Micky Duncan looked pleadingly at Brodie, and for a moment his tears seemed real. 'We'd no grass on ye, Chibber, ye know that.'

'Shut up.'

The only movement in the room then was Brodie's fingers tapping against his thigh. They were all looking at MacNair.

'So ye come here the night tae find me,' Brodie said.

'Any harm in that?'

'Wi' the snouts on yer tail. Two jeeps, ye said, Chippie?'

'Aye, an' a car,' said Chapman.

'That's a helluva lot o' snouts tae be after one auld bum like you.'

MacNair, cornered, was saved by a suggestion from

Micky Duncan: 'Mebbe they seen the Derry.'

'Whu the hail asked you, ya mus'rable little runt?'

'That's right,' said MacNair quickly, 'there was a bunch of Irish down by the canal, but they beat it when they saw the jeep, and I got picked up. No so quick on my feet as I used to be.'

After that it had been downhill. He had told them about the explosive, and that had impressed them. He had told them what he could do with it, and that had impressed them more. The prospect of smashing something more than a few windows had them rippling with excitement. Brodie had retreated into a sulk and MacNair had caught a glimpse of a deprived little soul behind the flat pale eyes. Pressed by the others Brodie had admitted that the situation had possibilities. But first he would have to make a phone call. He had taken them all out with him and locked the door.

Scared I'll take them away from him, MacNair thought. Poor sod, that's all he's got left . . . Watch it. He'll be most dangerous when he's jealous. And he's still suspicious. He's not clever, but he's got an instinct, he can smell a threat to himself, and that's what he smells on me. He could do a man in for less.

Feet pounded on the stairs, the door banged open. They were all grinning like children at a party, but Brodie had them back in control.

'Where's the gear?' he said to MacNair.

'Kingston tunnel. I stashed it by the lift.'

'Can ye find it?'

'I suppose so.'

'Ye're gaunny dae a job.'

'To-night?'

'Aye, an' we'll see if ye can dae as big as ye talk.'

'Whatever you say.' Sorry, Hart old chum, no time to consult. 'Are you coming?'

Brodie hesitated. 'Ah'm no tae show ma face. Chappie an' the ithers'll be handin' ye. Micky, you stay.'

'Aw, Chibber . . .'

'The fuzz isny that stupid. If they see that mark they'll shop ye.'

MacNair saw that if Brodie was fond of any living thing it was Micky Duncan. 'What's the job?' he said.

'Ye'll know sune enough. An' when it's done ye're no tae come back here. Get loast.'

'Okay.'

'Get oot o' Glesca the morra, go tae Stirling on the fast bus.'

'I'll do that.'

'An' MacNair—'

'Yes?' Getting warmer. Five hundred if I find the top man.

'If ye're no' on the level, ye're deid, d'ye hear? Sure as Christ Ah'll find ye an' cut yer bliddy throat.'

You would too, oh, I know you would. And now I shall have to ask you where the toilet is.

VII

When Brodie had rung off she stood for a whole minute pressing the receiver close to her ear, listening for the faint mush and second click which would mean the phone was tapped. But there was nothing—just the unfathomable silence of a disconnected line.

As she listened the towel slipped from her shoulders and fell to the floor, but she let it lie, enjoying the feel of the fan heater blowing across her dripping limbs, then completed the process, pulling off a frilly shower cap and tossing it across the room. Released by a flick of her head, a rich mane of copper hair tumbled down, glinting under the unshaded bulb which hung from the ceiling. And even under that clinical light she had nothing to be ashamed of: a creamy skin, spattered with freckles around the base of the neck, a body slim enough to show the outline of ribs and backbone but soft and full where it mattered, and considering its length, remarkably proportionate; and above it a head to match, held high in a long neck, straight uncompromising features framing tawny eyes and ending in a slightly prominent jaw.

Body and head proclaimed a pedigree. In the ranks of the Scottish Liberation Army she was known by her Gaelic codename, *Seonaid*, special courier for *An Ceannard*. More for romantic than practical effect: within the organisation it was fairly common knowledge that *Seonaid* was Sukey Dunmayne, daughter of the eighth Earl of Dunmayne. *An Ceannard*, the Leader, was a different matter; his identity was known only to her and three others, a secret not to be put at risk.

Putting down the phone she stared at it for a moment, like someone who has dropped a reckless letter into a pillar box. Normally when Brodie rang she referred back for instructions, but to-night there had not been time. Later she would have a chance to report, but if he disapproved it would be too late to go back.

Brodie was a personal project of *An Ceannard*, who believed that all the youth of Glasgow lacked was a purpose. Every Scot was eligible for the cause, and the cause would ennoble them all. Panicked protests from the SLA officer corps—a closed shop if ever there was —had been stilled with an assurance that there would be no uncontrolled violence. Sukey herself had been doubtful, but had to admit that so far it had worked. Three of the major gangs had united under Brodie, and no one had yet been hurt—though if he got them through to the election without slaughtering the Derry it would be a miracle.

She picked up the towel and crossed to the window. The flat was as bare as its owner: new white paint from top to bottom, rush matting, two see-through plastic chairs and a tiled coffee-table, telephone and fan heater. Stacked against the wall in one corner two unframed canvases, a thousand guineas' worth of Anne Redpath, waited sadly to be hung. *An Ceannard* had wanted his courier in Glasgow, so a month before she had left home and taken a cover job at SNP headquarters.

Crouched below the sill, she lifted the corner of the blind. Beyond the Necropolis the bulk of Saint Mungo's cathedral loomed against a pale night sky. The street was deserted. She did it every night, but knew it was a useless gesture. When the time came Special Branch would manage something better than a mackintoshed loiterer.

Dropping the blind she moved to the door of the flat and took it off the latch, then pulled a scratch pad from under a pile of party literature and scrawled with a felt pen:

'Where are you? Crusaders should take better care of their ladies. Gone to bed. Coffee in the kitchen.'

VIII

The Queen stared at the Bank of Scotland, her slim form erect and proud on the proud young horse. The horse was lifting two of his hooves in punctilious dressage while what looked like a poultice was applied to each of his other legs, just below the knee and the hock. Crouched under the belly of the horse MacNair connected the charges, pressing the gun cotton into the soft plastic, then backed away, paying out the Cortex from a reel to a point behind the tourist information bureau, where he cut it. Without haste he moved to the other side of the bureau and did the same for the Prince Consort, returning to the same point. He threaded the two ends of Cortex through two more reels of gun cotton, knotted them together, added another reel, then attached the detonator and the fuse, crimping them firmly together with pliers. His hands worked quickly, with complete assurance. The whole job took him four minutes. He did not look up until he had finished.

The square was empty. No diversions had been necessary. The only sound came from a flock of pigeons, cooing and strutting round the feet of Robert Burns. Dawn was still an hour away.

MacNair waved at Chapman, who was standing by the car in front of the Post Office. Chapman put two fingers in his cheeks and whistled, and the Zulus ran towards the car from their positions around the square. MacNair waited till they were all in, then signalled again, and lit the fuse, which was cut to a length of one minute. Chapman took the car to the far end of the square. Without looking back MacNair walked quickly into Queen Street station and was out of sight in fifty seconds.

The air quivered under a blurred thudding bang, which killed three of the pigeons and sent the rest clattering into the sky. The Zulus yelled with delight, MacNair smiled and kept on walking. The windows of the bank caved in. The Prince Consort went over backwards, clutching his plumed hat. The Queen fell sideways, her neck snapping on the pavement as the horse came down on top of her in a hollow clanging of bronze.

IX

Mackie had not reached her flat until after midnight. He had parked his car half a mile away and approached on foot by a round-about route. All their meetings were surrounded by the most elaborate security precautions. Sukey was still awake, so they had sat drinking coffee for a while, then he had sent her back to bed. Crouched awkwardly at the coffee table, he had worked for two hours on his speech, the most important of his life. Schoolteacher, ex-Labour MP, City Councillor, spokesman of the shipyards, SNP candidate for Glasgow Central—if tomorrow's rally came off this fragmented career would come to a head; he would be established as the leader of the movement on Clydeside, the Pied Piper of the Left leading the abandoned armies of social democracy into the Nationalist fold.

But now he was exhausted, inspiration was failing. Leaving the last sheet in her typewriter, he walked softly into the bedroom.

The room was warm, and full of her own particular clean soapy smell. She had thrown off the blanket and in the half-light he could see her form under the sheet, legs apart. She never wore anything at night.

A hand reached out of the gloom towards him.

'Finished?'

'Still looking for a climax.'

'Try me.'

'*Seonaid*, you're an evil woman.'

He slumped on the bed beside her, kissed her once, then pulled back the sheet.

She smiled up at him, unabashed. 'Going over your property?'

'You know I don't like absentee landlords.'

Her skin was a constant fascination to him. He had never seen anything quite so fine—the product, he liked to imagine, of centuries of careful breeding, nurtured on wholesome food and moorland air, untouched by drugs, drink, housework or any man's hand but his own. Alternative perorations tumbled into the back of his mind. He began to fumble with his clothes.

John Mackie was not the first champion of the working class to prefer upper-class girls, a taste justified by the principle that until you could beat them it was all right to join them. It was the challenge which appealed, and viewed as a challenge, Sukey Dunmayne had been irresistible: tall enough to look down her nose at him, Catholic, a virgin, and daughter of the richest laird in Scotland. An icy Highland peak, to be climbed because she was there.

At least that was how it had started. Now it was not so simple. He had expected a quick lunge into self-abasement followed by a tearful rush back to daddy; but she had stayed, and under that lofty exterior he had found a brain and a conscience, and a disconcerting strength of character. 'A true refugee from her class,' he said to himself, thinking of the rather sad quality which he glimpsed in her sometimes. But he knew that she was more complicated than that. Never being quite sure of her, he had fallen in love with her.

And vice versa. Her original motives were something Sukey preferred not to think about. She had defended her honour through four long London seasons, so what had made her say yes to a rabid schoolmaster from Pollokshields, ten years older than herself? The truth was she had gone slumming. John Mackie didn't care about her, and that had suited her well; he was a sock in the eye to the Jesuits and those presumptuous relatives who were always marrying her off to some kilted bore with a castle. Then, to her shame, she had discovered that he did care. Behind the demagogue she had found a gentle, self-mocking man, with a taste for slap-stick. But although he was now clearly devoted, she saw that she would never come near possessing him, most of the time he was simply too preoccupied to notice her. No woman would ever hold more than a corner of that endlessly energetic mind, crowded with its private visions of power and revolution. And that she found riveting.

Watching him undress, hands clumsy on the buttons, she wondered if it would be better this time. Now that the taboos were broken, sex was something of a let-down. He was too quick, that was the trouble. Franny Blair-Guthrie said Miles could go for twenty minutes by thinking about grain prices, but that wouldn't do for John.

'Please, John, gently.'

'What's the matter?'

'Talk to me.'

'Okay. Tell me more about your MacNair. Where did he come from?'

'He was getting a raw deal from this English firm, so he pinched their explosives and came to join us.'

'Aha, a member of the proletariat, that's what this movement needs. How's that?'

'Better.'

'He could be the man we want. We've got all that stuff at Loch Ailort and no one knows how to use it.'

'That's what I thought. But we need to test him first.'

'What will you do with him next?'

'I've arranged for him to be passed on to Donald Levi . . . to-morrow.'

'Isn't that risky?'

'A new recruit . . . always a risk . . . and I thought . . . well, Donald's the most expendable . . .'

'Clever girl, that's good, very good, he should be doing it about now.'

'Yes. Almost ready . . .'

'I can't wait.'

'It's all right. Now!'

The explosion seemed to come from below, shaking the walls of the house with a dull subterranean thump, rattling the windows, shock waves billowing into space.

'Oh.'

'Fabulous.'

'We did it.'

X

Hart pushed aside the fronds of a palm and rubbed a patch on the glass with his sleeve. The pane was green with dirt, but beyond it a wide expanse of grass was dimly visible.

'Another open space,' he said.

'And a crowd to get lost in.'

He followed the line of Rennie's finger. A throng of people was gathered round an obelisk about three hundred yards away across the grass. Two pipers were counter-marching round the edge of the crowd, the thin thread of their music rising and falling on the wind.

'Mackie?'

Rennie nodded. 'It's where the old Clydesiders used to speak. We had a ban on meetings there, but he got it lifted. He knows how to set the stage.'

'You're not so bad yourself.' Hart stepped back and peered up through the dust-coated tropical plants reaching high into their glass cocoon. Weak sunlight filtered down through the leaves. The air was hot and dank, but there must have been a hole somewhere: a small bird was getting hysterical trying to find the way out.

'This is closed to the public now?'

'Yes. The roof'll come down any day.'

The crowd round the Nelson Monument was already several thousand strong, and growing. Behind and about them church bells pealed, summoning the faithful into cold pews. But still they came, across Albert Bridge, from Gallowgate and the Saltmarket, through the gates of the Green and down the broad paths to that great stone totem by the river—a carnival crowd, carrying banners and placards, bawdy, garrulous, convivial, and as Scottish as those prim congregations. Swept along in that human tide, MacNair found it hard to keep up an appearance of destitution. His deeds were the talk of the town, it was a fresh gusty day; for the first time he was glad to be back in Scotland.

The boy with red hair had him well in view and was keeping his distance. As they reached the edge of the crowd he closed in, but the task was beginning to bore him.

At the foot of the Monument a wooden platform had sprouted overnight, its basic carpentry shrouded in flags. Above it a trio of amplifiers pointed outwards. A dishevelled student was coming to the end of a dishevelled harangue; his stock of phrases and gestures exhausted, he began to shout, as if reiteration alone would establish that elusive common ground between intellectual and worker.

MacNair and the red-haired boy exchanged simultaneous glances. The boy blushed, and turned quickly back to the platform.

A lukewarm clap for the student, an expectant hush,

then a roar of approval as the head of John Mackie appeared above the photographers.

MacNair examined him with interest: a short, lean, sallow-skinned man in his late thirties, carelessly dressed, with poor teeth and a shock of spiky black hair. Hard to see what the fuss was about, until he spoke. Then that skinny body seemed possessed by a force greater than itself, and suddenly that undistinguished voice, that face you would never notice in a train, were commanding your whole attention. MacNair was not a man of words, but often in his life he had watched simple people responding to oratory, from striking lumberjacks to African tribes, and he knew how it was done. One moment you are just a listener, the next you are in the magnetic field; the force is in you, short-circuiting the brain, and you're ready to jump off a cliff if that's what the fellow wants. Yes, Mackie had the gift. It looked like divine inspiration, but it was all technique, and beautifully controlled.

He had started slow, barely audible, until they were straining for every word. Late-comers, sensing some excitement, began to run towards the Monument across the grass.

'. . . Many of you here to-day are Socialists. You have come to this place, to Glasgow Green, with memories of other battles and other speakers, and you have your doubts.'

'That's right!' shouted a burly man in front of MacNair, and glanced about sheepishly for approval.

Mackie threw him another crumb. 'You ask yourselves what can the National Party do for you, the workers of Scotland?'

'Bloody nothing!'

'Tartan Tories!' yelled a voice at the back.

But the crowd was against them, and Mackie had finished with the humble approach. Raising his voice, he moved to the attack. 'Let me answer that with another question. What did the Labour Party ever do for you?'

If there was a reply, it was drowned. Mackie surged on.

'You devoted your lives to that party, you put your faith in it. I put my faith in it. And what happened? The promises turned to excuses, and the men we sent to Westminster came back talking like Treasury mandarins and Swiss bankers. And this, don't forget, was the party of Home Rule—another promise conveniently forgotten. Surely we have learnt our lesson by now . . .'

MacNair edged backwards. The boy had forgotten him; he was staring open-mouthed at the platform in a state of deep hypnosis. For a time his bright red hair could be seen riding like a buoy above the sea of heads, then it sank from view. MacNair reached the fringe of the crowd and turned away, and thought he felt Mackie's eyes burning into his back. The ringing nasal voice pursued him across the grass.

'. . . You may not find everything you want in our programme, but of this you can be sure, the radical principles for which most Scots have always voted will stand a better chance in a Scottish parliament . . .'

MacNair quickened his pace.

Ahead of him a girl, standing apart; tall, expensively dressed in tweed unisex, a long mane of copper hair blowing in the wind.

And then he was free. Patches of sunlight chased across the empty grass, catching the Venetian façade of the Templeton works in a sudden blaze of gold. Walking as fast as he dare, MacNair headed for the solid brick pile of the People's Palace, set in its hollow at the centre of the Green, and behind it the sagging greenhouse of the Winter Gardens. His mother had taken him there once to see the tropical plants. In those days Glasgow had seemed like the centre of the world. He wondered what it would be like now. Rennie was a man to go in the jungle with, Hart he was not so sure of.

'You lost him?' Hart said.

'Aye, a young lad. Hair like a traffic light, and not very clever.'

Hart added another cigarette butt to the pile at his feet. He was wearing a dark suit. Hart would always wear a dark suit on Sundays. 'We're in trouble,' he said. 'That scrap with the Zulus did us no good at all.'

'Was he hurt?' asked MacNair.

'Lost an ear.'

'The fireworks didn't help,' said Rennie.

MacNair looked put out. 'Just a couple of statues. What more do you want?' Rennie saw that he was genuinely proud of the job, and a small worry was born at the back of his policeman's mind.

'I thought I told you to consult first,' said Hart.

'I didn't get a chance.'

'All right, but for God's sake don't do it again.'

Rennie explained. 'I had an hour with the Chief this morning. He's doing his nut. He wants to pull Brodie in straight away.'

'You've got an address?' Hart said to MacNair.

'Yes,' said MacNair, 'but wait a minute . . .'

'That should make Blair happy.'

'Hold it, Hart, now just hold it. If you pull Brodie in you can pull me out. These people are not completely stupid.'

Hart looked sharply at MacNair, seemed about to slap him down, thought better of it. 'Point taken. We'll delay it as long as we can, and we'll warn you first.'

'We can put a cordon round the estate,' said Rennie, 'do it with a sweep. That way it'll look as if we're guessing.'

MacNair kept his eyes on Hart. 'Give me a week,' he said.

'Impossible, old boy. Three days at the most.'

'Five, or I quit. And I want to know when it happens.'

Hart dismissed the subject. 'Okay, we'll try for five. That gives you till Friday. Ring me on Tuesday to confirm. What's your next move?'

'They're passing me up the line.'

'Good. Now we may not meet for a while, so let's go over what we've got . . .'

XI

'They tell us we're too small. And you know the answer to that—we've got a bigger population than New Zealand, Norway and Denmark . . .'

Mackie paused to wet his throat from the cup of water which someone had passed up to the platform.

'They tell us our economy will never stand it. And you know the answer to that—the only thing wrong with the Scottish economy is English tax and English trade figures. Get those two loads off our backs and we'll be all right . . .'

It was the biggest audience he had ever had, perhaps the biggest ever to gather at this spot, a dense mass of up-turned faces stretching down to the bandstand, behind them the brown waters of the Clyde, flowing fast, and the Hutchesontown flats against a sky full of moving clouds. A current of excitement was running through them; all he had to do was tap it.

' "What about the Common Market?" say the English. Well, what about it? What has the shored-up bulwark of capitalism ever done for Scotland? It was hard enough to make ourselves heard in London, now we have to go to bureaucrats in Brussels.' (A collective shout of indignation. Xenophobia never fails.) 'There's a law at work in that organisation, which we can see if others can't. The farther you are from the centre, the greater the pull you need there. In which connection it has not escaped our notice that Luxembourg has an independent seat on the Commission with a population smaller than Edinburgh's.'

A long clap. Enough economics. Time to warm them up.

' "At least you'll stay in NATO," say the English. "If you left that, you'd be done for." Would we? It doesn't seem to do Eire and Sweden much harm. If collective security means fighting American wars, then NATO is something we're better out of.' (Cheers from Scottish

Student Power, in a phalanx down by the river.) 'Then the English get really bothered. You might almost think it was us they were worried about. "But you're too weak," they say. "How will you defend yourselves?" '

Pause. This was the rawest nerve of all.

'I'll tell you the first thing we'll do. *We'll get rid of those bloody submarines!*'

A universal cheer. Cut it short, no premature climax.

'Poseidon missiles are the sort of protection Scotland can do without. They were too dangerous to put in the Thames, so they put them in the Clyde—well-known to be a desert region.' (Laughter.) 'They told us the things would never be fired. They forgot to tell us what would happen if there was an explosion in the hull. Well last September we found out the answer to that one—fifty miles of Scottish beaches closed to the public, and some of our best fishing grounds lost for a decade . . .' (Applause swelling, time for a quick chop.) 'No more of that, thank you!'

Now let it come, loud and long.

'But the English are never satisfied. You go through all the arguments, and still they ask why. Why—when a quarter of our houses are condemned, why—when Chrysler move the Linwood plant to Ostend, why—when unemployment in Scotland is double the English rate, why' (soft and final) 'when two million people have left this country in the last hundred years. Yes, my friends, two million. We were the blood donor to the British Empire. And now it is the English themselves who are bleeding us white, pumping our life force into their ailing industries and overcrowded cities. And still' (very quiet) 'they have the nerve to ask us why.'

Pause. Sock it to them.

'*Because Scotland is dying—that's why!*'

A mixed reaction. Too tough.

'Of course they could see we were sick. They've tried several prescriptions. First they made us a Development Area, then they cut us up into Regions, then they injected a few extra powers into the Scottish Office. No go. So

50

then they sent for a bunch of specialists, calling themselves a Royal Commission. And what did those specialists recommend? A Regional Council of State.' (Boos.) 'Well that may be enough for the Welsh, but it's not enough for us. Scotland is *not* a region.' (Cheers.) 'We are a living, breathing nation, yes, still just breathing thank you, and with our last breath we say enough of English doctors!' (Cheers, rising.) 'We know the cure. I know it, you know it, our party knows it . . .'

Bulbs popping, cameras whirring in the hush.

'*Independence!*'

Storm breaks. Let it run. Time to look at the notes. A dangerous paragraph.

'Total, unqualified independence. And I mean total. It may be that, to save a few highly-placed faces, the new Scotland will have to call itself a Dominion. All right, we can accept that. But if, when they are free, the Scottish people vote to be a republic, a republic they shall be. And it'll take more than a few troops of the King's cavalry to stop them.'

A hammer and sickle waving under the trees. Thank you, the Scottish Workers' party.

'Yes, my friends, independence is the only cure. If the English had any sense they'd have seen it years ago, when two million Scots signed the National Covenant. But "No," they said, "run away and play. We've looked up the rule-book, and there's nothing in it about petitions." So we went away, and we played it by the book. We built this party up, step by step, against the odds, and in two weeks' time that long effort will have its reward. If more than half the Scottish constituencies go to the National Party —and who now doubts that they will?—the English will have to look up the book again. And this time the rules are clear. They will have to let us go.'

Applause, dying. They talk about it, work for it, but they can't believe it will happen. And now that it might, they're frightened. Give them a bit of Churchill.

'Some of you may be asking yourselves, what if they

refuse? What if they use force? Well, they might, it's possible. Ask the Irish.' (Nervous laughter.) 'All I can say to-day is if that happens, none of us here can answer for the consequences. It's no secret there are people in Scotland who have been preparing for that contingency for many years. I believe they had a word with Queen Victoria last night.' (Laughter, more confident.) 'I am not of their number. But if the time comes, I know bloody well whose side I'll be on!'

Loud cheers all round. Reassume responsible face.

'But that time is not yet. It may never come. And I would like to say to our young champions in the streets' (not that the little bastards will understand a word of it) 'by all means paint the walls of the city, it'll help to keep them up. By all means, shout, march, argue, persuade. But no more than that, not yet. This fight will not be won with bombs or razors, no more than it was by signatures. It will be won by voices, and above all, votes.'

Applause. Work them up for the end.

'The world will soon know those votes . . . but now let them hear your voices.' (A swelling sound, but undefined. Give them something to pin it on.) 'A simple demand from the people of Glasgow—we want our freedom, and we want it now. How's that?'

A roar of assent.

'Let's see if we can get it into their thick Sassenach skulls . . . What do we want?'

Scattered shouts of 'Freedom!' from the crowd, spreading as they cottoned on. Jab them with the hand, Kennedy-style.

'I don't think they hear you. What do we want?'
'Freedom!'
'When do we want it?'
'Now!'
'What?'
'FREEDOM!'
'When?'
'Now!'

'Thank you.'

Cut, finish. Turn away quickly, too modest to face that barrage of sound. Down off the platform into flushed laughing faces, hands reaching out to touch, thump, shake. Protest, but let them push you back up. A smile of embarrassed delight, then arms above the head. Flags, banners, placards waving. Crescendo. Climax. Oh you lovely people, oh Sukey . . .

Hart and Rennie stood at the edge of the mob. On either side of them a score of youths, Cong, Hawk and Zulu together, were leaping about the grass. Hart was wishing his suit didn't look so English, Rennie was gazing at the platform. Mackie was up again and the crowd were screaming for more. Mackie raised his hand for quiet.

'Once more then, and this time I want Patrick Harvey to hear it. *What do we want?*'

Hart answered before the crowd, with the sly smile of a man who rarely makes a joke.

'You,' he said.

XII

MacNair felt conspicuously scruffy in the inter-city bus. The interior was designed to look like a plane. He wondered what made them think he could afford the fare. But Brodie had specified the fast bus, and this was the only express running on Sundays, and the thatch of bright red hair three seats down told him there was no mistake.

They weaved through a multiple clover-leaf and took the flyover to Stirling. Glasgow faded to a blur of identical back streets, thinning slowly into factories and blocks of flats built on a Russian scale, then abruptly into open country. The driver switched on the television, projected on a large screen behind his back. A blizzard of white dots cleared to reveal George Scullard, in mid-commercial:

'The Conservative government has spent more on roads than any government in our history. Expenditure per head on roads in Scotland has been twelve per cent above the national average . . .' Plain speaking from a plain face. MacNair fell asleep.

He was woken by a hand on his arm.

'Dèan seirbheis d'on t-sluaigh.'

'Come again.'

The boy had moved to the seat alongside. His face was a mass of freckles, almost matching his hair.

'Dèan seirbheis d'on t-sluaigh.'

'Sorry, pal. Speak English.'

The boy leaned closer, speaking in a desperate whisper.

'Didn't they tell you the password?'

'No, they didn't. And who are you?'

'Hamish Stuart, Stirling Platoon.'

'Well, Hamish, if you don't know who I am by now, you've wasted a lot of time.'

'You noticed? I'm sorry . . .'

'Next time wear a hat. And what was that mumbo-jumbo?'

'It's Gaelic for Serve the People.'

'Sounds like a thought from Chairman Mao.'

'It is.'

MacNair glanced at his watch; he had slept longer than he thought. Stirling Castle was already rising from the plain ahead, but dwarfed by a massive complex of concrete and glass to the left of the road, commanding the field of Bannockburn. 'What's that?' he said.

'Caltech. Caledonia Institute of Technology. I'm a student there.'

'In guerrilla warfare?'

'Shh, please. Electronic engineering.'

MacNair suppressed a smile. He had expected a villain or a crank, not this earnest young face. 'Sounds good,' he said. 'So what makes Hamish run?'

'The same as you, I expect. I want to work for a society I believe in.'

'I just want to work.'

'It'll come to the same thing. You heard John Mackie, he puts it better than I can.'

The bus wheeled into the Stirling terminal with a hiss of brakes. MacNair reached up to the rack for his satchel, still smeared with brick dust from its cache by the tunnel, and lifted it carefully over his shoulder.

Stirling was a town abandoned to American widows going about their duty in transparent macs and plimsolls. A thin mist of rain was sweeping down the streets. Mac-Nair's mood had deteriorated with the weather; betraying this silly boy would be less fun than blowing up statues. 'What next?' he said.

'I've got you a room in my digs. The Section Commander will be down to see you to-night.'

'Who's he?'

'I'm afraid I can't tell you that.'

'Still checking, eh?'

'We have to be careful. You'll be cleared in a day or two.'

Later MacNair had a chance to search Hamish's room, but the only unusual thing for a student of electronics was a bren-gun behind the wardrobe. No list of names in his books and papers, no order of battle. On the floor beside his desk was a stack of unread notes for the extra-curricular seminars of Donald Levi, Assistant Professor of Political Science at Caltech.

XIII

The room was cold and mercilessly lit through a marbled pot hung from the ceiling on chains. Second time round, it occurred to Hart that not a single thing here was designed for comfort. Conversation stopped while the brass clock struck ten.

After half a day on the hot line the Chief Constable now held a better hand. Rennie was out of the game. Hart was calculating the odds. London had not been as helpful as he had hoped, the decision had been left to him. Brodie free was a risk: he might do more damage, and Mac-Nair could still be drawing blank at the end of the week. And Brodie nabbed was a risk: it could mean the end of the mission, and worse for MacNair. In either case he, Hart, would be blamed. It was a time for compromise.

'To-morrow night it is then,' he said. 'A quick raid on the house—no fuss, no publicity. But our men, not yours. They'll hold him somewhere quiet till Friday then let you know where to pick him up.'

Blair's eyebrows lifted in surprise. 'You can get authority for that?'

'It's been done before. Brodie won't know what hit him, and the gangs will think it's a London mob settling scores. We can leave a few pointers in that direction.'

'What do we say in court?'

'Anonymous tip-off, leading to arrest.'

'All right. As long as he ends up behind bars, I don't mind how it's done.'

Once again the interview left them with a thirst. Rennie knew a place in Townhead, full of smoke and the clack of dominoes. Hart ordered a large Scotch and got a pint of beer. 'Busy week-end,' he said.

'Yes.' Rennie's handkerchief was out again. 'I hope MacNair's as hard as he looks.'

'He can take care of himself.'

'What will you tell him?'

'Nothing.'

'Nothing? You gave him five days.'

'Brodie won't be formally arrested till Friday. There'll be nothing in the press till then.'

'Come on, you promised more than that. I was there, remember?'

'Look, Rennie. We're not going to win this game on moral principles. If I tell MacNair we're taking Brodie in, he'll make a run for it, and I want him to stay on the job. They'll grill him, yes, but they can't prove a thing, and if he doesn't know what's happened he'll tell a better story.'

'An Englishman's word is his bond.'

'A good police force catches more crooks than it employs. My round, I think.'

ELECTION

I

In the big hexagonal room on the first floor of the North British Hotel the curtains remained undrawn though it was past midnight. Through the tall windows the floodlit mass of Edinburgh Castle seemed to float in the night sky, chained to the ground by the line of lights leading down the ridge towards the Palace of Holyrood. The Lord Provost was a good Nationalist and, scenting victory, had ordered this special illumination on election night.

Inside the room the leaders and party workers of the SNP gathered as if in worship round the thirty-inch television. Their attention wandered as a well-fed Nuffield psephologist delivered his latest calculation of the swing. Glasses were refilled from the bottles which stood massed in rigid order on the white tablecloth in the corner. Suddenly the psephologist was dissolved in mid-sentence, and in his place the screen carried the simple message:

South Aberdeen—SNP elected (*recount*)
SNP GAIN

A loud cheer, glasses raised towards the high Victorian cornices, and someone clicked the big indicator in the corner from 31 to 32. Above the indicator, beneath a portrait of Henderson was a poster with a simple device—the number 36 on top of a thistle. Everyone in the room knew that Scotland had 71 parliamentary seats. The SNP needed four more to get the majority, and there were eight Scottish seats still to come: a close run thing. Aylesbury, Swansea West, Bassetlaw, Dudley—several Labour gains, but on the whole the Tories were hanging on well, better than the polls had said. In that room they were not interested in the English results.

Hamilton—Labour elected, no change. A murmur of disappointment.

Moray and Nairn—Conservative elected, no change. Another murmur.

Mrs Merrilies shouldered her way through the crowd to where Henderson stood alone and thrust her large face into his. The veins in her cheeks were purple. 'So it's up to the Highlands after all.' She made no pretence of politeness. 'I told you MacIver was too weak for the job.' MacIver, SNP candidate for Moray and Nairn, was Henderson's research assistant and protégé.

'We shall see.' Henderson turned away from her towards the window. There lay his city before him, a capital city, to-night perhaps within sight of becoming a capital again. To the left the ancient murderous ridge of the Royal Mile. In front, Princes Street, brash and prosperous, crowds drifting under the glare of the bright white street lights, bursts of ragged noise reaching upwards to the window like the aftermath of a good game at Murrayfield. To the right, the squares and crescents of Tory Edinburgh, spread in sober darkness towards the Water of Leith, grimy, elegant, unchanging.

It must be the second whisky, thought Henderson, I'm becoming romantic. He thought suddenly of a dinner given to his father by his father's employer, to which he had been taken scrubbed and awkward as a boy of fourteen. His father had served for forty years as clerk to a firm of Edinburgh lawyers, and to celebrate the anniversary there had stood the tall white-haired Writer to the Signet in a plum velvet jacket carving grouse on a tall sideboard in the tall cold dining-room of the immensely tall house in Lynedoch Place. When the port circulated the glass of the fourteen-year-old had been filled full.

Henderson looked across the room of the North British Hotel at Mackie, talking volubly to a throng of cronies.

Mackie had never eaten grouse. Mackie was a revolutionary, but then in Glasgow revolution came easy. To Henderson all of Edinburgh, left, right and centre, was his city.

The announcer was giving the total results, and Henderson turned quickly back into the room to watch them:

Conservative	292
Labour	280
SNP	32
Liberal	5
Welsh Nationalist	4
Results to be declared	12

As Henderson did the arithmetic in his head, three more Scottish results tumbled in:

> *Argyll—Conservative, no change.*
> *Western Isles—Labour, no change,*
> *Inverness—SNP gain from Liberal,*

A ragged reception as the indicator clicked to 33. The SNP had needed all three of those seats if it was to pass the magic 36, and canvassing returns throughout the Western Highlands had been good.

Mrs Merrilies was upon him again, breathing flame, plucking in her disappointment at the brooch with the large smoky stone at her shoulder. 'I told you, we should have promised to redistribute every estate over five hundred acres. That would have brought the crofters in.'

'And we'd have been compensating the lairds for the rest of our lives.'

This was an old argument, and Henderson saw no point in pursuing it. He did not like Mrs Merrilies but she was genuinely distressed, and exhausted.

'Don't worry, Margaret,' he said, 'we're doing fine.'

'Doing fine? But even if we win both Ayr and Orkney, we'll miss it.' She had spent forty years in the cause, and though she would never admit it, at sixty-five it was more of a strain to drive the endless twisting Highland roads from one tiny hall to another.

Henderson realised that she simply had not taken in the important fact. She had hypnotised herself with the figure 36. The first victims of propaganda were usually the propagandists.

Ayr—Conservative elected, no change (recount).

A groan of dismay, and in one corner a pretty girl wept into her glass. Mackie came over to Henderson. 'Idiots,' he said. 'You'd better say something before they all throw themselves out into Princes Street.'

Henderson motioned to the stewards, and in a few seconds there was silence.

'Fellow-Scots'—his voice was still husky from the night before in the Usher Hall—'it seems that we have failed, by a narrow margin, to win a majority of the Scottish seats; and that, I know, is a great disappointment to you. But we have won a decisive success. We've polled more votes and won more seats than any of our opponents in Scotland. Thirty, thirty-three, thirty-six—it no longer matters. Some of you can't have been watching the figures for England and Wales. Whatever happens now, Scotland is going to get her way. And Scotland means the SNP. We can keep the Tories in, or put them out. Neither of the London-based parties can muster a majority without us.'

Heads turned towards a blackboard noting the total results, and a rustle of excitement swept through the room. Henderson held up his hand for silence.

'We hold the balance, so we hold the power. And we shan't be interested in a few cheques from the Treasury or odds and ends of devolution. I can promise you this: none of your SNP members elected to-day will set a foot in Westminster until the full rights of Scotland are recognised.'

While they cheered a young man plucked at Henderson's elbow, and he left to confront the television cameras.

Out in the darkness the floodlit Union flag still flew over the Castle.

'Not clear enough,' said Mackie, pointing at the door through which Henderson had left.

'He says what he believes.' Mrs Merrilies found that her eyes were moist.

'But is it what we believe?' Mackie turned to go home. There was work ahead.

A stout waiter in a tiny white jacket jostled through the room looking for Henderson. 'It's the Prime Minister himself on the telephone . . .'

II

Donald Levi, Profpol Caltech, thumped his desk with an empty bottle of Moroccan red.

'All right, darlings, settle down. Hush please, let's have some hush.'

The Extra-Curricular Seminar on Conditions for Activism in the Late Neo-Capitalist Economy came to order, sixteen youthful faces of indeterminate sex. Levi noticed that Hamish was looking for a place next to Cindy Drummond.

'Plenty of room over here, Hamish.'

Plates of half-eaten paella were passed from hand to hand and stacked among the cacti. An emergency meeting, disguised as lunch, had been called for the morning after the election. The bill would eventually reach the paymaster of the Scottish Liberation Army as Item, Expenses, Section 3 (Caltech), Stirling Platoon, Lowlands Area. Levi was fussy about his accounts; a pacifist and lifelong opponent of the profit motive, he loved playing businessman as much as he loved playing soldier.

'Hush please, Donald wants to speak. Thank you. Now, sitrep as at 1300 hours June third—bloody shambles.'

The room exploded into laughter.

'Surprise, surprise.'

'Sock it to us, Don.'

'When's demob?'

'Very satirical, sweethearts. Now will you shut up or do I have to crack the whip? I'm talking about the bloody election.' Silence, or something near it. 'The last results have just come in, and the SNP is stuck at thirty-three seats. That's three short of what Henderson was bleating for, so it looks as if we're still in business.'

Levi himself was quite pleased by the election results, partly because the SLA was still in business, partly because the only qualification a cause needed for his support was that it should be a loser. At the first hint of success he would move on. He was touching forty, but no generation had yet outflanked him; a big flabby man with a little voice, permanently dressed in a black leather boiler suit. He claimed a Scottish mother.

'The question is, what's going to happen next, and speaking personally I hae me doots about Comrade Henderson, who I think we can safely say is not a million miles from a trimming bourgeois shithouse . . .' (Cheers.) 'No. I'm sorry, bad taste. Donald is running on . . . I cede the platform to this lovely lady. Her name is known to your commander, but you lot can call her Seonaid.'

Levi, whose Gaelic had never really got off the ground, pronounced it the way it was spelt.

'Shawnetch, for Christ's sake,' said a voice at the back.

But for quickness on verbal feet no one could beat Donald Levi. 'Look, Iain, I'll make you a promise. When this is a free country I'll learn your beastly language. The point is "Shawnetch" hath a message from the boss. Now before I upset you again just tell me how to say that.'

'*An Ceannard*,' said Iain, subdued. For the first time the room was completely silent.

Sukey stood up.

'Thank you Donald, I'm sorry to interrupt your banquet . . .'

The ones on the floor could see up her skirt. On an ordinary day those long legs and that clipped voice would have had them baying, but to-day they listened.

'I've been sent to tell you that a meeting of Area Commanders was held this morning to consider what action would be needed after the election. And here we have to confess to a failure of contingency planning; the Staff had calculated for failure or success by the SNP, nothing in between. So we're now responding to events. *An Ceannard* thinks the most probable first step will be some kind of deal between Henderson and Harvey. We can't prevent this, but we must do what we can to discredit it, and you're the best people for that. There's been no word yet if they'll meet, but as soon as it comes you can make your plans. We leave it to you what form the action takes—some fairly dramatic gesture, if you can, to make the point that Henderson is breaking his mandate.'

Sukey sat down.

'Thank you,' said Levi, not risking *Seonaid* again. 'Please tell him that Caltech Section is proud to accept this responsibility and won't let him down.'

'I'll do that.' Sukey leaned towards Levi and dropped her voice. 'Can I have a word with you before I go?'

'Surely. I'll walk you down. No, perhaps that's not very clever, you and me parading across the campus . . .'

Levi straightened up and addressed the room.

'All right, children, that's it. Dismiss. The seminar will meet to-night as arranged. We should have news of Henderson's plans by then. And don't get slack about your cover—bring your notes on the French Revolution.'

The establishment of a Popular Front government in France had given hope to leftists all over Europe. But the British worker was proving particularly obtuse: for the moment there was no danger of Donald Levi moving on.

'Coffee?' he said to Sukey when they were alone.

'Thanks.'

Levi busied himself with a percolator. 'Always drink Cuban, hope you like it.'

'Tell me, how's MacNair doing?' Sukey said.

'Very well. Doesn't say much, but he knows his stuff.'

'Do you trust him?'

'Look dear, if I didn't trust him he wouldn't be in the Section. I mean, you know—all right?'

'He wasn't here this morning.'

'I can't have him up to the seminars, he doesn't go with the décor.'

'Do the others get on with him?'

'Hamie Stuart shares digs with him and he says he's a gas, a walking encyclopaedia of the destructive arts. Look, I'll tell you, Hamish is the only one in this outfit with anything which goes bang. Of course we have the usual supplies, I don't let the little brutes get their hands on those. But Hamish has this bren which daddy brought back from the war or something, and he's got his own ammunition. Of course he didn't have a clue how to work the thing, but MacNair's taught him all that, turned him into quite a little soldier.' Levi handed Sukey a cup of steaming black fluid. 'Why the interest, anyway?'

'Brodie's disappeared.'

'Brodie?'

'Didn't you know about Brodie? Damn, I forgot.'

'You don't mean that boy the *Herald* has been going on about? Is he one of us?'

'Don't shout about it.'

'Oh but that's marvellous—*marvellous*! I mean, that's what it's all about, isn't it? I mean, you know, sometimes I wonder, and then I see those deprived little faces on the streets of Glasgow, and I *know*. Like the sheer *violence* of this society. When I see that I want to go out and burn every bank in Sauchiehall Street . . . Marvellous! But what's the tie-up with MacNair?'

'He came to us through Brodie, and now Brodie's gone.'

'What, defected?'

'Perhaps. Someone tried to grab him, we don't know who. Maybe Brodie doesn't know himself. Maybe he thinks it was us. We paid him quite a lot of money, and we made him promises . . .'

'I had no idea we were so enterprising.'

'But he never knew much about us, he never met a senior officer. So why should he trust us?'

'He'll be back. Where can he go?'

'I hope so. If the English get hold of him they'll make a meal of us.'

'Yes, I see that. And you think MacNair's a plant?' Levi appealed to some invisible witness. 'So *now* she tells me . . .'

'Now, Donald, don't flap. It's just a small worry. As you say, MacNair's passed all the tests. But I think you should leave him out of this operation, don't let him in on the plans or anything. And by the way, you're to keep out of it yourself.'

'What—send those boys over the top while I sit here on my fanny?'

'You know the rule. No unnecessary risks for officers.'

'But Sukey, darling, that's awful. I mean, leading from behind . . .'

'Donald, darling, I thought you always led from there.'

'Now that, my girl, was a naughty remark. I'm not sure I like that at all.'

III

Outside in the Palace garden the lilacs tossed and twisted, expecting the rain. Harvey waited for the King in the yellow drawing-room; on the wall two Landseer beasts, feet in a stream, gazed dimly at a huge blue mountain.

Harvey had always disliked the Scots, a formal long-winded lot, boasting about their scenery but living in fact in grim damp cities and terrible villages, consumed with unending quarrels and complaints. And now they had trapped him.

As the election campaign wore on he had come to terms with either victory or defeat. Eight years as Prime Minister was enough by any civilised standard. It would be good not to be tired. It would be pleasant to have time for commonplace things, to walk, to read, to notice physical objects round about him; time to explore his battered marriage and see if there was enough left in it to repair. But waiting for sleep on hotel pillows after each election meeting, he was equally ready to win. The colleagues in Cabinet, the Whitehall mandarins, the arrogant press, his backbenchers, the Opposition, even the King—he had tamed them all, one after the other. He was an experienced ringmaster now, sending these great beasts through their hoops, enjoying the whiff of danger and the applause of the anonymous crowd. He would miss the game if it was taken away from him.

But the actual outcome had come as a bitter shock. Not victory or defeat, but this botched and mischievous freak. His programme was at risk, he would have to bargain with the Scots; the Harvey administration would end, not cleanly at the polls, but in a tangle of compromises. More work, more exhaustion, fewer results. Driving up the Mall, glimpsing the tulips and the band playing under the plane trees, Harvey had almost decided that enough was enough: let Labour take a turn under Wellbeloved— or failing that a new Tory Government under one of his colleagues . . .

Almost, but not quite. He knew it would depend largely on the King, and the King was now in the room. Working together for so long in that strange relationship they had in fact become friends. It did not show outwardly; neither believed in unnecessary preliminaries.

'I asked Bradley to explain that this would be simply an informal talk,' said the King.

'Yes, indeed.'

'Wellbeloved told him yesterday evening that in his opinion Labour would agree to a coalition.'

Harvey shifted in surprise in his fragile gilt chair. The first spurt of rain blurred the window. 'But Labour couldn't ditch their own supporters in Scotland to do a deal with Henderson. Without their Scottish seats Labour could never come to power.'

'Quite so.' The King still got some ironic amusement from the mystifications of politics. 'But what Wellbeloved has in mind is a coalition between the Labour party and yourselves. He added that he would willingly serve under you.'

Harvey had trained himself not to show surprise on political occasions. He absorbed the note of hope in the King's voice. The Sovereigns of England always hankered after coalition, the stilling of discordant voices, the rallying of loyal subjects to the common good. He thought for a moment of the election campaign: wet market places, draughty halls, the noise of aircraft engines, perpetual movement, tense and sleepless nights. And his supporters, the ranks of cheering blue rosettes, the devotion which made any honest politician feel humble. They had fought on a good programme—the European defence scheme, the final acts of denationalisation, a massive interest-free loan to found new fee-paying grammar schools. A fine Tory manifesto, to crown eight years of Tory prosperity. Everyone agreed they had done well and they would have won outright, had it not been for the Scots and a certain boredom everywhere with familiar faces. But of course a coalition with Wellbeloved would mean abandoning the programme, which was poison to the Labour dinosaurs. The King must be brought to see sense.

'It wouldn't work, sir. I like Wellbeloved, but there's no common ground. There'd be constant trouble, and the extremists on left and right would gain ground quickly. Of course you could ask someone else . . .'

'Wellbeloved made it clear he would only serve under you.' The King paused for a moment to absorb his disappointment. 'What do you suggest then?'

'If you ask me to form a government I will find out from Henderson on what terms he would support it.'

'You've already been in touch with him?' The King's tone was sharp, and Harvey knew he must be cautious.

'Yes; for the moment he is sticking to full independence.'

The King walked to the window and looked out into the garden. Harvey could not see his face clearly. 'I must tell you that I should find it virtually impossible to approve an act conferring independence on Scotland.'

The burden of history. Every monarch rightly carried it, but so did a Tory Prime Minister, and Harvey felt he must make this clear. 'We are the Unionist Party, sir, and we will not destroy the Union. Henderson is a reasonable man. He hasn't won as many seats as he hoped, and I think he'll settle for a good deal less than his opening price.'

'I hope so, I certainly hope so.' The King turned from the window. 'He has some wild men about him, and so far he hasn't stood up to them. He says he and the other elected members don't come south of the Border until his demands are met. Why can't you leave them to stew up there and carry on at Westminster without them?'

'No government would risk that, sir. Its legislation would be at the mercy of men it knew nothing about. Within three hours they could be out of Edinburgh and into the No lobby. It wouldn't do.'

'But surely you wouldn't go to Edinburgh yourself to treat with Henderson?' The King was almost pleading.

'No, if I meet him, it'll have to be in England.' Harvey already remembered an undergraduate walking holiday, torrents of rain on the Roman Wall, shoes full of water, an abbey and welcoming pub. 'The Compact of Hexham' —it would sound well in the history books.'

'And the Act of Union?'

'I don't know, we should have to see. But of course your own position, sir, doesn't depend on the Act of 1707. Your ancestors were Kings of Scotland long before . . .'

The King cut in, visibly annoyed. 'I wasn't thinking of my own position. I know perfectly well that I can call myself a Stuart when I want to without consulting any Act of Parliament. Indeed, I feel more like a Stuart every day.' He got up to close the interview. 'Bradley will be in touch with you, probably this evening . . . But in any case it wasn't the Union with Scotland that your Unionist Party was formed to defend. And whatever became of the Union with Ireland?'

Royalty had a right to the last word: Harvey left the room.

IV

Business was slow at the Gaza Strip. An afternoon's effort by the doorman, backed by a lavish photo display of Shemona, Scourge of the Desert, had raised an audience of five: a couple of pink-faced farmers in front, horsing about with Alice and Beryl, two Chinese, heads together in the psychedelic gloom, and that miserable young Jock standing at the side. He had been there for half an hour, refusing to sit or buy a drink. He said he was waiting for Skinner.

A waste of her talent, Shemona thought. Without an audience it seemed disgusting. At least she had the Jock's attention; she could just see his face beyond the footlights, a pale smudge against the velvet wall. He might not talk much, but he knew how to look. She wrinkled her nose and blew him a kiss and wondered what it took to light a spark in those fish eyes.

The answer to that would have sent her running all the way to Cambridge Circus. As he watched the clothing drop from her plump white body, Brodie had an urge to mark it, split it down the middle like the belly of a pig. Soho made him uncomfortable. There was something offensive about such easy pleasure. Those northern streets were his home ground, an arena for simple games with brutal penalties, but cleaner somehow, more manly than this land of neon and sex and carpeted pubs full of Negroes with big gold watches.

Lord Thorganby felt much the same way whenever he stepped off the train at King's Cross, forsaking his ancestral glen for the uncertain subtleties of London.

Brodie belonged to Glasgow. But he couldn't go back until Skinner came up with the answer. He began to feel trapped in the dark cellar, but forced himself to wait. The air smelt of damp carpets, with an overlay of perfumed deodorant. Shemona was flinging herself about on a stuffed camel. The two Chinese exchanged small paper packets, shook hands and left separately. Alice was on the phone.

The ultra-violet light picked up teeth and a shirt, advancing down the edge of the room.

'Aboot bliddy time.'

'Don't get narky with me, mate. I've spent a week on this.'

Skinner led him into a small office at the back and closed the door. The walls were plastered with signed photographs, coy messages scrawled over mammary landscapes, implying that the manager of the Gaza had personally sampled all employees. Skinner sat in the only chair. 'It'll cost you a tenner,' he said.

'Ah havny got it.'

'Don't be daft, you can't be that short.'

Brodie swore, and banged a wad of Scottish notes on the desk. Skinner counted them. 'Prefer 'em green, with 'Is Majesty on the front. Still, can't be choosy. Right, now listen. You were right. Remember that outfit Lumleys where MacNair said he nicked the stuff? Well we got a bird there to take a butcher's in the files.' Skinner pulled a sheet of photostat from his pocket. 'She found this—letter to the boss from a bloke called Hart . . .'

A telephone rang.

Skinner picked it up and listened, stiffening slightly in his seat. Brodie stood tapping his thigh. Skinner slammed down the phone and jumped to his feet, pushing the photostat into Brodie's hand. 'Move it. Visitors from West End Central.' He hustled Brodie along a passage and into a lavatory. 'Out the window, over the wall and through the betting shop.'

Brodie was on his way with the speed of an alley cat. Skinner closed the window, folded the Scottish notes into his shoe, pulled the plug and wondered about Alice.

V

A warning light flashed, and a new table of times and charges came up on an illuminated panel below the mirror. MacNair scooped a pile of new pence into the Automatic Selector, cupped his hand for the change and waited for the electronic music to stop. Putting a man on Mars was simple compared to a British phone box.

Hart came through again. 'Sorry old chap, can't transfer —bad security. You were saying . . .'

'That's the plan, and those are the names. All Caltech. They're leaving to-night.'

'Any idea where they'll do it?'

MacNair dictated a reference and gave the number of Hamish's Ordnance Survey map.

'Good work.' Hart allowed a trace of admiration into his voice.

'They're just boys,' said MacNair, 'so go easy.'

'Anything else?'

'Watch out for a Hamish Stuart, laddie with red hair. Keep him away from the rest. He told me the plan, very cut up because they were leaving me out. So he's the only one who could point the finger.'

'Roger. That's it then?'

'Aye, that's it.'

'We'll go carefully with Levi. Special Branch have had their eye on him for some time.'

'Och, come off it. The fellow's a pansy. What about Brodie?'

'Not to worry, he's still running loose. We managed to hold off the law.'

'Thanks.'

'Keep in touch then. And MacNair, try to move it along, there's a good fellow. I'm getting stick from the boys upstairs. Any leads at all?'

'Hamish says there's a girl running errands for the top man. They call her some fancy codename. Tall, goodlooker, and daddy's not a miner.'

'There's a dozen of those in every SNP office. Still, better than nothing. We'll work on it.'

MacNair signed off and slid the receiver back into its slot. As he stepped off the floor of the box the lights were out. He stood in the darkness for a moment, looking up the street, then headed back to the house.

When he got in Hamish had gone. He was upset by this. He realised that he had hoped to say something, but was not sure what. He lay on his bed and stared at the wallpaper, patches of damp submerging the flowered pattern like big brown clouds, until he drifted into sleep and dreamed of a village in Korea, a squat stone house crouching close to the hillside. Andy Gemmill had gone in first, kicking in the door. Boom, puff. Roof falls in, brown dust billowing out of the windows . . . They put the pieces in a bucket.

Jumping from his bed he ran to Hamish's room and looked behind the wardrobe. The bren had gone.

COMPACT

I

The government team had arrived in Hexham the night before, a squad of black Humbers decanting rumpled suits and red dispatch boxes into the Royal Hotel. That of course was a misnomer; they represented only the Conservative Party, come to seek alliance with a minority group. But the line is often hazy.

They had taken the whole top floor of the hotel, leaving the press to scramble for the rest. The 'advisers,' conscious of prep still to be done, had asked to be woken at eight, Scullard, who needed his sleep, at nine, and Harvey, with coffee and all the dailies, at seven—norm for Prime Ministers. They were all woken at half past six by the leaking baffle plates of a Jensen Interceptor. The car had survived several owners and belonged now to Jack Kemble, chief pundit of BBC Current Affairs. Kemble had arrived from London a few hours earlier, squaring the night porter with an extravagant tip, and after short ministrations from Jenny Stevens, Research Assistant of *Twenty-Four Hours,* was on the road again.

Joynson, the Prime Minister's Press Secretary, who knew the car, wondered what he was up to. He had noticed several messages in Kemble's pigeon-hole the previous evening.

As soon as a quorum of pistons were firing Kemble let the Jensen loose on the narrow streets. It was barely light, but several people were about. Someone was hoisting the Saltire on the roof of the Percy Arms, where Henderson and the Scottish team were due to arrive that morning.

He decided that he rather liked Hexham, a collection of dour but handsome buildings, faced with stone and anchored to their rolling landscape by the Abbey of Saint Wilfrid. Something endearing about the British provinces: that confident refusal to make the slightest concession to metropolitan tastes . . . If you must take a holiday here, do what you're told and leave the place tidy.

He took the A68 through Corbridge and headed north. The road swooped over bare brown moors, sliced through forests of spruce, skirted a reservoir and climbed slowly to the border at Carter Bar. Dripping cattle stared vacantly at long-distance trucks, grinding upwards in bottom gear. The verge became studded with warnings: *Sharp bends for Five Miles, Douse that Match, Danger—Artillery Range, Last Petrol Station in England* . . .

The crest of the Cheviots loomed ahead, nudging a sky full of low cloud. A last heave, then the road flattened, pausing briefly before the long descent to Jedburgh. Topographically speaking, a dramatic frontier; otherwise disappointing. No wire, no striped boom, no sentry box or flag, no multilingual warnings or words of welcome; just a small white sign, the sort which stands at the entrance to any country town, and a terse announcement scarred with rust: SCOTLAND.

Kemble stopped and lit the first cigarette of the day. The lay-by was surprisingly crowded. Two busloads of young Scots already lined the road with placards urging Henderson to turn back. A solitary Englishman, purpose obscure, was singing 'Land of Hope and Glory.' Police and press of both nations looked on, stamping in the cold.

Kemble walked towards a military jeep parked at a discreet distance. A young soldier jumped to attention beside the vehicle. He wore the uniform of the Scottish Division, glengarry and green battledress, with a plaid stripe down the trousers. The work of a royal hand, it had been acclaimed as a masterpiece of modern design and political expertise, preserving in its flashes, cap-badge or complicated tartan vestiges of all the uniforms of all the Scottish infantry regiments. Old soldiers still talked about the Black Watch and the Highland Fusiliers; but in the documents of Whitehall and NATO it now just was The Second and Third Battalions, Scottish Division.

'Mr Kemble? Colonel Cameron's expecting you, sir.'

'Where do I find him?'

'Drive on about half a mile, as far as the hairpin bend. You'll see a dirt track leading off the road. The command post is in the trees about four hundred yards up.'

'Thanks, soldier.'

'I shouldn't take the car up, sir—rather low clearance on those jobs. But leave it out of sight if you can.'

'Quite a climate you've got up here. No wonder the Romans quit.'

Kemble did as instructed, parked behind a gorse bush and put on a sheepskin jacket. A night's rain had reduced the track to a strip of yellow mud, which seeped over his Hush Puppies and into his pink nylon socks. As he climbed, head down into the wind, his breath came in shorter gasps. At that time of day his face gave the impression that if cut it would bleed black coffee. Poor Kemble; he looked quite good on television; hundreds of women wrote to him every week. It would have given them a terrible shock to see him on that barren hillside, locked in unequal battle with the elements, stripped of every essential prop.

He headed for a clump of trees, bent permanently sideways by the prevailing wind. Another glengarry appeared above the undergrowth, followed by the barrel of an offensive weapon.

'Halt! Identify yourself.'

'John Richard Kemble, of Shepherd's Bush and that Ilk.'

Silence, broken by a rasping voice from the centre of the trees. 'All right, Corporal, let him through.'

Kemble clambered through a thicket of brambles. At the base of the trees a patch of clear ground was littered

77

with equipment: mapcase, radio, megaphone and Very pistol.

'Down here, Jack.'

Cameron was lying under a bush at the far end of the clearing. Even in that position he looked incredibly smart. Wrapping his jacket closer, Kemble settled beside him on the poncho cape.

Cameron was good with journalists. Every exploit of his early career had set off a flare of Jingoistic publicity, which was good for recruiting but not so good for Cameron. Self-advertisement was the privilege of wartime generals.

Among the press corps Kemble was a special fan. In the end Kemble preferred men to women, and Cameron was the sort of man he liked best—vain, boyish, arrogant, good-humoured, and none too clever. 'What's this then?' he said.

'Internal security. Ever heard of the SLA?'

'You're joking.'

Cameron shook his head. 'Wish I was.'

'So where's the enemy?'

'Twelve o'clock, two hundred yards.'

Cameron pointed forwards. They were looking down the north face of the ridge. Below them a steep escarpment of rough brown grass tumbled down through patches of bracken, heather and rocks to an undulating plain. The road which Kemble had left passed across their front about eighty yards below, went into a sharp bend, then doubled back farther down and disappeared to the right. On the lower level it passed a thick copse of pines, at a point directly beneath the command post. Kemble realised that no traffic had passed since his arrival; the road must have been sealed above and below.

'In the trees,' said Cameron.

'Strength?'

'A bunch of students from Stirling. They're going to jump Henderson's car, put him in one of their own. Henderson, Mackie and old Aunty Merrilies. Here.' Cameron passed Kemble a pair of binoculars. 'You can see it.'

Kemble focused the binoculars on a grey Dormobile parked at the edge of the copse, out of sight of the road. Branches had been laid across the bonnet but he could read the words daubed in vivid red paint on the side:

CONTENTS—THREE QUISLINGS, DELIVERED UNDER PROTEST. DO NOT BEND, DESTROY OR RETURN TO SENDER.

Kemble thought of the photographers at the border. It seemed a shame to deprive them. 'A police matter, surely?' he said.

'Para-military operations require a military response.' Cameron smiled a devilish smile. 'Or so the argument runs. Don't blame me.'

'And with your usual concern for citizens' rights you've asked Jack along to see fair play.'

'That's my boy, attack on two fronts—I'll take care of the Nats, you look after the Bolshies in Portland Place. I don't want to hear any whining about fascist brutality.'

A red Very light snaked into the sky.

'Hold it. Here we go. Ready, Corporal? One green when I give the word.'

'Sir.'

A large black saloon came into view, climbing fast towards the copse, a police motorcyclist in front.

It was all over in less than a minute.

The Dormobile lurched forward and barred the road. The black car, now recognisable as an Austin Princess, approached, slowed, came on; then braked sharply, a sitting duck. The outrider climbed off his bike and walked forward. The students charged from the trees, then stopped dead as helmeted khaki forms erupted from all four doors of the Princess and ran straight at them with riot sticks and shields. The students turned and scattered, but they were trapped.

'Now!' shouted Cameron, and the corporal fired a green Very light over the scene. At the signal more troops rose from patches of bracken and heather around the copse and walked inwards in open formation, which quickly coalesced into small struggling groups as one by one the ambushers were caught.

'So where's Henderson?' Kemble said.

'Diverted to the A1. Any complaints?'

'No, one or two broken heads I should think, but they asked for that. No, very neat, very professional.'

Cameron took the compliment. 'If there's one thing I hate it's amateur soldiers.'

Kemble wondered what exactly he meant by that. One of the nicest things about Cameron was the way he seemed to consciously caricature himself, but sometimes he left you wondering how much of it was an act. A police Jaguar, rooflight flashing, had arrived on the scene, followed by two Black Marias. Funny thing bout the Scottish fuzz, they were hooked on Jags.

Cameron was getting to his feet when Kemble grabbed his arm. 'Just a minute—who's this?' Cameron reached for the binoculars.

A boy with red hair had slipped through the cordon. He was running straight up the slope towards them.

'Damn,' said Cameron.

And now Kemble noticed for the first time that two soldiers were lying concealed a short way below the command post. One of them had half risen from his cover and was looking back towards them, but getting no signal he resumed his position.

'Corporal, the megaphone. Jump to it.'

Cameron dropped the binoculars and Kemble picked them up. A white face under tousled red hair; mouth open for air. He had crossed the upper loop of the road and as the hill got steeper began to zigzag, leaping every obstacle like a stag . . .

Kemble's head jerked forward. 'He's armed,' he shouted, and adjusted the binoculars to a shorter range. 'Christ! He's carrying a bren!'

And then the boy fell. Kemble had him clearly in view.

Something had caught his foot and flung him into the side of the hill, and his finger must have caught in the trigger. A whip cracked once, a small sound on the wind. An answering shot came from the soldiers in front.

'Over his head!' yelled Cameron, but the megaphone was dead. His fingers fumbled for the switch.

The boy was on his feet, dazed, searching for the source of the shot. In one quick movement, which could have been anger or could have been panic, he dived down and came up with the bren, held at his hip, and fired again, a single shot aimed at random.

'Hold your fire!'

Cameron's command, booming from the megaphone, drowned the soldiers' shots. The boy sat down, hard, then toppled backwards. The bren skidded across a rock and dropped out of sight.

They waited, but the only movement was the tail of a hare bounding to safety. Kemble looked at Cameron, but Cameron was glaring straight ahead, a muscle working in his jaw. The two soldiers advanced and bent down. One of them straightened up and made a negative sweeping sight with his rifle. Cameron lowered his head until his brow was resting on the ground.

'Fair play?' said Kemble quietly.

Cameron took a deep breath and lifted his face; his eyes were closed. 'Bloody young fool,' he said.

'About nineteen, I'd say. '

'He fired first.'

'Yes, he did. Into the bloody bracken. Let's comfort ourselves with that.' Kemble looked at Cameron with genuine concern. 'Look, Douglas, I know you, I know you weren't meant to sit behind a desk, but watch it. That little corpse has an MP.'

'Do I need you to tell me that?' Cameron was on his feet tugging his uniform into place. A knot of police and troops was collecting round the body.

'He probably cared as much about this country as you do.'

'Oh shut up. Corporal, clear up here, then follow me down.' Cameron started down the hill, then stopped. 'I'm sorry, Jack, but I really can't take that sort of stuff from you. Just do what you can. You saw how it was.'

'Of course. Take care then.'

'Are you coming?'

'No. That's about my limit for pre-breakfast activity.'

Cameron thought it was squeamishness, but in fact Kemble's brain had already made several detailed calculations. One: they would be lucky to clear up the mess before the press arrived. Two: he did not want to be photographed with Cameron, dangerous company now for a political commentator of well-promoted liberal views. Three: if the Outside Broadcast people in Hexham were hooked up, he could still get a spot on *The World at Eight*.

II

Levi lay on a cluster of pillows, leading from behind.

The ambush: no problem there, provided no passing motorist had a go. The border: Strathclyde had laid on a demo to make sure of the press. That would draw some police, but Iain would be there with his box of tricks to jam their radio. Dormobile passes through, slow for the cameras, then fast down the hill and away. Strathclyde lie down in front of the police cars. On to the fork at Otterburn: dump the Dormobile, locking Henderson in, off with the gloves and headsocks, switch to the Minis and back through Newcastle. No absentees for the afternoon lecture . . .

It might come off. But probably not; more likely the ninnies would make a boo-boo, and damn near certain they'd blab when it was over, which would mean a spell in the cooler for all concerned, a disciplinary board, and after the usual sit-in another move for Donald.

Perhaps to Guantanamo this time. Reader in Marcusian Studies at that glossy new university. A neat little villa on the old American base, lithe brown bodies frolicking over the beaches . . .

He folded the map and swung his feet off the bed.

Yes, they'd need a bit of help with Marcuse.

Stepping out of black pyjamas, he put on a caftan and moved to the sitting-room.

And they don't speak bloody Gaelic.

The room was good for almost anything except sitting; a bare white box, with tribal masks overlooking wall-to-wall cushions. Glancing at his watch, Levi punched a button on the television, then swivelled as the door of the flat banged open.

'MacNair! What the hell . . .'

'Where's Hamish?'

'I told you never to come here.'

'Shooting a few English for breakfast, is he?'

'If I wanted you to know I'd have told you.'

MacNair advanced into the room, picking a path through the cushions. 'Look, Levi, stop faffing about. If you don't move fast we've had it—you, me, Hamish, the lot.'

'What are you talking about?'

'The law, they're on to us.'

'What! How do you know.'

The television came to life, eight strokes of Big Ben booming through the room. MacNair stalled. 'I was going to send Hamish up with a message, but he didn't come in, then I saw he'd taken the gun. '

The World at Eight . . .

'Gun?' said Levi.

'The bren.'

'Oh my God.'

Good morning . . .

'So I came straight over.'

'Shush.' Levi held up his hand and turned towards the set.

Troops were in action to-day at the Scottish border, where a party of students attempted to hijack the delegates of the Scottish National Party . . .

Levi sank to his knees. 'Oh no.'

'*One of the students, who was armed, was killed. There were no other serious casualties . . .*'

'Oh no, no!'

'*Later in the programme we shall be going to Hexham for a special report by Jack Kemble, who witnessed the incident . . .*'

'Bastards!' Pounding a cushion with his fist. 'Murdering, fascist, English bastards!'

That's it, thought MacNair, that's really it.

'*It seems that the dead student, who has been identified as Hamish Stuart of the Caledonia Institute of Technology, made a frontal assault on the troops, only two of whom were armed, across open ground . . .*'

Lie, thought MacNair.

'*A shot was fired over his head, and he was warned by loudhailer to drop his weapon. He continued to charge and opened fire. Fire was returned and Stuart was killed. He was found to have been carrying a light machine-gun of the type used in the Second War. The gun was loaded with a full magazine. Throughout Scotland there were demonstrations last night at the news that James Henderson had agreed . . .*'

Levi turned down the volume and stood up. 'So much for your little soldier.'

'I'd like to know the truth. He was no as daft as that.'

But Levi was no longer thinking of Hamish. He began to walk in small circles, holding his head with both hands. MacNair watched him absently. He was sick of them all. 'So what next?' he said.

Levi went on walking. 'Calm, Donald. Think, think.'

'You could get your nightie off for a start.'

'The papers! I must burn the papers!'

'Leave it, they know it all already.' MacNair started for the door. 'I vote we get out of here as quick as we can.'

'Seconded,' said a girl's voice behind him.

MacNair had half turned when a hand grabbed his

hair and pulled him backwards, yanking his head to the front.

Levi gaped and cried, 'Sukey!'

Before MacNair could recover, another hand was holding the blade of a knife across his throat. 'Careful now,' the girl said, her voice rising in alarm. 'Donald, this is James Brodie.'

III

They had hardly taken their seats when Mackie repeated almost word for word the speech which he had made at the opening session the previous afternoon. Harvey switched his mind off; better to let Scullard handle the procedural matters.

He looked round the friendly room where the Hexham Urban District Council usually met. In the eighteenth century the Rector must have hung his ancestors on those solid walls; now there were photographs of past Council Chairmen, and HMS *Loch Eck* sailing a choppy sea, strong in the knowledge that in 1942 she had been adopted by the Hexham and District National Savings Committee.

Behind the central U-shaped table at which the principals sat the room was packed with advisers. But at the head of the table one chair was empty, the red leather chair with arms reserved for the chairman.

'I repeat,' said Mackie, 'the representatives of Scotland cannot accept that the English Prime Minister should take the chair at these proceedings. This is a conference between equals. We have come to negotiate, not to hear respectfully the latest arrangements worked out in London for the future government of Scotland. That colonial relationship is at an end. On behalf of the Scottish delegation I formally propose that the chair be taken by the leaders of the two delegations, Mr Henderson and Mr Harvey, at alternate sessions.'

Mackie sat back from the table, and the morning sun

caught his pale face. Harvey had learnt that a man's true character usually shows during the few seconds after he has finished a speech; but Mackie was expressionless. A lonely man, probably, with a private vision of a ruthless new Scotland. How far would he go to force it on Henderson? Perhaps Henderson was asking himself the same question.

Scullard cleared his throat and began ponderously to read his reply. An unimaginative man, he had managed to pass three years as Secretary of State without popularity or odium. He held his text stiffly in front of him, and his hairy wrists looked red with constant scrubbing.

'I cannot accept the description of this meeting put forward by Mr Mackie, which in no way accords with the facts. This is not a conference between sovereign states, it has been called by the Prime Minister of the United Kingdom to discuss certain aspects of the situation created by . . .'

Harvey unfolded a note passed forward to him from Joynson, his Press Secretary:

N.B. The boys won't stand much more of this.

He left his seat and crooked a finger at Joynson, who joined him at the back of the room. Joynson exercised the right of very free speech.

'What the hell am I going to say at the press conference to-night? You're supposed to be Prime Minister, and you've been sitting in this god-forsaken hole for two days listening to Scullard and Mackie make speeches at each other about whether you're fit to chair the meeting. The Sundays will boil you alive if this goes on.'

'What about *Panorama* to-morrow night?'

'I told them no one on our side would play. They'd got Mackie lined up, but he backed out as agreed. So they've scrapped it and put in a piece on Old People's Homes. But they're hopping mad, and minting wild new phrases about a conspiracy of silence.'

'Let them. They'll have forgotten about it by next week.'

'Sure they will, provided you're up to something on the

side. But if you've brought the whole London press up here for the fresh air and the sound of Scullard's voice, then we're in trouble.'

'It's all right, Bill, I'm up to something. Stick to your job and don't bellyache.'

'And what's my job? I'm beginning to wonder.'

'To make the spectators think they're seeing all of the game.'

IV

Hart stood alone in the government conference room on the top floor of the Royal Hotel. The bed had been moved to one side; three tables of not quite equal height had been put together and ringed by miscellaneous chairs. No one had emptied the ashtrays and balls of paper littered the carpet.

He walked to the window and looked down. The street was a traffic warden's nightmare: imported demonstrators, local onlookers, official cars, unofficial cars, a truckload of terrified cattle, television vans banked on the pavement. Hexham would never be the same again.

He closed the window, then turned nervously as the door opened.

'Ah, Rennie.'

Rennie flopped into the nearest chair. He had spent the day interrogating the captured students.

'Anything new?' Hart said.

'A few scraps. They know more about police procedure than they do about their flipping army. MacNair's right, it's the girl we want.'

'He'll get on to her.'

'If they don't get on to him.'

Hart pulled out a chair and sat down. 'He's cooked up a lovely story for Levi.'

'It's Brodie bothers me,' Rennie said.

'Brodie's thick.'

Rennie smiled. 'He made short work of your men.'

Hart nodded dejectedly. He was tired. His wife had written to say the roses had black spot. 'I've got great faith in MacNair,' he said.

'Let's hope he returns the compliment.'

'Not again, Rennie, please.'

'He'll be upset about the boy.'

'MacNair is a man who works for money.'

'He's a Scot.'

'Precisely.'

Hart was saved by the door. Rennie did the introductions; he and Cameron had had several meetings.

'Nice work,' Hart said. 'That business on the border, I mean.'

'Thanks to your information.' Drawing on a lifetime's experience of British hierarchies Cameron had already assessed Hart completely, and knew he was small beer. 'More like that, and we'll crack 'em.'

'What about the other bunch in Dunbar?' Rennie said.

'Yes, I wanted to have a word about that.' Cameron turned back to Rennie. His service dress was beautifully pressed, shirt and tie exploiting the permitted deviations of senior officers. 'We moved on the house this morning, but they'd done a bunk.'

'Really?'

'Nary a trace. Looked as if they knew we were coming. No offence, Rennie, but are you sure all your people are sound?'

Rennie looked shocked. 'We've never had anything like that.'

'Well don't rule it out,' Cameron said. 'That's the trouble with this sort of show, can't tell the cowboys from the Indians.'

'I'll look into it.' Rennie was enjoying his job less and less.

Cameron looked round the room, assessing fields of fire. 'What's this about then?'

'Hanged if I know,' said Hart,

'Hasn't he heard of chains of command?'

'Must be urgent.'

'Pep-talk or dressing-down? Any bets?'

'He's late,' said Rennie.

The door opened again. 'The Prime Minister will be with you in a moment,' said a young man, and vanished. They waited. Hart and Rennie straightened their ties. Cameron sat, drawing patterns on the floor with his stick. A vague sound approached down the corridor, a rustle of urgent activity, like that which surrounds an accident: the familiar of important men.

'Good afternoon, gentlemen.'

Cameron snapped to attention. Somebody closed the door, and the rustle retreated.

'Please sit down.'

A small man, smaller than expected, with a slight stoop and a bald patch, and a work-worn face which was only a pale copy of the cartoons. Rennie felt cheated; it was like a bad impersonation.

'I won't keep you long,' Harvey said. 'I just wanted to have a word about these Scottish extremists, and I gather you are the people closest concerned.'

Hart and Rennie manœuvred for the humblest chairs.

'That's right, sir,' said Cameron, 'Rennie and Hart here on the intelligence side, myself the military. Wotherspoon in Edinburgh is handling the normal police aspects. I'm afraid they got him with a cobblestone last night.'

'Yes, so I heard.'

'He's asked me to speak for him, sir,' Rennie said.

'Good.' Harvey settled at the head of the table. 'Now what I want to establish, in as short a time as possible, is how serious a threat these people represent . . .'

They answered his questions with growing confidence. Cameron did most of the talking, but Harvey listened closest to Rennie.

'Thank you, gentlemen,' he said when they had finished. 'You paint an alarming picture. However I get the impression that, purely from the point of view of law and order, there is nothing there which cannot be handled under existing arrangements.'

'It might be wise to move all Scottish units north of the border, sir.'

Harvey looked thoughtfully at Cameron. 'That brings me to what I wanted to say. You see, this is not just a matter of law and order. There are delicate political and psychological aspects to be considered. Your opponents are certainly well aware of them, so you should be too. If we over-react we play straight into their hands. It's important that we put a stop to this business, but in doing that we must be careful that our methods do not offend moderate Scottish opinion. Do I make myself clear?'

Nods round the table. Harvey addressed himself to Rennie and Hart: 'I want the leaders exposed, and the sooner you can get the names the better. But I'd like to be consulted before any action is taken against them.'

Then to Cameron: 'And I want the Army involved as little as possible. Moving units across the border at this stage is just the sort of action we should avoid.'

'Yes, sir, I see your point, but . . .'

Harvey cut him short. 'For instance, who authorised the use of troops against those students yesterday morning?'

'The Joint Liaison Committee accepted our recommendation, sir,' Hart said. 'We thought they might be armed.'

'And in the event you were right. But it shows my point. If a boy fires on unarmed police, he's a hoodlum; if he's shot by a military rifle, he's a hero and a martyr to the cause. That might seem to you an unfair distinction, but that's how the public sees it.'

Rennie felt like clapping. There was a lot in that face the cartoonists missed.

Harvey smiled. 'I'm asking you to learn some politics, gentlemen.'

But Cameron would not lie down. 'If you're asking us to do this job without a few broken bones, sir . . .'

Harvey's voice hardened; there was no increase in

volume but the change in tone was startling. 'We're talking about a death, Colonel. If we can get it back to broken bones we'll be lucky. You've seen what happened to-day ·—violent demonstrations in every Scottish university, plans for a public funeral, even a monument I'm told. There may be reprisals. Before the week is out you could be leading a battalion over the barricades at Caltech.'

Yes, thought Harvey, you're the type who would enjoy that. Whoever picked you for this job needs his head examined.

'That, I repeat, would be a disaster. I have told the JLC that in future the Army is only to be used as a last resort, and then not without my specific consent on each occasion. And Cameron—'

'Yes, sir.'

'When it comes to dealing with the press it is you who are the amateur. I don't know how Kemble got to the scene in time yesterday, and I won't ask.'

'Thank you, sir. It won't happen again.'

'I hope not. A change of command at this stage would be a shocking waste of time.'

Back in his room Harvey looked through his notes for the press conference, then lay on the bed and thought about Hamish Stuart: a name to be lost in cuttings libraries or a sentence in the history books, subject of maudlin ballad and exaggerated reminiscence?

Cameron was a fool. Soldiers who lusted for publicity were all fools. Eight years ago he would have sacked the man on the spot. But now he was tired, and distrustful of snap decisions, and converted to the principle that Prime Ministers should not interfere in junior appointments. Anyway, how much of it was personal animosity? He had always disliked that type of military man.

He decided to leave it.

V

The bar was empty. After one round Hart and Rennie had mumbled excuses and left, as if scared that disfavour was catching. Either that or they thought it was an impertinence to drink in the Prime Minister's hotel. What a timid pair they were.

Cameron stared morosely into his glass. It was a bad time to be a soldier. Always some diplomat or politician looking over your shoulder, bleating about the other chap's point of view. Men like Scullard and Harvey. His career had been blighted by men like that; at school they had been the swots, creatures of no importance to be ducked and debagged and winkled from the library to score at cricket. But now they came back to haunt you; that forgotten face in the choir was behind a ministerial desk, demanding explanations.

'Barman.'

'Yes, sir.'

'Make it a large one. Is Mr Kemble around?'

'Just left, sir. I think he's gone to the press conference. Would you like me to . . .'

'No, never mind.'

Thank God for Kemble. Kemble had done a good job. Of course the boy had almost certainly fired by mistake; he had been killed by a pair of trigger-happy louts. 'And whose fault is that?' he would like to say to them. 'You took away the regiments, centuries of pride and tradition abolished with one little stroke of your computer. And you still expect decent soldiers?'

But that wouldn't do much good. Nothing he could say would do any good. Thorganby was right about Harvey. If the pressure built up, Harvey would sack him; he'd be back to recruiting at Perth or bundled off as Attaché to some African water-hole. Meanwhile he must bend to the wind, seek to give no offence. It was important to stay in the job. It was a stroke of luck that he'd got it and having got it, he must keep it, however painful. Damn Patrick Harvey. Damn Hamish Stuart. Yes, it was a sorry business, Scot against Scot, not what one had hoped for. But it had to be done and it was better than nothing, better than pushing up paper at Area HQ. Years gone to waste, but a chance for glory still . . .

The barman boggled as a fifty-pence piece clattered on to the counter. 'Thank you, sir. Thank you very much.'

Tugging his uniform into place, Cameron left the hotel. The small crowd still at the door murmured in recognition; his face had been on every front page that morning. A delirious Scot ran forward and spat before the police could catch him, but Cameron reached his car with dignity and started on the drive back to Edinburgh.

VI

Sukey had been driving all afternoon.

She had taken them straight from Stirling to the flat in Glasgow and there they had stayed for a day and a half, MacNair blank and silent, handcuffed to the bed, Brodie and Levi pacing restlessly about. Brodie wanted to get back to Blackhill, but wanted to kill MacNair first. Levi preferred the idea of Brodie to the fact; his only thought was to get out of the country. She had persuaded them both to wait for orders, but *An Ceannard* had been unobtainable. That afternoon she had got back to find MacNair bleeding from the lip, one of the Redpaths ripped and Levi on the phone to a friend in the City who knew how to dodge the Exchange Control. In despair she had packed them into the car and headed north, out through the suburbs in sullen silence, along Loch Lomond, Glen Falloch, Strath Fillan, and into the mountains.

Brodie sat in the back. As the city receded he had started to fret, jigging his knife up and down on his knee.

Sukey had watched him in the mirror. He was surprisingly neat, with short hair and clean hands and nothing flashy about his clothes; a narrow face and protruding eyes, which told you nothing except that it might be a mistake to laugh. Yes, that was what he would mind most. But otherwise perfectly ordinary—take away the scar and you could put him behind the counter of a bank . . . He caught her eyes in the mirror and asked where they were going.

She held her finger to her lips, gestured backwards at MacNair. He nodded and smiled. It was the first time she had seen him smile and it was rather touching—a small, clumsy disturbance of the lips, quickly suppressed. He seemed quite prepared to take orders from her; perhaps she was so far out of his world that the normal rules didn't apply. But it wasn't an advantage she cared to exploit. MacNair was lying trussed and gagged on the floor of the car. Whenever he moved Brodie leaned down and pressed the point of the knife on the back of his neck.

Levi had spoken once, tapping the front page of *The Scotsman*. 'I see the Army gets a roasting. What's his name —Cameron—that's the man you ought to go for.'

Sukey had noticed the 'you' and said, 'Quitter.'

Levi puffed and shifted in his seat. 'They know me now, I'm no use to you. But I could do a lot abroad—spread the word, raise some bread . . . Lots of mates in the States, you know.'

Someone had put the American telephone directories through a computer and came up with fifty-seven million Celtic names.

'There's a boat on the way,' Sukey said, and thought how much she would like to jump on it herself. Up to now it had all been rather unreal—a touch of scarcely credible danger to spice her life, perhaps just a rich girl's hobby, like raising money for impossibly thin babies who came no nearer than the colour supplements. But now she was scared to bits; she wondered what she'd got into and where it would end. 'We'll get you away in a week,' she said. 'I

94

don't suppose he'll object.'

MacNair listened, filing each clue in his head.

The road was following the course of a river, climbing slowly through a desolate valley. The last grey farmhouse vanished behind, 'Bed and Breakfast' in the window like a plea for help. Cultivation dwindled and stopped. The world was abandoned to sheep—motionless lumps of wool tugged and parted by the wind, which rose from the grass on black stick legs like a species of weather-proof plant. The Forestry Commission had been and gone, leaving puny trees to fight for their lives in furrows scored across the valley floor. At a distance the sheep looked more like maggots, infesting the brown hillsides.

'They made a desert and called it peace.'

This from Levi, who had exhausted the classified ads in *The Scotsman* and was staring mournfully out of the window. It had rained all day but now the evening was fine.

'Cliché,' said Sukey. Fatigue and the sunset had loosened her emotions. 'They'd call it genocide now.'

'Another cliché. Let's be frank. Most of them were murdering cattle thieves.'

'I know, I know, and they'd have starved anyway, and they're better off making money in Toronto than dressing up for the tourists. Still, it is sad. It used to make me cry just to think about it.'

'All the way to the bank.'

'What's that supposed to mean?'

'Well, you lot did all right, didn't you? Like no beastly clans to look after, and six million acres to play about in. Somebody worked it out once—two ounce of grouse to the acre.'

'Don't worry, I'm not proud of it.'

The road reached the head of the valley and came out on the Moor of Rannoch. For Sukey home began here. A penance of childhood summers had been the hike across the moor with botanical Aunt Florence, a wild-eyed figure in knitted stockings and discordant tweeds, gum-boots plunging through the lochans as she led the search for those tiny spots of colour with strangely indelicate names —Bog Myrtle, Lousewort, Bladderwort and Saxifrage . . . What did Donald Levi know about Scotland?

Suddenly she felt stifled. At the top of Glencoe she pulled the car on to the verge and walked to the edge of the gorge. Brodie stayed with his charge. She would have liked to be alone, but Levi came padding up behind.

They stood in silence, conversation crushed by the view. Aonach Eagach, soaring to the right, volcanic cliffs like ruins in the setting sun, to the left the dark buttresses of Bidean nam Bian, white threads of water falling to feed those still green meadows below. The Herdsmen of Etive, Ossian's Cave, the Devil's Staircase, the Loch of Blood . . . and through it all the road, life-line of the twentieth century, scooter and charabanc and caravan, scuttling from gift shop to camp site. It was difficult not to be corny about Glencoe.

'Where *are* we going?' Levi said.

'Loch Ailort. Ardnish Castle.'

'A castle! That's too much.'

'Not really. The old one was burned down, this is just a replica with turrets. It belonged to my aunt.'

'Don't tell me, the Young Chevalier slept there.'

'Yes.'

'Arrogant papist twit. One more word about him and I'll puke on the Macdonalds' grave.'

'You're a bore, Donald, did you know that? The sooner we get your fat carcass across the water the better.'

'Darling!'

'Well you asked for it. You bang on about the Stuarts and the grouse, but what do you care?' Sukey walked away and sat on a boulder, picking at the moss. 'It's my bloody country,' she said loudly, and burst into tears.

Levi followed and touched her shoulder. 'You're right. I'm a fraud.'

'Oh, Donald, I'm sorry. Aren't I awful? It's just that boy, sitting there all the time with his knife . . .'

'Yes, I know. He gives me the spooks too.' Levi waited for the storm to subside. 'You were saying, aunty has a castle . . .'

'Poor Aunt Florence. She went through three husbands and died in a Swiss convent. The family were horrid, they called her Scarper Flo. But she was the best of the lot.'

'A Nationalist?'

Sukey giggled weakly. 'Rabid. She used to fling bottles off the *Queen Mary* with messages—Gaels of the World Unite, that sort of thing. She never had children so she left the house to a committee of her chums called the Alba Trust, with a lot of instructions about preserving the Highland way of life. No one was sure what that meant, so they let the Commandos have it. Then there was a fish farm, but that went bust, so they handed it over to Outward Bound.'

'And now we're using it?'

'Yes, for the last two years. The Committee are Nats to a man, so it wasn't difficult. And the crofters are used to funny goings-on there.'

A tide of shadow was moving across the glen, over the birches and the river, across the shoots of scree and up the walls of rock; above the cliffs an eagle was doing aerobatics against a pearly sky. 'Tell me,' Levi said. 'Why are you in this thing?'

Sukey sighed and shrugged. She felt she could sleep for a week. 'It runs in the family.'

(The first recorded Dunmaynes had fought with The Wallace and The Bruce; the clan had turned out at Flodden and the third Earl had fallen on Drummossie Moor, legs mangled by grapeshot. Cumberland's dragoons had hacked off his genitals and left him to die in the night.)

Levi said: 'And what exactly runs in the family?'

(Ask the third Earl. He only wanted to be on the winning side. He played it both ways for weeks and was late for the battle; he could have turned back, but knowing he had calculated wrong he led the clan to their deaths on the guns of the redcoats.)

'Persistent, aren't you?' Sukey smiled and shook her head. 'I don't know. Style, perhaps—a taste for the grand gesture. Aunt Florence used to say that survival was the talent of the middle classes.'

'She was right.'

'I'm easily bored, you know. But to turn back almost three centuries of history and start again, that would be fun. That would be original.'

'You're all loonies.'

Sukey stared down the gorge. She was looking for the truth—as much for herself as Levi. 'Of course,' she said, 'you could look at it another way. It's always been difficult to find a man I could respect.'

'I've seen his sort before. If you got in the way he'd drop you in a flash.'

'Exactly.' She flung back her head and laughed. 'And what about you, Donald? Why?'

'No imperial power has ever been beaten by the vote.'

'Pause for loud music.'

'I never really fancied growing up—how's that?'

'Better.'

'The world is a club for the married and the fertile. The young aren't so choosy.'

'Poor Donald.'

'Poor Sukey.'

'Come on, you drive for a bit.'

VII

A mile to the east of Hexham the road was dominated by a garish neon sign. They called it the Borderers Motel, but no one was deceived: a squat Northumbrian farmhouse with the yard asphalted, parking bays marked out in white lines and a row of painted wooden huts where the chicken houses had been. One of the huts was occupied by two men.

'I would say that the taxation arrangements are the key,'

said Henderson.

It was only their second meeting, and personal relations had not really formed yet. With these two men personal relations would only come from working steadily together, and this they were beginning to do. The management of the motel had moved the twin beds into one corner and promoted the white dressing-table into the centre of the room, giving it a jug of water and two glasses.

'The Ulster arrangement works well,' Harvey replied.

'It wouldn't be enough. The Government of Scotland must have in its own hands the whole power of taxation. Then we could pass on to London whatever was necessary to pay our share of foreign affairs and defence.'

'I wonder if that's really wise. Taxation for these purposes is not exactly popular. Mightn't it suit you to have it levied direct by the Central Government?'

A girl came in with two cups of tea. She goggled and smiled, and seemed too shy to leave the room.

'How many people know we are here?' asked Henderson, when she had finally edged through the door.

Harvey noted the nervousness. 'That was the daughter of the house,' he said. 'Only she and her parents, and they've all been talked to severely. But of course it's bound to come out fairly soon. We don't have much time.'

'Quite so. I don't like talking in a corner. But anyway you must understand that if I'm to give up independence and have a chance of making this stick, the Scots must have complete control of all taxation. What they contribute to London must be the free decision of their own government and assembly.'

'But you're expecting London to spend a lot of English money on Scottish development.'

'Of course, because it's in your interest that Scotland should be prosperous.'

Henderson knew the answers, but Harvey saw that he was tired as well as uneasy. The freckles stood out on his face, and the hand on the white table slowly clenched and unclenched. People who seriously tried to govern

Scotland did not die old.

'Yes, I agree. The advisers will go into the details of development policy this afternoon. But you must see that I have my difficulties too. How can I persuade the English taxpayer to pour money into your factories when he can't even be sure that you'll pay your fair share of defence?'

Henderson paused to take the point. He was clearly looking for real solutions which would work. From that moment Harvey was sure that this was the man he was looking for.

'The money must be levied by the Government of Scotland. But there could be an agreed defence assessment which would then automatically be paid by us to London without any debate in the Scottish Assembly. If either Government wanted to change the assessment, then there could be some kind of independent court before which they could argue.'

Harvey was privately pleased, but it was too early to show it. 'I see some snags in that, but it may be worth examining. We'll get the advisers to draft a formula and see how it looks. Now, can we get on, the powers of the Governor-General . . .?'

In the bar of the Royal Hotel Joynson ordered a round of whiskies and sent up a silent prayer.

'Harvey's got a slight sore throat. He had his supper here, as you saw, and now he's gone to bed with about two dozen red boxes from London. It's nothing serious, no temperature, he'll be about to-morrow.'

The moment passed successfully. Only Jack Kemble of the BBC asked a question.

'How the hell did he get a sore throat? Listening to Scullard?'

A cell with a view, thought MacNair. Either these people are amateurs or they don't care because they're going to turn me into a fish meal. Levi had made the big slip.

'Holy Krishna, what a mess.' Down into second, water noises off. 'Tory jerry-builders . . . why can't they bring the ferry back until it's fixed?'

Ballachulish. The bridge had collapsed in April. So the girl had stopped in Glencoe. Soon after that a town—busy streets, a juke box, self-service petrol, and Levi had found a bar with a television. Fort William. Out on a decent road, then several miles of pitted surface and cattle grids. Take your pick . . . But somewhere on the coast: the loch below the house was tidal and the boat which had come in at dawn was an Admiralty MFV. He had made a note of the number—OB 014. That would be enough for Rennie.

They had locked him in a top-floor room on the front. One corner bulged out in a bow of tall slit windows; from there he could see the matching turret at the other end of the house. It was quite a place: a hallway full of guncases and crossed claymores, stags' heads on the panelled walls, and everywhere the smell of an unused church. A dense pine forest closed in behind, probably screening it from the road. In front an overgrown lawn led down to a jetty. To the right, at the edge of the loch, six Nissen huts inside a high wire fence and a second jetty, newer, with concrete fish tanks along one side. Parked beside the huts, two Land-Rovers and an old Army three-tonner.

Earlier on they had been very busy. He had counted about thirty of them, fit-looking types in kilts or khaki shorts, hurrying about with an air of secretive purpose. OB 014 had unloaded into the fish tanks and vanished into the mist, lights out, full throttle on her Kelvin Diesels.

But now no one was in sight. The house was silent.

Even the generator had stopped. And through the glass the landscape was lifeless as a postcard, rhododendrons hanging in the heat, flat-calm water stretching to an anonymous line of hills, everything bright and still—that peculiar stillness of a Highland summer day. MacNair had a sudden impression of what it would be like to be deaf.

He had searched the room for clues. It was full of sad junk: broken fishing tackle, stuffed birds, books full of pressed flowers, a zither, a wedding dress, boxes of yellow photographs and twenty years of the *Illustrated London News*. The books had a label inside: *Ex Libris Florence Dunmayne*. And in one of the photographs he had found the girl—grave young face under a bowler hat, skinny legs astride a barrel-shaped pony. If it wasn't for her Brodie would have carved him up. Did she know what a women's prison was like? Had she ever thought about it?

IX

'It's ingenious,' said Scullard, looking at the Compact of Hexham, 'but it won't be easy to sell to the colleagues.'

'No, it won't, but between us I think we can manage.' Harvey was determined to keep Scullard on the hook. 'I'm calling a Cabinet for to-morrow afternoon. Meanwhile it must of course stay a close secret.'

'The 1922 Committee won't like the financial clauses.'

'But the simple question is whether they want another five years of settled Conservative government without repealing the Union with Scotland. If they do, we've got it for them. The undertaking of SNP support for us at Westminster is unequivocal.'

'I suppose so.'

'I shall mention the part you played. If it hadn't been for your steady batting against Mackie, we wouldn't have pulled it off.'

Harvey had found that Scots of all parties were abnormally susceptible to flattery.

Henderson had decided to see his two lieutenants separately. The talk with Mackie had been short and quiet. Mackie had simply said that he would study the document, and of course it would have to go before the Party's National Council. Henderson had in his drawer a list of the Council with a pencilled tick or cross against each name. There was a small majority of ticks. Mackie's name had a cross: he would certainly vote against the Compact. Henderson had put a query against the name of Margaret Merrilies. She was important, and he was trying to handle her gently.

'As I see it, Margaret, this has been an exercise in saving the face of the English. What we've negotiated here is independence without the trappings.'

'I'm not so sure,' Mrs Merrilies moved her big frame restlessly on the hotel sofa. She was genuinely undecided, and her rheumatism was playing up. The sheets in the Percy Arms were damp.

'The financial clauses are particularly good.'

It was the wrong thing to say, and Henderson knew it at once. Something like an earthquake occurred within the mountain of tweed opposite him.

'That's your difficulty, James, you think of nothing but money. But it isn't money my people are worried about. They want a clean break and a proud new Scotland, and that's what I've promised them.'

'There's plenty here to be proud about,' said Henderson, holding up the Compact.

'Is there?' When Mrs Merrilies was excited, her thick yellow-white hair vibrated above the big face. 'What's all this about a Governor-General then? Will that be some fancy English Duke lording it over us in the King's name?'

For a moment Henderson had a vision of Mrs Merrilies herself, in purple velvet down to the ground, the Order of the Thistle undulating across her bosom, standing to receive the guests in Holyrood House. It was a tantalising thought, but, to do her justice, she wouldn't take the job.

'The duties and powers of the Governor-General are not yet fully defined . . .' Without much hope Henderson settled down to patient exposition.

X

As they waited round the television in the Prime Minister's hotel sitting-room, Harvey was quiet, Scullard nervous. Television had been invented by a Scot, Harvey was thinking. But so had penicillin.

For once in his life Joynson was outwitted and furious. 'And I'll tell you what really bugs me,' he burst out. 'Kemble had the bloody nerve to tell me they were keeping the outside unit here to do a schools broadcast on the Abbey.'

'What exactly was the message from Number Ten?' asked Scullard.

'They'd just heard that *Panorama* was putting Hexham back in because they'd got an interview with Ma Merrilies. I expect she'll weep in Gaelic and storm out on a broomstick.' Joynson lit a fierce small cigar.

Scullard turned to Harvey. 'But it's clearly a breach of your agreement with Henderson. I turned down an invitation to appear, so did you, and so did Mackie. Can't you get him to stop her?'

'I doubt if he could, and anyway the BBC have got the tape. When it comes to frustrating the public interest there's no one so determined as a public corporation. Too late now anyway.'

A portentous fanfare from the screen, white globe hovering against a shot of Hexham Abbey, then Kemble and Mrs Merrilies on a municipal bench. Joynson swore.

Mrs Merrilies was ill at ease, fiddling with her brooch. The medium was still strange to her, her conscience could hardly be clear, and the bench looked hard. She was groping for platitudes.

'. . . of course the document to which you refer is the result of confidential negotiation, and I am not yet at liberty to divulge its contents.'

'Attagirl,' Joynson said.

But Kemble wheedled. 'We all respect that, Mrs Merrilies, but you will understand the very great public interest, particularly among our Scottish viewers. There are parts of this so-called Compact on which you personally must have strong opinions, in view of all that you have said in the past. For example, the position of the King . . .'

That did it. Mrs Merrilies glared into the camera, and began to boom. 'Yes, indeed. It is always forgotten that the King is King of Scotland first, and King of England second. That's a matter of history, it can't be contradicted . . .'

As he listened Harvey was suddenly overwhelmed by the essential silliness of the whole business. Someone had said that SNP stood for Somewhat Naive People.

'. . . Now we're going to have a Scottish Prime Minister at last, that's quite right. But this paper says he can't go to the King direct as Harvey does. He must go and talk to some new creature called a Governor-General. I would like to know where in Scottish history they find any justification for a Governor-General. To me that is plain colonialism and I can't accept it.'

'But Mrs Merrilies,' Kemble said, 'Northern Ireland has a Governor-General, so do Australia, New Zealand and Canada. They're not exactly colonies.'

'I don't care what other countries do. They know what's right for them, I know what's right for Scotland.'

Kemble was now out to do damage.

'But, as I understand it, Mrs Merrilies, the proposal for a Governor-General is an essential part of the Compact. Are you saying that you reject the terms which the leader of your party has agreed to?'

Mrs Merrilies was in retreat. 'No, not all of them . . .'

'But unless this very important part of the document

was withdrawn you would vote against and oppose it?'

'Yes—yes, I would.'

'Mrs Merrilies, thank you very much.' Cut to Kemble alone against municipal tulips. 'And so, to-night at Hexham, despite three days of old-fashioned secret diplomacy from which press and public have been rigorously excluded, the conference is split wide open, and the prospects of agreement are dim indeed . . .'

'That's torn it,' said Scullard.

Joynson rammed his cigar into an ashtray. 'I'll just go downstairs and wring Kemble's neck.'

'Perhaps you would get me a line to Buckingham Palace first,' Harvey said. 'The sooner I can talk to the King the better.'

XI

RESTRICTED

Transcript of telephone call made to John Mackie at the Percy Arms, Hexham, by unidentified woman speaking from Fort William call box. Recorded at 9 p.m., June 6, Special Branch Authority Natpol S. 0057/80 refers.

Caller: Hallo.

Mackie: Hallo.

Caller: John? Damn this thing.

Mackie: Relax, I can hear you. I think we've got company.

Caller: Oh. I see. Well, how goes it?

Mackie: All over bar the communiqué. I lay low.

Caller: What did we get?

Mackie: Ulster with trimmings. Control of the purse, Governor-General . . .

Caller: Oh no!

Mackie: Maggie had a go about that. Did you see *Panorama*?

Caller: No. Is she holding out?

Mackie: Dithering, but the Doctor will win her over.

	He and Harvey fixed it all in a couple of private sessions. And of course she doesn't fancy me for a bedfellow.
Caller:	Don't blame her.
Mackie:	I'll remember that.
Caller:	So what next?
Mackie:	Henderson will have to sell it to the Council.
Caller:	Do you want us to . . .
Mackie:	Careful. Yes. I think some fairly loud entertainment . . . as soon as we get back. Can you manage that?
Caller:	What about that idea we discussed?
Mackie:	Yes. Yes, that would do very well.
Caller:	I'll pass it on.
Mackie:	Are you in touch?
Caller:	Off and on. It's getting more difficult.
Mackie:	Remember the night of the big bang.
Caller:	Oh you cryptic beast.
Mackie:	I must go.

[Unidentified sound, both speakers.]

Mackie:	This has got to stop.
Caller:	Tarra then.
Mackie:	'Bye.

XII

As she came into the room Sukey's nose wrinkled in disgust: the smell of decay was now mingled with the reek of male sweat. She asked Brodie to leave them alone. He stared at her, then turned away slowly and closed the door. Each time the stare got a little longer and he now had a gun. Duguid had issued him with a Browning automatic; whenever he wasn't with MacNair he could be found blasting away in the cellars. He was no good at all, but if the range was short enough it wouldn't matter.

'What are we going to do with you, MacNair?' she said.

MacNair shrugged and said without much conviction, 'You could let me go.'

'Please, be practical. You've seen me, you've heard my name—and you've seen this house.'

'It could be anywhere.'

Sukey smiled wryly and shook her head. 'You could give a fair description—they'd find it in a week. I'm afraid we've been rather careless . . . No, we can't let you go.' She walked to the window, and looked out. 'I expect you can guess what else has been suggested.'

'Yes.'

'We don't want to do that.'

'You don't,' MacNair said.

She turned back to look at him. 'There is an alternative, and I hope you'll take it. We have some explosive here . . .' MacNair nodded. He had been expecting that, counting on it. 'We're not out to cause casualties, you understand. Just something to remind our politicians that it's too late for deals with the English.'

'When?'

'To-morrow. Brodie will stay with you.'

'I'm getting used to that.'

'If anything goes wrong he's been told to kill you.'

'And afterwards?'

'You'll be brought back here. We may need you again. We'll have to keep you locked up, I'm afraid, but I'll see that you're more comfortable than this.'

'Thanks.'

'Will you do it?'

'I don't have much choice.' The look of relief on her face was pathetic. And now MacNair smiled too, not much movement of the lips, but a definite glimmer in the eyes. A chance to live, a chance to put the skids under Hart: what more could a man ask?

They all looked up as he came into the hut. Someone

switched off the radio and conversation stopped. Three of them were kneeling on a tarpaulin littered with pull-throughs and flannelette, their hands and forearms black with grease. They had set the manual in the centre and laid out the parts of the machine-gun according to the diagram. Two more were unpacking rifles from a crate. The wood was sodden and green, without markings, but the box inside had a waterproof lining and the rifles were packed in polythene. About a hundred had been cleaned already; they stood in a rack along the wall, with a chain threaded through the trigger guards. Three more racks were standing empty. At the far end a pair of mortars. All standard NATO issue.

Sukey let MacNair take it in. 'You see, we're well prepared.' She sounded embarrassed, as if the whole thing might be a preposterous joke.

A man in khaki drill and a beret came up to them. Pinned to the beret was a plastic disc, Saint Andrew's cross with a red lion rampant in the centre. They were all wearing them.

'This is Robert Duguid. He's in charge in here.'

If Robert Duguid had never quite persuaded anyone that he was a man it wasn't for lack of trying. He was bursting out all over: barrel chest, shirt sleeves rolled high above the biceps, a show of muscled leg between shorts and long woollen socks. A rugged pipe curled down from his handlebar moustache.

'So you've agreed to do it,' he said to MacNair. 'Well don't expect any favours. If this was Ireland we'd have wrapped you in barbed wire and dropped you in the loch.'

Brodie sniggered. He was leaning cowboy-fashion on the door with the Browning stuck in his trousers.

Duguid pulled out a bunch of keys and led them into the next hut. A skull and crossbones had been painted on the door. It was dark inside; all the huts had black-out painted on the windows. Duguid pressed a switch and MacNair saw more crates, larger, with a splash of red paint on each side, stacked from floor to ceiling.

'We haven't touched it yet,' Duguid said.

MacNair nodded and held out his hand for the hammer in Duguid's pocket. Duguid handed it over. MacNair told him to put his pipe away and started on the nearest crate. They watched him in silence as the side of the crate came away with a squeal of nails. Enjoying his moment MacNair asked for Brodie's knife, gently cut the layers of padding, then another, then stood back. Whoever had packed this stuff was a pro.

'Same in all of them?' he asked Duguid.

'As far as we know, yes.'

MacNair made a clucking noise with his tongue. 'You're well prepared all right. You could blow the Forth Bridge with this lot.'

Duguid looked at Sukey. Sukey looked at MacNair. 'You didn't tell us you were psychic,' she said.

XIII

The helicopter swooped above the slate roofs of Newbury, over the regiments of parked cars reflecting the sunlight back in a metallic glare, then swung over the faultless turf towards the low line of wooded hills. For a moment, seeing the Standard droop above the royal box, Harvey felt again the twinge of irritation with which he had first heard that the King would still go racing that afternoon. But of course it was irrational. For he was not only or mainly Harvey's King; he was King of all those thousands happily gathered in their differently priced enclosures below. To them the political crisis was far less important than Connemara's chances in the Highclere Stakes. Heaven forbid that it should be otherwise, thought Harvey, as the helicopter settled on the turf beyond the members' car park. Politicians and journalists had to pretend that Britain was permanently in a state of fever; everyone else knew it was nonsense. A country which worried more about politics than racehorses would be in a poor way.

'I suppose the lure of the box was too strong for her.'

The King poured Harvey a glass of hock. Plates of mangled lobster littered the royal box, but the King had sent his guests down to the paddock while he talked.

'I think Henderson must have rubbed her the wrong way.'

'He'll learn.' The King was much more relaxed than at their last interview. Through his binoculars he watched the mass of two-year-olds canter up to the starting-gate for the first race, brilliant colours against the green. An unimportant race, and he only bet on his own horses. 'Well, what will you do now?'

'Of course we'll have to publish the Compact. Ideally, I'd like to leave the Scots to stew for a bit, let them see they won't get anything better. But I'm afraid events will run the other way. There's an ugly lot of violence brewing up there, and if I don't give Henderson something quickly, he'll lose control. That brush with the students was badly handled.'

'Let me give you some advice.' The King lowered his binoculars. 'Don't fuss around with the financial clauses, they're not relevant any longer. All you politicians worry too much about money, and that silly Merrilies woman has shown you up. What we need is some gesture which will make the Scots feel they really count.'

Harvey noticed the 'we' with relief. This was going better than he had expected. Thanks to the racecourse.

'I had an idea, sir, very much on those lines—though I'm afraid you may not like it. I wondered if you would agree to spend say three months a year at Holyrood, the powers of the Governor-General being in abeyance while you were there. I think it would have a great effect.'

The King laughed. 'It would have an effect all right. I'm not sure if the cold rooms or the smell from the brewery would kill me first—or the sermons at Saint Giles'. I had a different idea. The Prince of Scotland—how does that strike you?'

Harvey was not sure, and the King went on.

'It came into my mind the other day when the Duke of Norfolk started talking about an investiture at Caernarvon next year. Why always Prince of Wales? It was a political gesture in the thirteenth century. Six hundred years later we need a new gesture in the other direction. And anyway he has been Steward of Scotland and Duke of Rothesay since the day he was born. He could be invested at Stirling, spend about half his time in Scotland, and gradually take over the duties of Governor-General.'

'There'll be trouble with the Welsh.' Harvey was never quick to take new ideas.

'Isn't there always trouble with the Welsh? They take too much for granted. They can wait a generation, or they can have the younger Prince in five years' time.'

The lad would look well in a kilt, thought Harvey, he had the figure for it. Old Merrilies and half her crew were Jacobites at heart. It might work.

'And now, if I've solved your problem,' said the King, 'would you like to come and see Connemara in the paddock?'

XIV

The nationalism of Sir Alan Blair, Chief Constable of Glasgow, was less a vision of the future than a compound of small complaints about the present—the inconvenience of British Standard Time, the King's infrequent visits to Balmoral, letters franked 'Pick an English Apple.' The appearance of the Forth Bridge now reminded him of another.

'And if you ask me what I resent most, it's this damn toll. The English get their bridges out of their taxes, so why on earth shouldn't we? If Henderson doesn't put that right the man deserves to fail.'

Rennie made a non-committal noise. One of the more loathsome things about Blair was his habit of granting audience to non-playing subordinates on the golf course. The inaccessibility, like the golf, was intended as proof of social standing. So far Rennie had managed to avoid the fairway, but had been forced to accept a lift as far as Kinross to get a word in.

'So you've no objection to my proposals for staff transfers, sir?' he said.

'No, go ahead if you must, though I fail to see why we should accept complaints from that numbskull Cameron.'

'There's a leak somewhere. This lot in Kinross is the second to get away.'

'What about Hart's little spy, hasn't he come up with anything?'

'Nothing on the leaders, no.'

Blair was listening carefully. 'And you still think it's Mackie?' he said.

'You saw that transcript from Hexham.'

'That didn't prove much.'

'No, and it's the last we'll get. Downing Street have ruled out all direct surveillance of Nationalist MPs. The girl's the key to it, the courier MacNair mentioned—she could be the one who phoned Mackie. But they protect her well.'

'I want you to keep me fully informed,' Blair said.

Rennie looked over the Firth, improbably blue in the clear morning light, and above it that miraculous mile of girders hanging from its filigree of cables. 'Of course,' he said, 'I'm marking all the papers to you.' The motorway dipped behind low hills as they left it and veered north. 'I suppose you couldn't spare a moment to support me in Kinross? They won't take kindly to suggestions of incompetence.'

'I'm afraid that's quite impossible. I'm due at Saint Andrews for lunch. Hallo, what's this?'

The approach road to the bridge was clogged with a

queue of stationary traffic. Several drivers were out of their cars and peering forward in exasperation. Nobody knew what was wrong. Rennie offered to investigate; Blair agreed and said he would wait in the car.

The queue started at a bend two hundred yards ahead, still out of sight of the entrance to the bridge, though the southern tower now loomed close above the hills. Police were barring the road.

'What's up, Sergeant?' Rennie said.

'Bomb scare, sir.'

'Nats?'

'Aye, I expect so. Probably a hoax, but ye canna be too careful these days.'

'Who tipped you off?'

Rennie had not identified himself but the sergeant knew a senior colleague when he saw one. 'Glasgow—they'd had some joker on the line . . .'

'How long ago was this?'

'About half an hour. We've cleared the bridge—the Army are down there now.'

'The Army?'

'Bomb Disposal Squad.'

'Oh. Quick work,' Rennie said, 'well done.'

'Not us, sir—Glasgow.'

'Who did you speak to there?'

'Special Branch, Chief Inspector Rennie.'

'That's interesting. What sort of vehicle are they using?'

'Excuse me, sir . . .' A group of drivers had begun to complain loudly. As the sergeant started towards them Rennie caught his sleeve and yanked him back. 'Stay where you are, man, and listen to me. What were the Army in?'

'A Land-Rover . . .'

'How many men?'

'Hard to tell, they didn't stop. Three, I think.'

'Right. Here's what you do. Call up the other side, tell them not to let it through, then . . .'

'As he listened two patches of yellow developed on the

114

sergeant's cheeks and through the mental mist, competing with Rennie's orders for attention, came the outline of the awful truth, quickly followed by visions of demotion and ridicule. The whole thing was just about clear when the ground kicked under their feet.

'Down!' yelled Rennie, and had time for a four-letter word before he hit the road.

XV

Henderson had hardly slept for three nights, and he wished desperately that the National Council would come to an end. They were meeting in the Concert Room on the first floor of the ancient house in Edinburgh called Gladstone's Land. The windows were shut to silence the noise of the demonstrators in the Lawnmarket outside. They had started an hour and a half ago, and it was not going well.

'Of course I accept many of the criticisms which John Mackie and Margaret Merrilies have made,' he said, keeping his patience. 'But this isn't a statement of our demands, it's a negotiated document. Already Harvey and the King have gone beyond the Compact, with the plan for a Prince of Scotland. I'm quite sure that we can't go back to Harvey with a list of further demands—unless of course we're aiming for a breakdown and the violence which will follow. But I haven't heard anyone advocate that openly this morning.'

Something hard thrown from the street below hit the window-frame, and they heard a muffled shout. Mackie smiled. All morning he had been relentless and skilful, quietly pointing out each ambiguity in the Compact and interpreting it in the most pessimistic way.

'I think we'd all agree that James Henderson has done his best,' he said. 'But equally I'm sure that we can't recommend this document to our members as any kind of substitute for the full independence to which we're pledged.'

Henderson's patience broke. 'I'm sure we can, provided we stop bickering and squabbling about it. It gives us everything of substance that we need for Scotland, far more than we could reasonably have hoped for. And I must add that I wish John Mackie had made some of these points earlier. He was mighty quiet when he first saw the Compact at Hexham.'

They had all been speaking from their seats, but now Margaret Merrilies got to her feet. She had criticised but not so far committed herself against the Compact, and had agreed warmly with the idea of a Prince of Scotland. Instead of speaking she strode to the window and opened it. Below in the Lawnmarket a single line of police protected the entrance of Gladstone's Land from a crowd of about three hundred, mostly students. At the sight of her they gave a ragged cheer and flourished their banners, COMPACT = COLONIALISM, REMEMBER HAMISH STUART, SCOTLAND SAYS NO SURRENDER, and a montage of Henderson, complete with glasses and stiff white collar, hanging from a gallows. Four of them carried a blue blanket, the traditional symbol of Edinburgh protest.

'There is the Scotland of the future,' proclaimed Mrs Merrilies, raising a second cheer with a downward sweep of her massive arm. 'Those are the people we must persuade, not sitting here behind closed doors, but out in the market places and on the moors.' She closed the window and resumed her seat with an air of satisfaction, as if she had said something decisive.

Mackie spoke again. 'I suggest we have a ten-minute recess. I think that within that time my friends and I could work out a proposal which would be generally acceptable.'

It was agreed. Mackie and Mrs Merrilies went upstairs with their supporters. The rest of the members hung about, chatting in low voices, at the far end of the Concert Room. Someone brought Henderson a cup of coffee, but otherwise he was left alone. He did not get up from his chair, but looked up at the dark timbered ceiling, with its paintings of birds and flowers. In all his political career he had never felt so drained of strength. The careful calculations made at Hexham had been knocked askew by the Merrilies broadcast, the stupid incident with the students and now the explosion on the Forth Bridge. The SLA were nothing if not inventive: posing as an RE Bomb Disposal Squad they had demolished the toll gates on the southern approach and driven off the northern end.

Henderson jotted down his latest calculation, but got no comfort from it.

In favour of the Compact, seven: his own men, east-coasters mainly, shrewd and middle-class. Against, five: Mackie's Clydesiders and a militant Lallans poet. Un-decided, five: Mrs Merrilies plus a ragbag of Highlanders and trade unionists. He had noticed Mackie and Mrs Merrilies exchange notes: five and five made ten. But he could do no more; if they wrecked the Compact they would have to find a new leader.

When they took their seats again, Mackie spoke with new authority.

'That was ten minutes well spent. I think that all of us round this table can now accept the Compact as it stands.' Henderson was too tired for surprise. 'But a majority of us ask you, James, to write a letter of clarification to me as our spokesman. We have worked out a draft, which is short and simple.' Mackie passed a sheet of paper down the table to Henderson.

Henderson read it once, then a second time, and relief flooded through his mind. It was blather, simple blather, of the kind he had heard spouted from Nationalist platforms for a decade now. Margaret Merrilies had stood firm. Mackie must have realised he was beaten and worked out a face-saver. The Compact was agreed, that was all that mattered.

'This will be a confidential letter?' he asked Mackie.

'Of course. It is simply an assurance to those of us who would have liked the Compact to go further.'

'Then I agree.'

Letter from James Henderson to John Mackie.

On the occasion of the acceptance of the Compact of Hexham by the National Council of the Scottish National Party I write to confirm that:

(a) The party's commitment to the principle of complete independence remains;

(b) the party will continue by every means to work towards the realisation of this aim.

SHORT COLD SUMMER

I

'But John, he's won.'

'The letter, woman, read the letter,' Mackie said.

Sukey looked again at Henderson's letter. 'So. Where does that get us?'

'First rule for revolutionary leaders, forgotten alas by the great Guevara—never entrust policy to your mistress.'

'First rule for a man losing an argument, try to be funny.'

'Henderson is finished.'

'He's run rings round you, he and Harvey together, and all the great John Mackie can do is sit cracking jokes in his Y-fronts.'

'Harvey is finished.'

'Seriously,' Sukey said, 'I've got to take something back to them. What do we do now?'

Mackie began to walk about the room. 'We wait,' he said. 'Stir the pot, turn up the heat in September. We've lost the first round, so now we box clever, wear the other fellow down till he starts lashing out.'

'Trying always not to mix our metaphors.'

'The important thing is to keep the organisation intact. That goes for everyone, you and me included. Especially you and me. Now sooner or later someone is going to cotton on to these little meetings . . .'

Sukey's head sank in disappointment. 'I wondered when that was coming.'

Mackie came back to the bed and sat beside her. 'Look, love, we know they're after a girl, we know they've got their eye on me. If they find a link we're in trouble.'

'Yes.'

'It's not for long. We'll keep in touch through McShane.'

'Whatever you say.'

'Thought from Chairman Mackie: Abstinence makes the heart grow fonder.'

'You *are* full of beans, aren't you?'

'You could call it that. One more time then . . .'

'What about Levi?'

'Oh, yes, Levi. I've got a little job for him. I've been doing some letter writing myself.'

II

'Ah, you're back.' Levi jumped to his feet as she came through the door. 'Look, darling, I don't want to be a bore but I'm getting a tiny bit sick of aunty's chateau and your boy-scout friends. Not Donald's scene at all.'

'You're leaving,' Sukey said.

'You said that weeks ago.'

'To-morrow.'

'To-morrow!' Levi clapped his hands with delight. 'Oh, bless you.'

'There's a condition.'

'Anything.'

Sukey handed him an envelope. 'We want you to deliver this.'

'No address?'

'Here.' Sukey took a crumpled scrap of paper from her bag. 'Commit to memory.'

'Bucholz . . .' Levi looked up in astonishment. 'What—not *the* Bucholz?'

'No questions. Just memorise. You're to hand the letter to him personally, no one else. If anything goes wrong destroy it.'

'Will they let me through?'

'It's a private villa, he'll be on holiday. Just hang about

till you can see him. After that you can do what you like.
I expect he'll help.'

'Oh, but this is marvellous. I mean, I had no idea . . .'

III

Minute to Director-General, Security Service, August 28th

CONFIDENTIAL

Scottish Extremists
Following our talk, I visited Glasgow last week, and I
regret there is little to report. Our inquiries there fall under
5 main heads:—

1. *SLA Command.* Special Branch consider Mackie the
   likeliest candidate but have no evidence. On the surface his activities are consistent with normal political
   duties, and he is careful to avoid any public statement
   of support for violence.
2. *Local Branches.* SLA Sections in Stirling, Lanark and
   Galashiels have been uncovered, resulting in a total of
   28 arrests. Similar operations in Dunbar and Kinross
   were forestalled by the disappearance of all principal
   suspects. Steps have been taken to tighten Police
   security.
3. *Penetration.* In May we succeeded in installing an in-
   formant within the SLA, which led to valuable information at Hexham. Since that time he has failed to
   make contact, and we must now accept the possibility
   that he has been compromised. He has no dependants.
4. *Arms.* Cameron informed me that these continue to
   be found in substantial quantities. All weapons are of
   the standard types now used in NATO, with markings
   removed. UK Ordnance factories and depots were

checked in July without result. An overseas source now seems probable. Coastal authorities have been informed.

5. *Communications*. The SLA Command use a female courier operating under a codename, and her identification would be a major advance. CID are lending full assistance, but failing a fuller description rapid results are unlikely.

I attach a letter to Hart for your approval.

S. G. Harrap.

Letter from S.G. Harrap, Curzon House, W.1 to Graham Hart, September 3rd

CONFIDENTIAL—BY HAND

You will not be surprised to learn that my report to the DG was greeted with some disappointment. As you know, we are under the strongest pressure to resolve this business before the end of the Parliamentary Recess. An outbreak of violence during the passage of the Scotland (Devolution of Government) Bill could have the most serious consequences. Despite the apparent failure of your original mission, I cannot accept that your presence in Glasgow is no longer justified; it is essential that we maintain the closest contact with other security forces on the spot, and our own effort should certainly not be less than theirs. I repeat, we do most emphatically need some more positive result before the end of this month.

IV

Levi waited in a cool sparsely furnished room with a tiled floor. Through the window a jumble of pink roofs shimmered in the sun, and the sea was a dazzling blue. After a time the woman came back and led him through the villa and out on to a terrace, where a short bald man sat beneath a vine. As they came towards him he rose without smiling and held out his hand.

'Sit down, Mr Levi.'

'Thank you.'

'Here, in the shade.'

'Thank you.'

'This letter you have brought me . . . I would like you to take a reply.'

'A reply? But I'm not going back.'

'You will use the same route, and give it only to the girl. The boat leaves in ten days. Until that time you will be our guest.'

'Now wait a minute, please,' Levi said, his voice shrill with protest. 'No one told me about a reply. I mean, surely, you have other ways . . .'

'Yes, but for the moment you are the best.'

'I'm sorry, I can't. I'm finished there.'

'Mr Levi, you force me to remind you that your choice in this matter is restricted. You entered this country illegally, without papers. You are wanted by your own police. I have only to pick up that telephone . . .'

'Wouldn't that be rather embarrassing?'

'Ah. You mean that you could inform the British authorities of my support for the Scottish autonomists. Yes, my friend, you could. But that hypothesis depends on the assumption that you would still be alive, does it not?'

Levi sank back on the little iron chair and his mouth dropped open. 'I see.'

'I'm glad.'

'Don't beat about the bush do you?'

'I merely present the facts. Your co-operation on the other hand will most certainly be rewarded—in the form, shall we say, of papers and immediate passage to Havana? If that is what you want.'

'When I get back.'

'The day itself. So with those limitations you have a choice.'

V

The mad scene from *Lucia,* in a concert performance, was trying to the limit the patience of the burgesses of Edinburgh. The woman had lost her senses, and to spend twenty-five minutes illustrating the point in a foreign language imposed a strain which even the presence in dinner jackets of their Lord Provost, the Secretary of State for Scotland and Mr James Henderson did not remove. It was a hot evening, and they were glad to spend the interval relaxing on the terrace outside the Usher Hall. In the gardens below the fireworks had already started. As between fireworks and Donizetti the choice of Edinburgh was clear.

'A grand error to hold the Festival this year.'

The statue of Sir Walter Scott, bathed in pink light beneath his canopy, was suddenly surrounded by leaping rockets.

'I beg to differ. We could not let ourselves be flummoxed by a bomb or two.'

'I was thinking of the deficit.'

'Ah, the deficit . . .'

The two citizens observed a moment's silence for balance sheets in distress. To their right beyond Sir Walter Scott and the line of shops in Princes Street a warm glow became visible.

'That's a new variety of illumination, is it not?'

The glow swelled and brightened.

'The burden on the rates will be terrible.'

A man standing to one side of them turned, and they saw it was Henderson. 'Look again,' he said and moved quickly away into the darkness. They looked again. A column of flame shot into the air and outlined against it they could see a crumbling roof.

Extracts from The Scotsman, *September 12th*

PLAYING WITH FIRE

The fire which last night destroyed Saint Andrews House, seat of the administration of Scotland, may have been accidental. It is a sign of the times that until that is proved, the assumption must be that it was arson, the latest in a series of increasingly violent incidents mounted by extremists to discredit the Compact of Hexham. If so, it is an act which all decent Scots will condemn. Wisely, the SNP has already done so, and it is good to see that even Mr John Mackie felt compelled on this occasion to associate himself with the party's statement.

That said, it must also be said that the loss of this bastion of Westminster will not be mourned by the bulk of the Scottish people. Nor is it an architectural loss to the city of Robert Adam. A certain jubilation in the crowd which collected in Waterloo Place was both predictable and understandable and there can be no excuse for the behaviour of the police. The occasion called for calm and tact, not the indiscriminate use of batons and gas shells. The arrival of Colonel Cameron and his now notorious stormtroopers merely worsened an already explosive situation . . .

VI

Mackie waited for five minutes then followed her out of the pub and across the courtyard to the small double room above the old stables. He came in noisily, slammed the door behind him and locked it. Their suitcases were still on the bed unpacked. 'And who the bloody hell was that?' he said.

Sukey turned to face him with a look of terror. 'Oh, John, I'm so *sorry*. I just never expected . . .'

'Well who, for Christ's sake?'

'Gerry Plumer . . . I used to know him slightly in London.'

'Did he see us together?'

Sukey shook her head miserably. 'He didn't say.'

'Would he know me?'

'No, I don't think so.'

Mackie walked to the window and looked down into the courtyard. A gaggle of geese had collected outside the kitchen window for scraps. It was a cheerless grey afternoon, the summer had gone. 'I thought you said this was the safest pub in Scotland.'

'Janet would never breathe a word.'

'Bully for Janet. Why did you drag me up here, anyway?'

'I wanted to see you. It's been a long time.'

'You *had* to see me.'

'Oh, forget it. I'm sorry.'

'Now, please—you're not the crying type.'

'It's just . . . this hanging about. I just wish the whole thing was settled, one way or the other. That's all. I'm weak and silly, and I'm sorry.'

Mackie put a hand on her shoulder. 'We must keep it going till Blackpool.'

'Blackpool?'

'Let's get out of here. Will they mind if we cancel the room?'

'Janet will understand.'

As she patched up her face Mackie said, 'Plumer . . . Haven't I seen him on the box? What does he do?'

'Gerry? I'm not sure. He's a sort of retired satirist, something to do with that magazine . . .'

VII

Extract from Private Eye, *September 30th*

THERE'S MANY A MACKIE MAKES A MUCKIE
(Scots proverb)

Rumours that John Mackie, SNP Member for Glasgow

Central, is to marry Lady Sukey Dunmayne, only daughter of the Eighth Earl of Dunmayne, are to be discounted. It is thought that a temporary interest in the Highland fling is not sufficient to overcome the barriers of class involved, as indeed could be said of the movement to which they belong.

'Seen this?' Rennie said.
Hart nodded. 'Bloody little rag.'
'Required reading at the Yard, I'm told.'
'I'll stick to *Punch*.'
'Dunmayne—we ruled her out.'
'Too respectable, you said.'
'To work then.'

SB CYPHERTEL GLAS 003 DTG 1430210 PASS IMMEDIATE HARRAP CURZONHOUSE FROM HART BEGINS CONFIRM SUSAN DUNMAYNE OPENED SECOND ACCOUNT FEB 78 NATIONAL LINEN AND COMMERCIAL BANK EDINBURGH SUPPLIED BY MONTHLY TRANSFER £2000 (TWO THOUSAND) FROM NUMBERED ACCOUNT INTERBANK GENEVA WITHDRAWALS REPEAT WITHDRAWALS CASH ONLY STOP SUGGEST I PURSUE URGENT GENEVA RENNIE CAN HANDLE HERE ENDS

SB CYPHERTEL LON 157 DTG 1703210 IMMEDIATE HART FROM HARRAP CURZONHOUSE BEGINS YOUR GLAS 003 AGREE RETURN HERE SOONEST PREPARE ONWARD FLIGHT GENEVA GOOD SHOW ENDS

VIII

'At Blackpool this year, isn't it? The papers say Harvey will have trouble putting across that Compact of his.'
It was a pity that Ian Dunmayne insisted on talking politics. Thorganby did not want to have to think about the Conservative Conference. Dunmayne's dinner had been surprisingly sound, and instead of port there was a malt

whisky which Thorganby remembered from his last visit.

The strenuous day on the moor was paying its dividend: he would be stiff in the morning, but now his body felt pleasantly exercised and his face fresh where the rain had lashed it. The candlelight flickered over the silver, hardly reaching the panelled embrasures and the high ceiling with its stiff Victorian plasterwork. Thorganby noticed that the splendid carpet from the Summer Palace at Peking had disappeared; most of his friends lived tolerably by selling something good every two or three years.

'What does Sukey say?' he asked. His god-daughter had said little at dinner; but she had looked superb, no jewels, long green dress setting off her neck and shoulders putting to shame the smudged smoking jackets of the men.

'Oh, you've heard?' Dunmayne was for the first time downcast. 'About this fellow Mackie, I mean.'

'There's been some talk.'

'You can probably tell me more than I know myself. When she told me we had a frightful row. But it got us nowhere, and if I'd gone on she'd have stopped coming home. So I shut up, and she shut up, and we're rubbing along. But I wish . . .' Dunmayne stopped in mid-sentence. He had no other child.

'She looks very well.' By which the Earl of Thorganby meant, and the Earl of Dunmayne understood, that Sukey despite her unfortunate connection was not scruffy, long-haired or loud-mouthed.

'Oh, she's got her mother's looks, and her mother's style.' The Countess now lived in Long Island with a man who owned twelve bad and profitable newspapers. There was a pause, then Dunmayne returned to political gossip. 'But what about the Blackpool Conference, David? Do you mean to speak?'

'I haven't made up my mind whether to go.' In fact Thorganby was almost sure he wouldn't go. Even at the height of his career as a Cabinet Minister, Blackpool and Brighton had been a penance. Now he was out, forgotten, a face people would just notice as they passed on the front, a face they could not quite put a name to. They would all be talking about Scotland, and he hated listening to speeches on subjects which he cared about. There would be a lot of claptrap about 'moving with the times' and 'this day and age.' His wife would insist on going with him, and would then be offended because she wasn't asked to the smart parties. No, it would be better to stay at home.

'But what about the Compact?' asked Dunmayne. '*The Scotsman* says there'll be a big row.'

'I doubt it,' said Thorganby. 'Harvey will have the Conference sewn up, and they'll approve the Compact with a standing ovation. That's the way the world goes.'

It was a thick soft night without stars. The two Labradors scratched and snuffled in the rhododendrons, reluctant to end the last expedition of the day. It had seemed a good idea to offer to share this duty with his god-daughter, but now that they were alone on the sandy path Thorganby did not know what to say. Sukey had put a coat over her dress; he could not see her face.

'We talked politics after you'd left us at dinner,' he said lamely.

'I thought you would; the Laird is always longing to.'

The use of her father's old nickname encouraged him. 'I hear you're pretty well involved yourself.'

She stopped. They had reached the end of the garden, where the ground fell away to the loch below. 'Yes, but not in your way. You talk about elections and compacts and majorities, but all that's irrelevant now. We're just not interested in it any more.'

Her voice was harsh, almost insolent. At dinner she had offended them both with an astonishingly abusive tirade against Cameron and the Army. Thorganby thought of a pretty girl in white, a smile of uncomplicated enjoyment on her face, dancing reels into the dawn in a castle in Skye. Eight years had passed, and the smile with them.

'What is important to you then?' he asked.

'To get our way, by any means necessary. We know we're right, and the people are behind us. So why should we wait?'

'Is that what Mackie tells you?'

'What's that supposed to imply? I can think for myself, thank you.' Then she controlled herself. 'I'm sorry, but it's no use talking to you, Uncle David, we could be at it all night, and you wouldn't begin to understand.'

She turned, and they walked back up to the massive porch in silence. He had failed. But that night, looking out of his window to catch a glimmer of the loch, Thorganby decided to go to the Conference.

SWINGING BLACKPOOL

I

Article by Political Correspondent of The Times, *Tuesday October 5th.*

HARVEY SET TO WIN BLACKPOOL BATTLE
SCOTS COMPACT UNDER FIRE

Blackpool is known for its brisk breezes, and it looks as if the Prime Minister will be packing his sou'wester for the Tory Conference which starts there to-morrow. Heavy stormclouds are building up from the direction of Scotland, and Mr Harvey will need his proven powers of navigation to steer the conference safely into port.

Before Parliament rose for the summer recess the omens for this year's conference were good. In a masterly feat of diplomacy Mr Harvey had secured at Hexham the promise of Scottish Nationalist support while managing to preserve the Union. The Scottish Tories were enraged, but at Smith Square protests from north of the border have never counted for much. The stage seemed set for a personal triumph at Blackpool, and a standing ovation for the leader who against the odds had won for the Tories the gift they most wanted and least expected —another five years of power.

But now the weather has changed for the worse. The rising swell of violence has scandalised the party of law and order. Tories have long been accustomed to bombs and similar nonsense from the Irish, the Arabs and other lesser breeds; but Scottish terrorism has come as a rude shock. The impression has grown that Henderson is not master in his own house; yet if he cannot control his supporters, what is the use of the celebrated Compact of Hexham? These misgivings have been strengthened by the recent speeches of the SNP leaders John Mackie and Mrs Merrilies, who have clearly indicated that they will press for amendments to the bill which will come before the Commons in November—this despite the fact that the bill will carry out the undertakings given by Harvey and accepted by Henderson at Hexham.

Doubts and suspicions are now rife in many sectors of the Tory Party. Will they find a leader who can turn this discontent into a full-scale revolt? Here the composition of the Blackpool Conference is important. It is a conference of the Tory Party of England and Wales. The Scottish rank and file, many of whom are now virulent against Harvey, will not be there. The Chairman of the Scottish Tory Party is invited as a matter of courtesy, but he is a Harvey appointee and a safe man; Scullard, the Secretary of State for Scotland, has put his name to the Compact and has no personal following—which leaves only the Deputy Chairman of the Scottish Party, Lord Thorganby. Thorganby has been virtually out of politics since the Rhodesian crisis, and though he has held on to the office of Deputy Chairman this has been simply a recognition of his distinguished personal position. His views on the new turn in Scottish politics are unknown, and it seems unlikely that he will break this silence at Blackpool.

The omens are for a lively debate on the Scottish question, then a closing of ranks and a reluctant but unanimous vote in favour of Harvey's policy. Tories hate not to follow the Leader; more important, they need the thirty-odd SNP votes to retain a majority in the Commons, and no one has suggested any other way than Harvey's of keeping the Government in power. It will take more than the grumblings of lairds and backwoodsmen to persuade them to pack their tents and leave the Promised Land for the political wilderness.

II

Sukey was gay, Mackie silent as they drove south along
the front, past a row of floodlit hotels, first line of defence
against the Atlantic wind, the Winter Gardens, the Tower,
raking the night sky with its searchlight, and on down
the Golden Mile, kilowatts of noise and colour, land of the
pin machine and one-armed bandit. On the seaward side,
between the tramlines and the beach, the illuminations
bobbed and glowed—Disneyland, Zootime, Astronauts,
Bikini Girls—a continuous frieze to shut out of sight and
mind the works of Nature beyond. At Blackpool the sea
is the enemy. The sea is free.

Harvey's portrait, carefully bronzed and dewrinkled, was
scattered about above the legend 'The Man You Know'.
Along the promenade cohorts of the faithful hurried from
cocktail to cocktail and the sideshows of politics fused
with the razzle-dazzle: MONDAY CLUB, LUNAPARK, PEST,
PLAYLAND, IMPACT, JOHN BRAINE, GIPSY PETULENGRO, CROSS-
BOW, NOVELTIES, FREEDOM, ROCK, CONSERVATIVES MAKE
LIFE BETTER.

Sukey kept up a running commentary. The more she
laughed the crosser Mackie got; he wasn't sure which
offended him most, the sneering at working-class taste
or the revelation that she considered all politics ridiculous.
He had an urge to say something wounding. She was so
damnably self-assured. Tories in the mass made him nervous.

'Where is this place?' he said.

'Fleetwood Drive, I've got it on the map. Keep going.'

'Are you sure he's there?'

'Yes, and hating it as much as you will.'

'I find that hard to believe.'

Sukey looked over her shoulder. The Vauxhall was
still behind. Since the story in *Private Eye* she had been
followed day and night. A student from Strathclyde

had taken over as courier, and she and Mackie had decided to brazen it out. 'Our friend doesn't give up easily,' she said.

'Never mind about him, tell me more about this godfather of yours.'

'Like what?'

'I'm wondering what to do if he accuses me of forgery.'

'I'm sure he wouldn't believe anyone capable of such evil. Anyway, he can check it with Henderson.'

'The debate's to-morrow,' Mackie said.

'He could telephone to-night.'

'Henderson might deny it.'

Sukey thought. 'Well, couldn't he listen in while you phone? You could ask Henderson if he objects to the letter being published—something like that.'

'Yes, that's not bad. Henderson will object, of course, but that should be enough to prove I'm not a liar. Just when I decide you're really stupid you go and say something rather bright.'

'Oh, John, *look*! You know, I think this place comes very near my idea of hell . . .'

Mackie let it go; he was feeling more cheerful. Blackpool faded into Lytham St Anne's, empty streets lined with dolls' houses in very red brick, tongues of sand drifting off the dunes to pile against neat garden walls. After the Golden Mile it was like a cemetery.

Which was part of the attraction for the Palmers. The Palmers loathed noise, hotels, public functions in general and Conservative Conferences in particular. As an MP Palmer could hardly escape, but having tamed his constituents and given up hope of office he could afford to keep his distance. His wife Lydia would venture from Belgravia only if guaranteed fun. Their solution was to hire a house on the edge of town and stock it with their own claret, servants and cronies from London. From this base the Conference itself could be raided for amusing or important dinner guests, and on a good night it was possible to create the impression that the centre of gravity had shifted to a semi in Fleetwood Drive.

To-night was not quite in that class. Crowded into the front room of the little house, among the glass giraffes and Tretchikoff pictures, were Hector Probyn, editor of *The Spectator*, Laura Mangold, novelist and star of *Any Questions*, the Countess of Islay, the Minister of Defence, Simonetta La Cruz, Lord and Lady Thorganby, and Gerry Plumer, court jester. Something was lacking, Lydia felt, and as if by telepathy the telephone had rung. Sukey herself was long missed, but Mackie was a bonus—that potential for embarrassment without which no good party was complete. Conversation picked up.

'What's he doing here anyway?'

'He's got a press card.'

'Blackpool correspondent of the *Scots Independent*.'

'That's just a cover.'

'A social-climbing Scottish Bolshevik—beat that for a nauseating combination.'

'Actually he's awfully sweet.'

'Bad teeth.'

'But quite sexy, don't you think, in a sort of lean, mad way?'

'Sukey must be out of her mind.'

'What happened to her anyway?'

'Perhaps she got tired of people like us . . .'

The event was less dramatic than Lydia had hoped. Mackie was quiet and conventionally dressed, didn't ask for beer, didn't rant; and indeed had no cause to take offence. Whatever might be said of the Palmers' salon they were not bigots; their undeniable capacity for nastiness was only really set in motion by a boor or a toady. Mackie was neither, and soon had a following—cause for needle in the breast of Gerry Plumer. Since both were working for it, it was only a question of time before they were stranded in a corner.

'You're quite a success,' Plumer said.

Mackie was genial. 'Off the record, that makes my evening.'

'What's this, a last fling before the revo?'

'Strictly business. You?'

'Pleasure, all pleasure.'

'The pleasure of servicing Lady Islay during the afternoon debates?'

'What a tasteless remark.'

'Ah, taste—now there's an elastic word. Lucky for you I have the taste not to repeat it in Greek Street.'

'Mr Mackie, you have the self-satisfied look of a man who's on his favourite subject.' The Countess of Islay was between them with a rustle of silk.

'I am, Lady Islay, I am.'

'And what's that?'

'Protecting your reputation.'

A malevolent angel was overhead; the remark lobbed into the silence like an unexploded grenade. No one dared to pick it up. Lady Islay's reputation survived to the extent that everyone knew about her and Gerry but no one was sure who else knew. Rescue came unexpectedly from Lord Thorganby, who banged down his glass on the Kosiglow fire and placed a hand on Mackie's back.

'Come on, let's take a walk. Excuse us, Lydia—it's not every day I meet a man I completely disagree with.'

Sukey could have kissed him.

Inhaling the cold sea air, they strode along the pavement together. There was common ground there somewhere, but neither felt the need to seek it out. Across the street a man sat smoking in a Vauxhall. 'Thank you,' Mackie said finally.

Thorganby made a dismissive sound, somewhere between a chuckle and a growl; his favourite substitute for speech. 'A glutton for punishment, aren't you?'

'I like to get a look at the opposition.'

Thorganby, cautiously: 'If you and Sukey are to make a go of this—and personally I wish you well—you'll both have to lose a few friends.'

'Actually I came looking for you.'

'Me?'

Mackie pulled an envelope from his pocket. Thorganby opened it and stood reading in the lamplight, looked up, seemed about to give it back, then read again. 'Can I keep this?'

'That's the idea.'

'When was it written?'

'After Hexham.'

'The price of your support?'

'Yes.'

Thorganby examined the taut young face before him, sickly green in the lamplight; a nervous, tigerish man, impervious to argument. But not dishonest. 'You're a politician,' he said, 'so I take it you know what you're doing. And I think I understand your motives . . .'

'This alliance is based on a complete misreading of popular feeling in Scotland.'

'You're beginning to sound like me.' Thorganby smiled. Deep below his solid exterior he nursed a sympathy with the flamboyant. 'And you'd prefer an open fight?'

'It'll mean less trouble in the end.'

'I'm inclined to agree. But with respect, before I can act I must be convinced that this is genuine.'

Mackie laughed. 'I thought you'd say that. Let's find a telephone . . .'

III

As George Scullard left the Young Conservative Ball and walked towards his car he was thinking that of all the jobs in the Government, Secretary of State for Scotland must be the least rewarding. He was in the Cabinet only because the Scots insisted that his office carry Cabinet rank; if Harvey dismissed him the Scots would howl for joy, no colleagues would object and everyone would forget him in a week. Whatever went wrong north of the border was his fault. Whatever went right was nothing to do with him. The Nats had labelled him Plastic Mac, and the name had stuck. His own party was scarcely more grateful; to-morrow morning Harvey would take the credit for Hexham, while to-morrow evening he, Scullard, would fulfil his only official task of the week—a lecture to the Conservative Political Centre.

Already the papers were commenting on Harvey's decision to handle the Scottish debate himself. The Chairman of the Party had taken Scullard aside during the supper interval and told him how highly everyone thought of him. Scullard had let the man pay for his whisky, but he was not deceived.

The strains of the last waltz pursued him across the car park. That would be followed by the Gallop, Auld Lang Syne and three cheers for something or other. He had got away just in time.

Pausing, hand on the door of his car, Scullard wondered what it was about young politicians that he found so depressing—all that energy and ambition, the love of organisation, the moralising pomposity . . . Perhaps what rankled most was to be reminded so precisely of his own beginnings, the patient progress through years of Gay Gordons and Hokey-Cokeys to that first trembling kiss, Wedding of the Year and a son-in-law's place on the board of the drapers in Princes Street. In those days success had been fun.

The moon shone bright and still on the roofs of the cars. The air was turbulent, full of the roar and salt smell of the sea; the tide must be coming in. A man in a dinner jacket appeared on the ballroom steps; he seemed to be waving to someone. A car horn blew twice. Scullard recognised the juvenile councillor from Aberdeen who had dogged him all evening with obsequious conversation. Time to be away; he opened the door and sank wearily on to the seat.

'Dinny muve or ye're deid.'

Power is relative to the situation. What use a place in the Cabinet to a man with a Browning automatic in the back of his neck? At least he has more than the usual right to a cry of outraged authority:

'Look here, what is this?'

'Okay, Micky, get his hands.'

'Do you know who I am?'

The gun rammed into the base of his skull, crushing his face against the wheel. His nose began to bleed.

'Aye, we know. Noo gie us yer hands or Ah'll belt ye.'

'Certainly not . . . Oh!'

Nylon cord cut into his wrists. A car pulled into the space alongside.

'A' reet, oot. We're tekkin a trip.'

'I suppose you people are Nationalists . . .'

'Oot, Ah seid.'

'Well this sort of thing gets you nowhere, you know. If you'll all come back to my hotel I'm perfectly willing to talk this out . . . Oh. Oh my God. Oh. No, please . . .'

'Hey, Chibber, lay off. The bastard's bleedin all over me suit.'

IV

Much of the work of a Party Conference is done in the corridors, a great part of it after midnight in the corridors of the main hotel. Here it is possible to see, each night for almost a week, the leading personalities of press and politics collected together in a remote seaside resort and deprived of any company but their own. The atmosphere is informal, the discussion long and intense: an exhilarating break from the Westminster routine, but exhausting in its way.

It was certainly exhausting Jack Kemble, who was propped in a phone booth outside the door of the lounge. As he listened to the thickly accented voice in the receiver his eyes, red with fatigue, stared back at him in the mirror.

'All right, Mac, we'll take a look,' he said into the receiver. 'But God help you if you're having me on.'

He hung up. Breathed deeply, leaned his head on the glass. Was it worth it? He was tempted not to bother. But a small voice was calling through the Highland Mist, and Kemble trusted that voice; it paid the rent, it had never let him down; it was his pride and his life.

In the lounge a male choir reached for the top note of 'Jerusalem'. Traditionally the evening ended with a hymn.

He picked up the phone again.

'Room 201, please . . . Jenny? Sorry to wake you, sweetheart . . . Yes, I know . . . Listen, I've just had a call from some Scottish berk. He says there's a story for us on the North Pier. Won't wait, he says . . . Yes, it could be, but Jack smells trouble. Can we rustle up a camera? Now please, don't get technical . . . I know that . . . Well where are the boys? . . . Thanks . . . No, you go back to sleep. I'll be up later . . . What? . . . Okay, please yourself.'

Insolent bitch.

Steady, Jack. Plenty more where she came from. Waiter, there's a ball in my booth.

'Change the bloody bowler.'

'Come on, Jack, give him a quickie.'

Kemble looked up the corridor. At the far end, barely visible in the sea mist, Joynson was crouched behind a ballroom chair; Chief Whip at mid-on, *Daily Express* in the slips, Ryder Bennett at the crease with a reversed umbrella.

A clutch of hotel staff were looking on, reluctant to intervene as long as the Chancellor of the Exchequer was batting.

Kemble stooped for the ball. The crowd roared. He started his run, fourteen paces, easy action, heavy artillery of the Corporation Occasionals; but to-night there was mist about and the pitch was of polished marble, the ball hit the Hall Porter between the eyes and the bowler went into the furniture. Six feet above his head a vase of chrysanthemums obeyed the laws of gravity. On the North Pier the story waited.

'I think we'd better begin,' said the Chairman of the Conservative Party.

It was 8.31 a.m. In the Dubarry Suite at the headquarters hotel several chairs at the long table were still empty, though round the edge of the room young men in dark suits were sitting on the window-seats or leaning against radiators. The Chairman's morning meetings during the Conference always began like this. As they proceeded the various dignitaries of the Party would enter apologetically and take their seats in a faint aura of kippers and marmalade.

'This morning of course is the Scottish debate,' the Chairman continued. 'We had a little difficulty with the motion, but I think it reads well enough now—not too enthusiastic. I gather you've had some amendments in, Sir Joseph?'

'None that I intend to call.' Sir Joseph Cockcroft, the Liverpool industrialist who presided over this year's Conference, used his large body and vacant heavy face as a disguise. 'But I'll have to give the opposition a fair crack at the main motion. There are quite a few names down to speak against. No one of much substance, and I propose to give them their head.'

'Good.' The Chairman knew that Harvey, winding up the debate, would make a better speech and get a better press if he had some open criticism to reply to.

'There's one point,' said the Central Office Press Officer. 'Some of the press are asking why the PM is taking this debate and not Scullard.'

'That's obvious,' the Chairman said. 'It's a matter of major constitutional importance, and there are plenty of precedents for the Leader of the Party intervening before the final rally. No difficulty about that.' Except of course for Scullard, with whom the Chairman had had that awkward late-night whisky at the YC Ball. 'Right then, let's move on to the afternoon debate on European agricultural policy . . .'

The Chairman broke off to read a note passed to him by his Private Secretary.

'A message from Lord Thorganby. He asks to be allowed to speak against the Scottish motion.'

There was a silence round the table. The Conference had been running with remarkable smoothness. But these were professionals who knew that politics was a matter of continuously assimilating lumpy indigestible facts. The smoothness had been too good to last.

'Surely it's out of order for the Deputy Chairman of the Scottish Party to speak at our Conference,' said the Chairman of the Young Conservatives, who had come to the top through unceasing study of the rule-book. 'Anyway he's too late to put his name down.'

Sir Joseph, cutting the first cigar of the morning, was the only one to laugh. 'There are times when you can use the rules and times when you can't. I'll have to call him if he sticks to it.' He turned to the Chairman. 'Can someone talk him out of it?'

In his mind the Chairman had already run through the list of people who might. 'No,' he said. 'He's been out of the swim too long. But we should be able to find out what line he's taking.'

On the stiff white card which he carried everywhere with him the Chairman wrote: Scullard to see Thorganby. It would give the wretched man something to do.

Sir Joseph was ruminating aloud: 'I'll call him just before Harvey, that way he won't influence the other speeches from the floor. Of course he'll only have five minutes, and as I remember, he's a fairly slow speaker . . .'

And so the Party prepared to digest the latest indigestible fact.

VI

Sir Joseph Cockcroft banged his gavel, and the shuffle of delegates returning from their elevenses was stilled.

'I shall now call on Mr Mitcombe, President of the Stretchford University Conservative Association, and after him I shall call on the Right Honourable the Earl of Thorganby, who will speak against the motion.'

There was a buzz of interest as delegates repeated to each other the information which they had all just heard. Lord Thorganby was a figure from the past linked with strong half-forgotten emotions, virtually silent for several years, and the more powerful for that. Unfortunately Mr Mitcombe interpreted the buzz as encouragement to himself and launched with extra vigour into his carefully studied speech. He was twenty-three but his style was middle-aged; he sported a watch chain and took off his spectacles to illustrate a point. Mr Mitcombe was against colonialism and old-fashioned attitudes towards Scotland; he had confidence in the Compact and the Leader of the Party; in this day and age he was in favour of new thinking and a fresh start. Nobody listened to a word he said.

As the light flashed on the rostrum to warn that his time was nearly up, Joynson, standing at the side of the hall, signalled to someone in the wings. A moment later Harvey emerged on to the platform behind the rostrum and took a carefully vacant chair next to Sir Joseph. It was his first appearance at the Conference, and his Cabinet colleagues on the platform began to clap. The applause was taken up from the floor, and Mr Mitcombe, in mid-peroration, beamed first excited and then confused, as he realised the sudden approval was not for him. He glanced behind, stumbled to a close, then down the steps in front of the massed blue hydrangeas and back to the little posse of stalwarts from Stretchford, who restored his morale with much back-slapping.

There was an expectant pause, then people began to recognise a big burly man, with an outdoor complexion and grey-silver hair, who was making his way up the centre aisle. The clapping began again slowly, then swelled. By the time Lord Thorganby was at the rostrum it was the loudest so far heard that year. On the platform the Cabinet too were clapping decorously.

'A bit ominous,' said one of the stewards to Joynson, as they stood together by a pillar at the back.

'Not yet,' said Joynson. 'So far they're clapping the man, not what he's going to say.'

Thorganby's first words were lost in a muzzy crackle because he spoke too close to the microphone. He withdrew a few inches.

'Sorry,' he said. 'Never quite got the hang of these things.' There was a sympathetic chuckle right round the hall.

'He did that on purpose,' said the steward. 'No,' said Joynson. 'But the effect's the same.'

Thorganby began in a conversational tone.

'This is the first Party Conference I have been to since I left office. They don't seem to have changed very much. So far as I'm concerned, there is one change, which is definitely for the better. Now that I'm speaking from the body of the hall, instead of from up there, I shan't be allowed more than five minutes.'

'I bet he speaks for ten without a peep out of old Cockcroft,' said Joynson.

'I am speaking to-day because I feel very strongly about the future of Scotland. That country has been my home all my life; and I think I know as much about it as those who have spoken earlier this morning. I want to tell you the simple conclusion I've reached about recent events there. I am sure that the stability and prosperity of Scotland depend in the future as in the past on the Union with England, and I am sure. . . .'

A short burst of applause cut into the sentence. Harvey

144

was listening carefully, no expression on his face.

'. . . I am sure that this Compact which the resolution asks us to approve spells the end of the Union. I'm not concerned with the provisions about taxation and capital investment, about which we've heard so much. I've read all those clauses, but I'm not sure that I understand them.'

A sympathetic ripple.

'I'm ready to admit that they've been cleverly and diplomatically negotiated. One would not expect anything less from the Prime Minister. But to my mind that's not the point.' Thorganby dropped the conversational tone abruptly. 'The point is that the Conservative Party, the Unionist Party, our Party, has made a deal with the SNP, a party which proclaims and works openly for the destruction of the Union between England and Scotland. I must tell you that throughout Scotland this is taken to mean that we are prepared to abandon the Union.'

No applause, but everyone was listening.

The television cameras swung round the hall, picking up intent faces.

'Now of course we have been assured that quite the contrary is true. We have been told that it is the Scottish Nationalists who have given up their principles and abandoned their campaign for complete independence. In those glossy little folders which we all receive regularly, Central Office have begun to say some quite nice things about Mr Henderson and the Nationalists. We are told that they have nothing to do with the violence which in these last weeks has been the scourge of Scotland. But we Conservatives in Scotland are a cautious lot. We have always felt that we would need a good deal of proof before we believed that the Nationalists had changed their spots. We were not sure that they had really renounced violence and extremism. You see, we know them quite well; we know what they have been saying, and are still saying, in the pubs and on the doorsteps. So we wanted proof. And yesterday, by chance, proof came into my hands. But, Mr President, it is proof in the opposite sense

145

—proof that the Nationalists are still bent on destroying the Union, proof that they have gulled us, proof that they will use every means without exception to gain their end. I have here a letter, which I believe on excellent authority to be genuine . . .'

Thorganby paused, fishing clumsily in his coat pocket. The cameras swung to focus on him. In the press gallery even the most blasé journalist had his notebook out. Slowly Lord Thorganby read out Henderson's letter to Mackie, the letter signed in exhaustion in the upstairs room above the Lawnmarket four months before.

'. . . the party's commitment to the principle of complete independence remains; the party will continue by every means to work towards the realisation of this aim.'

As he finished reading a murmur grew in the hall. Some delegates did not at once catch the letter's meaning; others began to show their anger; all were enjoying the unexpected meal of drama. A young man from Central Office handed Joynson a note in Harvey's writing: *Stop the press handout. I shall have to ad-lib.*

Lord Thorganby stopped the growing noise with a wave of his hand.

'Just a word in conclusion. We are all concerned this morning about the future of Scotland. I believe that future to be dark indeed unless the Government changes its present course. But we ought also to be concerned about the Conservative Party. I have always had a certain idea of our Party. We have made bad mistakes, we have left undone many things which we ought to have done. But cleverness isn't everything. I believe we have always had a certain good reputation—a reputation for looking beyond the quick trick and the tactical advantage, for safeguarding the true interests of the country, for standing by our principles and our friends. It is to this reputation more than anything else that we owe the success which we have had in my lifetime and in yours. I hope that this Conference will to-day show itself a wise and firm guardian of that reputation.'

Thorganby turned to thank Sir Joseph with a quick nod. By the time he turned to go down the steps of the rostrum the applause had started. He paused for a second, then continued his way back down the aisle to his seat. The noise swelled quickly. Hands were thrust out for him to shake. Isolated groups of people began to stand up, beckoning their neighbours to do the same. 'Standing ovation' scribbled the press, and one or two of them got out their watches. People began to look at the platform. 'Stand up, Harvey!' shouted a beefy young man with ginger hair at the back. A woman threw her hat into the air. On the far left of the platform the Minister of Housing and Local Government got half-way to his feet, glancing irresolutely down the line of his colleagues; most of them were by now clapping slowly. There was a crowd of people round Thorganby in the centre of the hall. Slowly, with a fixed smile, Harvey got to his feet. The few still seated in the body of the hall did the same, and the noise became overwhelming.

'It'll last for fifteen minutes,' said Joynson. 'What'll Harvey say now?' asked the steward. Joynson shrugged. 'Dodge a vote and play for time.'

As the demonstration continued Harvey was talking to Sir Joseph. The Chairman of the Party joined them, a piece of paper in his hands. All three were clearly desperately worried. They were not looking at the delegates at all. Finally Sir Joseph returned to his place and took up the gavel. The first bangs achieved nothing against the uproar. He banged again, and began to shout for order in his great bull voice. Something of his sense of urgency began to communicate itself to the hall. Gradually people began to sit down, and the applause died. Over the remaining claps Sir Joseph shouted:

'Order! Order! I have an announcement to make.'

'No tricks, Joe!' shouted the beefy young man, but his neighbours turned to shush him.

'I have a tragic announcement to make.' Sir Joseph's voice was hoarse. 'I have to tell you that the Secretary of State for Scotland, Mr George Scullard, has suffered a fatal accident here at Blackpool this morning. It appears that he was drowned. In these circumstances I propose to adjourn the session at once. I ask you to leave the hall quietly and in orderly fashion. An announcement about the time of the next session will be made shortly.'

There was a collective gasp. The delegates were no longer a body, but individuals reacting separately to the unexpected. Sir Joseph banged once more, and left his chair. People began to drift out of the doors at the back.

'Saved by the funeral bell,' said the steward.

But Joynson had already sprinted into the wings. He emerged two minutes later, and two journalists, defeated in the first rush to the telephones, seized on him. Death sold papers.

'What happened to Scullard then? Went out of his depth?'

'Too right, you bloodthirsty bastards.'

'Couldn't he swim?'

'It's difficult to swim when you're hanging by a rope from the end of the pier, wrapped in the flag of Saint Andrew.'

REVOLT

I

Hart was ready to burst into song. Beyond the window lake and Alps shone like a dream; inside the atmosphere of Whitehall prevailed, green filing cabinets, regulation carpet and the reek of duty-free Three Nuns. After five months of Scottish hotels and Scottish police stations Geneva was a foretaste of paradise.

'Any good?' he said.

'We do what we can.' Lomax put down the phone and turned on the condescending smile which he reserved for members of the sister service. 'I hope you people won't make a habit of this.'

'It is rather vital.'

'So Harrap said.' To Lomax the national interest was less important than protecting his sources.

'Well?'

'It seems the Lady Dunmayne has a tame Frenchman, one Philippe Le Chat. The money comes in regular transfers from an account in his name at the Banque du Nord, Saint-Brieuc. She transfers it to Edinburgh a few days later.'

'Saint-Brieuc . . . Saint Brieuc in Brittany?'

'I suppose so.'

'It fits. Celt speaks to Celt . . .'

'And now I suppose you'll catch the first jet to Paris. My God, if I had your expenses I could crack every bloody bank in Switzerland.'

II

The bundles of mail, originally addressed to the House of Lords, were delivered to the house in Eaton Place twice a day. Others came direct, thudding through the letter box in big enough packages to make the sealyhams bark. For the second time in his life Lord Thorganby found himself the hero of a large and vocal chunk of the nation. As before over Rhodesia, thousands of letters from unpolitical and very political people, inviting him to open fêtes, stick to his guns, lend ten pounds, make the King sack Harvey, get us out of the Common Market, send a British team to Mars, arrest Henderson, prepare to meet his doom. He had hired a small team of secretaries, and the letters now came to him filleted without envelopes. But this morning on top of the pile was a stiff white envelope marked Strictly Personal. Thorganby came quickly out of the study when he had read it; his wife was deep in her third cup of coffee and the *Daily Telegraph*.

'Harvey wants me to go and have breakfast with him to-morrow.'

'Don't go. He'll only try to get you to retract what you said at Blackpool.' Lady Thorganby, like most women in politics, preferred battle to compromise.

'I must go. He is the Prime Minister.'

'Then tell him for once to behave like one.'

Joynson saw the name on the list of next day's engagements and walked straight into the Prime Minister's room.

'Surely you don't want the Press to have this one?'

Harvey smiled, and Joynson noted that he was back on form after the trauma of Blackpool.

'Lord Thorganby is very respectable.'

'You know perfectly well I can't give them any guidance unless you tell me why you're wasting good corn flakes on the man who cut you up last week.'

'I don't want you to give any guidance,' Harvey replied. 'Just play it straight.'

'That's the best way of making sure the press plays it crooked.'

Harvey began to sort the papers on his desk. It was his usual gesture of dismissal.

III

The rendezvous was fixed for first light on Tuesday: longitude 7, latitude 57, Sea of the Hebrides, between Rhum and Eriskay. *The Western Isles,* OB 014, was on time, but the gale got there first.

Levi watched from the wheelhouse of *L'Appel du Large,* crammed between the captain and the echo sounders. Gouts of spray were arching up from the bows to slap against the glass. *Le Large* had never looked less appealing; black mountains of water rolling eastward under low cloud, whipped by a blast of polar continental air. The two boats circled at a distance, ducking and soaring through the spume, signal lights flashing as they rose from a trough together. The captain yelled at an oilskinned shape clinging to the outside of the wheelhouse.

'*Il a compris?*'

'*Oui, il s'en va.*'

'*Vive l'Ecosse!*'

'*Quelle merde de pays.*'

As he saw the Scottish boat turn away Levi gave a cry of protest and was almost flung down the gangway. 'You want to swim? *Allez, en bas.*'

Below was a narrow passage lined with fetid wooden coffins. Levi's was worse than the rest, his blankets encrusted with half-digested food; he had run out of Dramamine in the Irish Sea. Kicking off his boots, he lay in the mess and groaned. Everyone was shouting. They were cutting loose the crates and dumping them over the side.

It was chaos but was it organised? *L'Appel du Large* did not inspire confidence. For a start the sea came right through her belly: that kept the lobsters alive and was convenient for the rifles. He could hear them through the bulkhead, rolling from side to side in their waterproof bundles, sloshing through the helpless crustaceans to pile against the hull, and suddenly everything was sliding one way, the world was on its head, the sea was in the cabin, blankets, mattresses, boots, plates, mugs, everything airborne in search of the lowest point. Levi tumbled from his bunk. Thrashing wildly for a hold he lifted his head from the water and, as promptly as he had adopted him, deserted Krishna for his childhood faith.

IV

Extract from The Guardian, *Tuesday, October 18th*

HARVEY IN BID FOR PARTY UNITY

SURPRISE CHALLENGE TO THORGANBY PLANNED

By Cornelia Margoff, Political Correspondent.

Downing Street was tight-lipped yesterday over the news that the Prime Minister will give breakfast this morning to Lord Thorganby. It will be the first time the two men have met since Thorganby tore Harvey's Scottish policy to shreds in his sensational speech at Blackpool last week. Seasoned observers reckon that only the even more sensational news of John Scullard's murder saved Harvey from a dramatic Conference defeat. But the day of reckoning may only have been postponed. Scullard's death, still being investigated, has set off a muffled explosion at the grassroots of the Party. Middle-of-the-roaders who had been inclined to give Harvey the benefit of the doubt were yesterday openly urging Thorganby to head an out-and-out revolt against any further Tory dealings with Scottish Nationalist leader James Henderson. But Harvey has nailed his colours to the mast of a policy of conciliation in Scotland. At this morning's breakfast he is likely to give Thorganby a dramatic warning against playing with fire. Those who know the Prime Minister best believe that he will make a powerful appeal to Thorganby not to persist in a campaign which could tear the Tory Party to pieces. It remains to be seen whether at this eleventh hour such an appeal will fall on deaf ears . . .

The toastrack and the coffee pot were almost empty. The two men had been alone for ninety minutes.

'Then you will take it?' Harvey said.

'You don't give me much choice. After what you've said about future policy . . .'

'I'm very glad—and grateful. It would be best to announce it at once.'

The King has been pleased to approve the appointment of the Right Honourable the Earl of Thorganby KT as Secretary of State for Scotland in place of the late Mr George Scullard. At the same time it was announced that the Government intended to recall Parliament at once to consider a Public Order (Scotland) Bill to be published later to-day. The Bill will suspend constitutional guarantees in Scotland and grant special powers to the authorities to detail without trial persons suspected of instigating violence and disorder. The Bill already published for implementing certain measures of constitutional reform in Scotland will not be proceeded with.

'Now can I ask what it means?' said Joynson.

'Isn't it clear?' Harvey looked as if he had won a battle, and this made his Press Secretary mad.

'It's clear to the press. Sellout by Harvey, Scotland to go under colonial rule. You'll get stick from all the opinion-formers to-morrow.'

'The one thing the opinion-formers don't do in this country is form opinion.'

This was Joynson's own doctrine, and he switched the line of attack. 'But you're going back on the whole Hexham policy . . .'

Harvey got up and poured two glasses of sherry from the bottle in the cupboard behind his desk. It was a rare gesture. 'You'd better get this straight, Bill, if you're to be of any use. Scotland is a political problem, and it will only be solved by political means. That is what Hexham was all about.'

'Hear, hear.' Joynson sipped the sherry, a drink he detested.

'But the political answer is just not within reach now—not here, not in Scotland, not at all. The hooligans who tied up Scullard have seen to that.'

'So?'

'So we wait until the wheel turns again. For the moment diplomacy, constitutional reform and all the other long words are too dirty to use. It won't always be like that. The wheel always turns.'

'And meanwhile?'

'Meanwhile, don't forget that more people get killed under weak governments than under strong ones.'

'And that means Thorganby?'

'For the moment that means Thorganby, and since he is honest, we could do much worse.'

'But later, if the wheel turns, you'll try again?'

'Of course.' Harvey saw that Joynson was genuinely worried. 'You deal in to-morrow's headlines, Bill. It's a desperate job and you do it well. But heaven help us if you ever persuade me that it's my job too.'

V

In the Rue du Fauburg Saint-Honoré the Begum Aga Khan was trying to talk a Borzoi into a Rolls. In the office on the second floor of the British Embassy, Hart was having similar problems.

'Could you read it again?' he said.

'Philippe Le Chat, 56, retired fish merchant from Brest. Ex-Secretary-General of the *Front de Libération National Breton.* Still maintains loose contact with the movement. Headed FLB delegation to Conference of Celtic League, Dublin 1978. Now lives Rue Val-André 17, Erquy. Married, no children. Personal friend of Serge Bucholz . . .'

'Not much, is it?' Hart said.

'Frankly, I don't see what more you need. The Scots are getting money from the Breton Nationalists. All right, pull the girl in, but don't ask us to go stirring things up in Paris.'

'A hell of a lot of money. Weapons, too.'

'That's not proven.'

'Well I think it should be. It's no crime for a Frenchman to send a Scots girl money, and we can't tell how she spends it. I ought to go back with something more.'

'You mean you want to go back with something more.'

Hart kept his temper. 'Perhaps we should submit this to arbitration.'

'I agree. But I warn you, whatever my instructions, there's a limit to what I can do. To get to the root of this quickly we'll have to bring in the SDECE. And I'm strongly against that.'

'Why?'

'Our French friends operate under less constrictions than we do. And they tend to have a very precise view of the national interest, not always synonymous with that of their masters.'

'Doesn't that work in our favour?'

'Sometimes, sometimes not. One can never tell. We could get a bloody nose.'

As if to confirm the point, the street below suddenly echoed to the hee-haw of sirens as a convoy passed at speed towards the Elysée Palace, two black Citroëns with lavish motorcycle escort followed by a busload of kepis. The escort carried sub-machine-guns slung from their necks and Hart noticed that the flaps of their pistol holsters were tucked back.

'I think it's a risk my superiors will wish to take,' he said.

'Yes, well, if I have to pursue this, I'll hand you over to a good man there. Name of Berthaud. He's done us a few favours . . .'

VI

Mackie followed a circular route round the paths of Glasgow Green, leaning forward then back to keep his balance in the wind. He liked to walk fast and alone, more for mental than physical exercise, and this was where he liked to do it. Because this was a political park; a space between the slums where the poor had collected and had felt their collective strength. Here a man could refresh his faith and discuss his dream with the ghost of John Maclean —a dream not for Scotland alone but for all mankind, with Scotland as the model.

He passed the Nelson Monument and heard again that mind-blowing roar as he finished his pre-election speech. An old man was lying on the steps where the platform had been. The wind was terrific, coming straight off the sea, across the shipyards and the hollow acres of the housing schemes, ripping the leaves off the trees and swirling them across the grass; a brutal, cleansing blast, like the political wind which would blow through Scotland.

But some things were hard to blow away. An image lingered in Mackie's mind, and he wondered how long it would stay: a man roped by the feet and choked in water. George Scullard should have been alive and a fool, the news picture of the decade; instead he was dead and a hero. That had been a bad mistake. Brodie swore that he had done as he was told, that he had not noticed the tide, that Kemble had agreed to come at once to the pier. Brodie was a bad mistake. The SNP had rushed into a predictably hysterical denunciation, but this time the SLA too had put out a disclaimer, their first official statement to the Press, a sober letter from *An Ceannard* to every editor in the land. It had taken some writing.

Now they had a new chance, now the Tories had gone for repression. That was not Harvey's way, but presumably for the moment he had no choice. If the SLA played it right they could more than make up the lost ground. They could sweep every Scotsman off the fence, ditch Henderson for ever and drum together a united people to chase Thorganby and the redcoats out of the country.

They must think big, turn the wind into a whirlwind. At the back of his mind Mackie kept a map, vivid as the image of a mistress. Striding across the Green, he remembered the roads, railways, bridges and lochs on the body of Scotland, and saw how it might be done.

VII

'You!' said Duguid, as the beam of his torch settled on the face of Donald Levi.

'Yes, me.'

Levi stood carefully on the jetty with his feet apart. His face was unshaven and his whole body seemed to have sagged; he must have lost twenty pounds. 'Where's Sukey?' he said.

'She's not here.'

'I've got to see her.'

'She won't be back before *Latha-Luain*.'

It seemed to Levi a hundred years since he had commanded Caltech Section, but he recognised the codeword for D-Day, and burst into Gaelic himself.

'Oh, *shit*.'

Duguid switched off his torch. Behind him the moon glinted wetly on the turrets of Ardnish Castle. A human chain had formed and the rifles were being passed up from the hold by the light of a hurricane lamp. So they're going to do it, Levi thought, the idiots are actually going to do it.

MacNair came up, Brodie still at his elbow. 'Where's the gelly?' he said.

'Where do you think, ducky? We had enough problems staying afloat without that lot.' Levi snickered in the dark. To think that those two morons had spent the whole summer waiting to kill each other . . . He must get away as quickly as possible; the Frenchmen had said they would wait off Barra Head for two days, and he had slipped the Scottish skipper thirty pounds to take him back. 'But you'll see her?' he said to Duguid.

'Eventually, yes.'

Levi unzipped his boiler suit and pulled out an envelope wrapped in a yellow plastic wallet. 'When you do, give her this. She must get it to him as soon as she can.'

'You're not staying?'

'Not on your nelly.'

Duguid, who was eager for news of Brittany, suggested a dram, and they walked away across the lawn, talking of the gale. One of the chimneys was down and a beech had fallen into the billiard room.

But now everything was calm. Behind them the fenders of *The Western Isles* creaked gently against the piles of the jetty. Her engines had stopped, and the night was full of little plopping sounds, the sort you get on lakes, fish perhaps or dripping trees, perhaps quite close or perhaps a mile away.

MacNair stood on the deck and listened.

VIII

The following morning, Friday, a week to the hour since George Scullard's body had been discovered, Lord Thorganby arrived in Edinburgh.

Henderson stayed away, but a band of five hundred Scots had collected at the entrance to Waverley Station to greet their new Secretary of State. The train had been delayed by an attempt to derail it north of Berwick, and by the time it got in, the crowd was a good deal noisier than the authorities had bargained for.

Thorganby was met on the platform by Cameron and the police, and told that he would have to travel to the George Hotel in a police van. He refused indignantly and demanded his normal car. Cameron persisted and was told crisply that General Wade was dead.

The next time they met Thorganby listened to Cameron more carefully. As the car came up the ramp and turned towards Princes Street the crowd surged forward and trapped it. For ten long minutes Thorganby had to retain his composure while fists, placards and even, at one point, feet hammered on the roof, hands clawed vainly at the door handles, the headlamps were smashed and the view from every window was blocked by yelling faces, faces contorted with hate and then with panic as the pressure behind squeezed them up against the glass.

Finally, and none too gently, the police and troops cleared a way and the car accelerated up the hill. A running fight continued through the city all morning, stones and bottles versus shields and riot sticks. Fifty-two people were arrested and almost as many injured.

There was a crowd too outside Henderson's house on the Corstorphine Road, but he slipped out of the back door and walked through a neighbour's garden to find the undistinguished black car which took him to meet the new Secretary of State.

IX

The proprietor of the Café du Port in Erquy was a funny-man. He served a banana pancake called *Rêve de Jeune Fille* and recorded his best jokes on slabs of wood with a poker. Hart was taken through them one by one: *L'abus du vin conduit à la bière. Le vin c'est la France le lait c'est la Mendes-France*—that one had been there for twenty years—*Un jour 100-20 est aussi triste qu'un puits 100-0 . . .*

'Please, you must speak it. *Sans-eau . . .* It is a game of words, no?'

Hart fell about and got a free glass of Calvados. The café filled up. A small girl with a middle-aged face changed paper cloths with the speed of a conjurer and slammed plates of pancakes in front of grizzled fishermen. Having pushed her productivity to the limit, father went to the rescue and Hart went back to thinking about Berthaud, his ally from the SDECE (*Service de Documentation Extérieure et de Contreespionnage*).

Berthaud was a good man; a rugby fan, with an English wife. When he showed his card people jumped. In turn they had jumped, bank manager, Gendarmerie and Douane —without result. Le Chat was clean. He kept a separate account for the Swiss operation and came to Saint-Brieuc to make the deposits himself, always in cash.

But Berthaud wouldn't leave it at that. At some point he seemed to have acquired an interest of his own. After a monosyllabic drive to Erquy he had left Hart in the café and gone to reconnoitre Le Chat's house. Hart could see it from where he sat, a modest affair of Breton design, rather like a cuckoo clock, tucked into the hill beside the pink roofs of the Bucholz residence.

Time passed. The café emptied. Hart moved to the terrace and sat in the sun, that autumnal glow which seems peculiar to France. The tide was out. Brightly painted boats lay scattered like tops on the mud of the harbour floor. A white Peugeot passed in front of the café, turned at the Customs Office and came back slowly along the quay.

The point at which Berthaud had acquired an interest was when the Commandant of Police had mentioned Bucholz.

A small boy was drawing patterns in the sand of the boulodrome.

X

Henderson had insisted on having a man in the room to take a note of the conversation, but after two hours Thorganby was frustrated enough to forget that they were not alone. Outside the clear autumn light was sharpening before it faded; teatime descended majestically on Edinburgh. It was stuffy in Thorganby's suite at the George Hotel, with a whiff of new paint scorching on the radiators. He would not have minded so much if Henderson had been self-confident and bloody-minded. But Henderson was clearly scared; he didn't know any longer what was going on in Scotland and for a man who called himself leader of the Scottish National Party this couldn't be healthy. Thorganby felt that someone more skilled than himself, Harvey for instance, could by now have found the key to the man's fears and turned them to account. But after two hours he had failed, and his patience had run out.

'I don't understand you, Henderson. You and I don't agree about the future of Scotland, but I've tried to put myself in your shoes.' Thorganby was walking up and down, his bulky frame too big for the room. He was moved to unusual feats of imagination. 'If these violent hooligans came out on top, they would throw you aside at once. You'd find yourself in a bed-sitting-room in Earls Court, living on dreams and margarine, like the other clapped-out social democrats who thought they could do business with extremists. If you come out and denounce the violence and help me put it down, you have a chance. Otherwise you're sunk, man.'

Henderson sat awkwardly on the chintz sofa, saying nothing. Thorganby could see that he had failed again to break through the man's fatigue and obstinacy. He tried once more.

'For God's sake, you're a Scot, I'm a Scot. Scots first and politicians after. Do you *want* to see Scotland destroyed?'

James Henderson stirred. Several retorts chased through his tired mind. Thorganby was not a real Scot, he was a Knight of the Thistle, and that was a big difference. Thorganby was part of the ascendancy, shrewd perhaps, probably sincere—but it was not with such that the new Scotland could be made. He searched for words, but they would not come. He fell back on the formula which he had used half a dozen times already that afternoon.

'I can only repeat, Lord Thorganby, that the SNP will co-operate in bringing violence to an end if the Public Order Bill is withdrawn and responsible powers at once granted to an elected Scottish Assembly.'

'You talk like a gramophone. You know perfectly well that no British Government could do business with you on that basis.'

Thorganby stopped in front of the window which looked north across the Forth. The windows of his car had been streaked with saliva where people had spat. The wooded hills of Fife seemed to send a summons across the water; they at least were real. He turned back to Henderson.

'I don't think there is anything more to be said.'

He would accept Dunmayne's invitation for the week-end, he would get rid of the pasty-faced detective now drinking whisky in the ante-room of the suite. Maybe he could go out on the moor with his gun to-morrow. Maybe Sukey would be there. Maybe he could even forget to leave

Number Ten his telephone number.

He shook hands stiffly with Henderson and escorted him out of the room. As they waited for the lift they both searched for small talk, but none came.

XI

Paris Telegram No. 253 to Foreign Office, Friday October 21st.

IMMEDIATE   Dispatched 17.22

Consul Saint-Malo reports British subject Graham Hart shot dead from passing car at Erquy-Plages this morning. Assailant unknown. See my i.f.t. Please advise action soonest.

XII

Lord Thorganby knew the hill well and already it was doing him good. Now in the late autumn its whole surface was wet. Through the mist his practised eye distinguished between the hillocks of heather, which meant a solid foothold, and the reedy grass which looked firm enough but would quickly suck his foot into black stagnant water. The weather was too thick for stalking, and secretly Thorganby was pleased; though he liked MacDonald, Dunmayne's gillie, on this particular morning he was glad to be climbing the hill alone, his twelve-bore over his arm.

Not that he meant to think about politics: the whole point was that he should not think about anything at all, just let the sensations of the day flow through him, wind, rain, the movement of legs and arms. He would get back to the house just as the light failed. He would lie for half an hour in a huge old-fashioned tub and let the chill soak away in the hot peaty water. Then he would ring up his wife in London and there would be time for a glass of Dunmayne's special malt before dinner. Perhaps Sukey would be there. They had expected her the night before, but she had not turned up. Thorganby had often climbed the hill with her, and many years before she had shown him the quick way to the top. She must have been twelve then.

He stopped to get his bearings. The mist was closing in, and he could barely see twenty yards. There was no wind to shift it, just a thin fine rain so light that it hardly seemed to touch the surface of the brackish pools.

He must listen for the burn. The air was full of different watery noises, and at first his ears were baffled. But he picked it up, the deeper noise of fast water over stones. He moved towards it, stopping every couple of minutes to get its direction. Then he saw the shapes of the rowan trees which flanked the burn, and soon he was on the path which sheep and deer had made by its side. Thoroughly pleased with himself, he pulled the flask from his side, and thought briefly of Henderson. That man had never climbed a hill by his wits on a thick November afternoon: how could he seriously claim to know what Scotland was about?

A sudden scurry ahead, and a mountain hare bolted towards him out of the bracken. He had put down his gun against a rock; by the time he was ready to aim the hare had swerved and vanished into the mist. Just as well; it would be a nuisance to lug it downhill round his waist, and a pity to leave the corpse for the crows. He remembered showing Sukey an eagle hovering over the peak which he was now skirting. Her father was very upset that the girl had gone political; Dunmayne wanted a daughter who would dance reels all night and come up with the lunch at shooting parties. But most girls had always wanted more to life than that, and now they could choose, politics or anything else.

The rain had quickened and was finding a way between his neck and the collar of his mackintosh jacket. An unwise step had filled one boot with water. He remembered a deserted croft in a shieling higher up the burn. He would take off his boot there, wring out his stocking, then start back to the house.

A few minutes later the path brought him to an outcrop of rock about his own height. There was just room to squeeze between the rock and the knotted roots of the bushes overhanging the burn, which here formed a waterfall. Thorganby was at the narrowest point when a man stepped out on the path in front of him. He was so swathed in waterproof garments that Thorganby did not at first recognise him.

'No further, my lord.'

It was Jamie MacDonald, Dunmayne's chief gillie. Through the mist it became clear that he was carrying a shotgun, pointed half-heartedly at Thorganby's middle.

'MacDonald! What nonsense is this?'

Thorganby's first thought was that MacDonald was poaching. He remembered the hare which had bolted towards him from something farther up the hill. But that was nonsense; MacDonald had free run of the hill.

A cracking of twigs above the sound of the waterfall. Thorganby turned to see that two more figures now stood behind him, similarly armed. One of them strode forward and wrenched the twelve-bore from under his arm. His face was unknown.

'I'm sorry, it's orders,' said MacDonald. 'Will ye please come this way?'

It did not occur to Thorganby to resist. He was wet, tired and sixty-four. His mind could find no explanation for what was happening. He only knew that the hot bath was receding.

MacDonald led him on up the path, turned aside into the shieling which Thorganby himself had been making for. Smoke was rising from the chimney. MacDonald stood aside and Thorganby was edged in by the men behind him. He had to bend to avoid knocking his head on the lintel, and when he straightened up he understood.

Sitting by a peat fire, in jeans and a fisherman's sweater, was Sukey Dunmayne. She laughed.

'Come in and warm up, Uncle David. You're too set in your ways. Jamie and I knew at once which way you would come.'

'Sukey, what in heaven's name is this nonsense?' But he knew.

'No nonsense, Uncle David.' Her voice was harder. 'You've been formally taken into the custody of the Scottish Liberation Army, and will be held at the pleasure of *An Ceannard*.'

XIII

'John? Can you talk?'

'Yes, it's all right. How was it?'

'No problems; we're taking him to Janet's.'

'I'll be there to-morrow night. Anything from over the water?'

'Donald came back with a letter. Duguid's got it now, he'll bring it to the pub.'

'Good. All set then. Take care.'

'You too.'

XIV

'Colonel Cameron?'

'Speaking.'

'Rennie here.'

'Don't you coppers ever relax? It's Saturday night, man.'

'Something's up. I thought you ought to know.'

'Let's have it then.'

'It looks like a general mobilisation. Every SLA unit we've got our tabs on has upped sticks in the last two hours and headed north.'

'Have they now? Does Blair know this?'

166

'I tried to get him to put out roadblocks, but he won't have it. Says we must hold our hand till the Public Order Bill goes through.'

'The man's a ninny. Have you spoken to London?'

'All in bed.'

'Not to worry. We'll call it a practice alert.'

'Anything I can do?'

'Sit on that phone and let me have anything new as it comes in. I'll ring round the battalions now.'

XV

Captain Warburton-Mackenzie, duty officer at Fort George, Inverness, put down the phone and swallowed the last of his drink. He stood for a moment, Cameron's orders ringing in his ears, then moved quickly into action. The mess was deserted except for two lieutenants lying half-asleep in leather armchairs. He woke them both with a kick.

'On your feet, you two.'

'What's up?'

'SLA—Contingency B.'

'To-night?'

'Now.'

'Jesus.'

'Get your kit together as quick as you can. Roddy, down to the guardroom, and get the armouries open. John, ring the Sergeants' Mess. Tell Grehan I want all his men at the MT Park in half an hour. Where's the Colonel?'

'Still playing snooker.'

'Right. Synchronise watches . . . I'll meet you at the gate at 0200.'

XVI

As had been his custom every Sunday morning for twenty-five years the minister walked up the High Street of Fort William towards his kirk, a stately figure in black gown and white bands, the sheets of his sermon under his arm.

'It's a grand day, Minister.'

'A grand day for the Lord's work, Miss Macpherson.'

Miss Macpherson went on hanging up pink lambswool sweaters at the entrance to the Flora MacDonald Boutique. The minister disapproved of Sunday opening, but she didn't care. The season now closing had been spoiled by the foolish talk about trouble in Scotland, and who could tell if that particular shade would sell next year? Knitwear was a risky profession.

The minister walked on in the sunshine, enjoying the tone of his own church bell, silently practising his opening text. He hardly heard the police car draw up beside him.

'Sorry, Minister, I'll not be taking the bag round this morning.'

'Why ever not, Sergeant?'

'There's trouble at the pulp mill. One of the security men just rang.'

The Jaguar gathered speed up the street, swerving to avoid a convoy of three cars coming south, each towing a caravan. The police were so keen to get to the pulp mill that they did not notice the driver of the front car hoot frantically when he saw them.

By now the minister was climbing the granite steps of his church. At the top of the steps he paused to catch his breath and look back over Loch Linnhe. A stiff breeze moved across the glittering water; and just where the surface was ruffled, not far from the Corpach shore and the chunky outline of the pulp mill, he could see six motorboats moving fast in formation towards Fort William. He had often complained to the Lochaber Tourist Association about races on the loch on a Sunday morning.

The three cars trailing caravans came to a disorderly halt in Gordon Square in front of the boutique. The door of the leading car opened and a young man fell out into the gutter. The shoulder of his pink shirt was bright with blood. The woman who had been driving scrambled out and bent over him.

'A doctor!' she shouted at Miss Macpherson, half-question, half-order.

Miss Macpherson, mind trained by years of *Z Cars*, stumbled through festoons of scarves and sweaters to the telephone at the back of the shop. When she returned the caravans were still disgorging. Twelve or fifteen campers had tumbled out of each of them, in shorts mostly, men unshaven, girls blowzy, all talking.

'Came at us out of the dark, pulled down the tents on top of us . . .'

'Johnny hit one and he pulled a gun on him . . .'

'At least a hundred . . .'

'Pinched our cars and the boat . . .'

'Chap in a kilt told them to lock us into the caravans.'

'Will the insurance pay?'

'Ought to be in hospital with that shoulder . . .'

'Give me Minorca any day.'

'More like an army if you know what I mean . . .'

'Bloody hell! Here they are again.'

But this was not quite correct. It was not the main force, but the naval contingent which had crossed Loch Linnhe in their captured motorboats, and landed on the quay beside the railway station. The sleeper from King's Cross was not due for an hour, and the signal box and station were secured without noise or difficulty. The contingent moved in open order across Gordon Square towards the bus station, open-necked shirts above kilts or slacks, plimsolls, sub-machine-guns. The crowd round the caravans in the square began to melt. A small boy clapped and shouted. Miss Macpherson shut the doors of her shop.

For a few seconds Fort William was very quiet.

In the kirk the minister had prayed for the King and the Royal Family, for the High Court of Parliament, for those in sickness and distress, and was now elaborating on those in peril on the sea. The congregation shifted on their seats; he was strong on prayer, the minister, and it would be fifteen minutes before the next hymn.

A man appeared in the pulpit, behind and to the left of where the minister stood facing his flock. He wore a beret with a plastic disc and a sergeant's stripes on his shirt. Without noise he extended the bipod of a machine-gun and planted in on the lectern, swivelling the barrel until it pointed at the minister's back.

'Let us remember in silence all those who went forth from the Highlands in two World Wars . . .'

'May I have your attention please.' The voice from the pulpit was more matter of fact. 'You are requested to return quietly to your homes, and to remain there until further notice. Fort William is now in the hands of the Scottish Liberation Army.'

To the south of Gordon Square, the SLA had made a barricade across the Ballachulish road out of the three caravans. They had commandeered the Station Hotel, and the refugee campers were queueing for the single telephone box in the lounge. The Town Hall noticeboard carried the proclamation of a 24-hour curfew.

The four policemen returning from the direction of the pulp mill were too angry and scared to notice the empty streets. They had run into a roadblock at Inverlochy. There had been a volley of rifle fire when they tried to force a way through. When the Jaguar's windscreen shattered they had turned back.

'Savages, bloody savages,' said the youngest constable, who was at the wheel. He was proud of the Force. At the start of the High Street a sentry with a rifle motioned them to stop. The constable put his foot on the brake, then anger conquered caution and training. The others shouted at him as he accelerated, words were lost in the clatter of bullets. The car swung violently to the left and smashed into the Clansman Café. Glass cascaded into the street, followed by a shower of postcards, views of Ben Nevis, scraps of tartan, jokes about kilts and sporrans and hairy knees, spattered with the blood and brains of the constable.

The Managing Director's conference room at the aluminium works was crowded with the company's executives, some in grey flannel suits, some in sports jackets to mark that it was Sunday. The room had magnificent sheets of window, neither open nor openable, looking one way over Fort William, the other towards the lower slopes of Ben Nevis. For the rest it was pale oak, concealed lighting, and a thudding air-conditioner.

They had been invited to hear a presentation by Professor Sturm of Programmatic Instinctual Engineering. The Professor had with great kindness flown supersonically from Ann Arbor, Michigan, and would return supersonically after tea. The Piper Comanche which had brought him from Prestwick lay with the company's other planes on the airstrip beyond the gate. All present had the sense of a historic occasion.

The Professor, a well-preserved physical specimen in rimless glasses and button-down shirt, proved with a wealth of diagram that all other systems of industrial management were obsolete since the invention of PIE. As he soared into a private stratosphere of unintelligible jargon, ballpoints flew across notepads and heads nodded in keen appreciation of each new point. Promotion could depend on this.

Finally it came to an end, and the Managing Director rose to thank:

'It is no exaggeration to say that after to-day industry in Scotland will never be the same again . . .'

As he spoke the window fell outwards, majestically and in one piece. The noise of the glass shattering on the pavement below was almost louder than the explosion. The lighting in the conference room went out, so that all present were exposed to daylight and open air. On the airstrip a cloud of smoke and falling debris showed where the planes had been.

The telephone buzzed by the Managing Director's elbow. When he had finished listening he was plainly scared.

'It's the police from Inverness—there's been a take-over by the Nationalists. They'll probably be here next. They've got small arms . . . The Army's on it's way, and we're advised to stay exactly where we are.'

There was babel in the room.

'My wife . . . on the golf course . . .'

'. . . promised to collect the au pair girl from mass.'

'. . . people coming to lunch.'

'I've always said they've got a case, but . . .'

'. . . bloody impertinence.'

A Land-Rover drove fast into the compound of office buildings, then a second, then two more. An officer in uniform jumped out and looked briefly round him.

'The Marines,' said the Professor.

'The Black Watch, I think,' said the Managing Director, smiling with relief.

The officer saw the faces above him and in a few seconds was in the room. He carried a swagger stick.

'Captain Warburton-Mackenzie, Fourth Battalion Scottish Division, at your service, gentlemen. I'm sorry you're having this spot of bother, but I hope we can take care of it. Reports are that there may be an attack on the company's installations within the next twenty-four hours, and I've been detailed to protect your property.'

'I'm sure we're all immensely grateful, Captain. You are of course free to make whatever dispositions you want . . . What would you like us to do?'

'Please stay in this room while I deploy my men,' Warburton-Mackenzie said. 'I can protect you here. If you try to return to your homes you may run into trouble. As soon as the situation is clearer I'll let you know.'

And so they waited, masking with cheerful talk some anxiety for wives and children. A cold breeze sprang up from Ben Nevis as the sun shifted. They moved to the Managing Director's room and munched olives and salt biscuits from little dishes on a side table. There was no sign of the rebels, though the telephone wires had been cut since the call from Inverness. The soldiers established four posts in different parts of the complex and seemed well prepared for any attack. It was hard to believe that anything more would happen. Soon they would all go home and eat the Sunday joint cold for supper. The Professor would fly back to Ann Arbor, and to-morrow they would fill in the hole in the airstrip and there would be production, profits, restrictive practices, all as usual.

'Thank God for the Army,' said the Managing Director, passing round his flask.

XVII

As soon as it was light Lord Thorganby had realised that he was being held prisoner in Janet Grant's inn. The courtyard with its gaggle of geese was unmistakable, though it was many years since he had last stayed there.

The knowledge was comforting; he was back in a familiar world. He admitted to himself that last night's journey had been unnerving as well as enormously uncomfortable. Odd how fears grow at night. Of course he had been thinking of what had happened to Scullard. When the daylight had faded up on the hill Sukey had said good-bye in a mocking sort of way, and MacDonald and the others had marched him down by a path he did not know. He was sure Sukey herself would do him no harm, but she was obviously obeying orders, and might not know what plans had been laid by whatever madmen were at the top of this outfit. At the foot of the hill he had been bundled into the back of a waiting butcher's van. No windows of course, and the two-hour journey had

173

seemed to consist of nothing but twists and turns. Then a sudden stop, and he had been transferred up a narrow staircase and into a simple whitewashed room with a bed, a chair, a washstand with a ewer. The door had been locked behind him. Common sense had told the Secretary of State for Scotland that the wisest thing in all the circumstances was to have a good night's sleep.

Now in the morning it was time to take stock. At one end of the room a small window faced the road and the bridge across the loch. The back window overlooked the courtyard. Looking down on the sunlit scene, Thorganby could not believe that he was in any physical danger. This was some charade which Sukey and that crazy bigot Mackie had dreamt up to make a fool of the Government. Of course his disappearance would cause a lot of stir. This morning Dunmayne and all his staff would be beating the hill to find him, led no doubt by that double-crossing MacDonald. Dunmayne would have telephoned his wife last night in Eaton Place. He could imagine the commotion which she would create, partly out of real worry for him partly from her innate sense of drama. '. . . I must speak to the Prime Minister himself at once . . .' And Harvey—how would he react? That was always hard to guess.

Thorganby's train of thought was interrupted by a clamour in the courtyard. The geese were being chivvied out into a small paddock rich in thistles, by a middle-aged lady in bright blue jeans and a green smock, above which tight grey curls rose in surprising formality. Confronted in this way by Miss Janet Grant, Lord Thorganby found it ridiculous to shout 'Help' or to expostulate in any way.

'It's a fine day, Miss Grant. What are you offering for breakfast this morning?'

Janet Grant did not turn her head. She continued to shepherd the geese, then went back into the house without a sign to her prisoner. Thorganby tried to recall what he knew about her.

She had kept the pub at Clovulin for as long as anyone

could remember. The inn had prospered on the traffic from the Loch Linnhe ferry, but a few years ago the ferry had been replaced by a bridge—part of the new Road to the Isles. The tourists now hurried on to Skye without a sideways glance, and the inn had survived only as a refuge for mountaineers and readers of the Good Food Guide. An Eton housemaster in charge of a climbing expedition had sought Janet Grant's hand at the same time as the Irish foreman of the gang which was building the road. A strenuous competition had ended in success for the Irishman, of whose soft white skin and prowess in the small hours she used to speak often and at length. But the road was made and the Irishman moved on. Miss Grant resumed her maiden name and with it a taste for solitude which was new. Living peacefully on her father's capital, she had settled back into the landscape of West Highland eccentricity.

Thorganby's thoughts were interrupted by footsteps in the corridor. The door was briskly unlocked, and a tray placed on the floor just inside it. To his own surprise Thorganby laughed; he was almost enjoying himself. On the tray were a full toastrack, a mound of pâté, and a bottle of Château Yquem. He remembered that Janet Grant's father in his early eighties had amassed a vast quantity of that wine as a sovereign aid to long life. Since his death a few months later no other wine had been served in the inn.

XVIII

Lord Thorganby would have enjoyed his lunch less if he had known that Clovulin and its pub were no longer, *de facto,* in the United Kingdom. By early Sunday afternoon the SLA controlled all of Fort William, its pulp mill, its aluminium works, and everything west of the town as far as the coast. It was well-chosen territory: a wedge of land bounded by the roads to Mallaig and Ardnamurchan, with Ardnish Castle more or less central; protected in the north by the roadless mountains of Morar and Knoidart and in the south by Loch Linnhe. With Fort William sealed, the only easy approach was by the bridge across Loch Linnhe to Clovulin.

The bridge was built causeway-style, running flat and low over the surface of the loch on concrete piles, with a lifting central section for shipping. The SLA planners had decided to establish a roadblock at the British end, to filter friend from foe, and a second post at Clovulin to overlook the bridge. This had been established in a hut beside the road, about eighty yards from Janet Grant's pub. If the first post was rushed, the second would destroy the bridge with an explosive charge.

McNair had been at it all afternoon, working from a small boat or suspended from the railings of the bridge in a harness of ropes. The point of fracture had been fixed a short way out into the loch. Twelve charges had been attached to the piles and a connecting strand of Cortex run back to a detonator in the hut. If it didn't work, Brodie had been told to shoot him.

Thorganby, watching from the front window of his room, assumed that this was routine repair work and went back to admiring the shifting patterns of shadow and light on Ben Nevis. But even this diversion was soon removed. The sun vanished, and it became what Highlanders know as a 'soft' day; the rain fell unceasingly, and by late afternoon Miss Grant's courtyard was a massive puddle. Thorganby feared that he was running a temperature, or it might be the Château Yquem. He dozed off, then woke unrefreshed and cold to see that a note had been pushed under his door. It was written on the back of a pink demand for rates from the Inverness-shire County Council: *Dinner at 7.30, J. Grant.*

Shortly after that a Land-Rover pulled into the courtyard and a man with a handlebar moustache got out. Thorganby thought of calling to him until he noticed the bizarre uniform: beret, polo-neck sweater under a safari jacket, webbing belt, revolver, kilt. The man's knees were smeared with mud and one hand was bandaged. He called to someone in the pub, then walked down to the hut by the bridge.

A few minutes later a youth in city clothes came up from the hut to the pub. He had been hanging about the man working on the bridge all day. As he came closer Thorganby saw that his face was scarred and that he too carried a pistol in his belt. He stuck his head in a window and asked Miss Grant for three bottles of beer.

Duguid lifted his head and looked at MacNair in bewilderment. A small trickle of blood was running from his nose into his moustache. MacNair picked up the Mole wrench and hit him again across the back of the neck.

The letter which Levi had brought was in the left breast-pocket of Duguid's jacket. MacNair undid the plastic wrapping, looked at the envelope inside, opened it, and read for half a minute. It was confusing, not entirely as expected; but enough. There was a name. At last he had a name.

John Mackie, you are *An Ceannard* and I claim my five hundred pounds.

A slight noise outside the hut made him dive for the revolver in Duguid's holster, but Brodie came round the door and dropped the bottles and reached for his gun all in one movement. He had practised it all summer.

XIX

Across the loch, at the other end of the bridge, there was a good deal of tension in the rebel roadblock. This was the southernmost SLA post and the most likely point for a counter-attack.

All day a stream of volunteers had come up the road from Ballachulish. Some of them had travelled quite a distance, dropping whatever they were doing as soon as they heard the radio, deserting families and jobs to join the cause, bringing vehicles, petrol, tents, food, odd bits of uniform and all manner of weapons. But each new batch reported the government forces closer, and in the late afternoon the stream had dwindled to a trickle.

Now it had stopped altogether, and the enemy were in view. A pair of armoured cars had appeared round the first bend to the south and pulled quickly across the road. The rebels had responded by revealing their full armoury —rifles, machine-guns and a rocket-launcher—above the two tourist coaches which they had overturned to block the entrance to the bridge.

The sun disappeared, the rain came down harder. Nothing happened. As the light failed a wall of sandbags began to rise around the wheels of the armoured cars and the rebels caught a first glimpse of blue diced caps and military helmets. Then suddenly a man appeared, in civilian clothes, walking confidently towards the bridge. A rustle of surprise in the SLA roadblock; fingers twitched on to safety catches. A sharp-eyed girl was the first to break the silence.

'It's John Mackie!'

The word spread, and by the time Mackie reached the gap between the coaches they were all cheering and waving, crowding round to slap him on the back.

'How did you get through?' someone asked.

'I said I'd come to visit my constituents.'

They cheered again. Mackie walked through them and stood on the bridge, lifting his face into the rain. He felt close to tears and did not want them to see. This was where the wind had brought him; now it was all or nothing, it would quickly succeed or quickly fail in this derelict belt of hills and lakes. He was making history or a complete idiot of himself, and in either case it was no cause for tears. He felt a bout of self-disgust, followed by a total lapse of confidence. They were all so bloody young.

Across the loch Clovulin was a huddle of squat white buildings, still just visible at the base of the hills where the road turned west to Sunart and Ardnamurchan. It did not look at all as he remembered it, but he was a notoriously unobservant man.

'Is that the pub?' he said.

'Aye, Janet's expecting you. Seven-thirty, she said.'

Mackie looked at his watch. 'We've time to walk it.'

'In this weather?'

'I'd rather walk.'

He started across the bridge with a small escort from the roadblock, who walked slightly behind him, as if he was Royalty, conscious of their weapons, not sure how to carry them. Someone produced a set of pipes and began to play, and the rest broke into song. Mackie was embarrassed and irritated. A culture based on romantic nostalgia was the ultimate proof of decadence. The new Scotland would need new songs. A line from Auden came to mind:

To-morrow, for the young the poets exploding like bombs
. . . but to-day the struggle.

But he let them sing and fell unconsciously into step, and as their ragged music carried across that great arena of rock and water, he did, reluctantly, feel a slight lifting of the spirit. What the situation really required was a quiet giggle with Sukey.

XX

MacNair tried again.

'Use your head, man. They don't stand a chance, and you'll be in deeper than you were before.'

'Ah'll no dae porridge again, so help me. Ye're a grass, MacNair—and Ah'm gaunny blow yer bliddy brains oot.'

MacNair was as still as a waxwork. He knew that Brodie wouldn't do it until he showed fear. He continued, in a neutral voice, without a trace of pleading. 'See this letter? Duguid brought it here for the top man. Help me to

179

get it out and the law won't touch you.'

'Ye're a liar, an' ye're pissin in yer pants.'

'I can prove it. As soon as we're out of this we'll make a phone call. There's a fellow called Rennie at Glasgow Headquarters, he'd give his pension to see this letter. You can talk to him yourself. And he's a big man—Special Branch. He'll see you're all right.'

'Drop it. Back. More. Okay, hold it theer.'

Brodie stooped for the letter. MacNair kicked him in the eyes and caught his wrist with both hands. The Browning fired once into the wall. MacNair lifted Brodie's wrist and brought it down on the floor with all his strength. The gun clattered free and MacNair felt a thump on his back. The sensation was obscure but he knew that a knife had passed in and out and was coming back for a second thrust, so he lashed sideways with his left arm into Brodie's head and scrambled free, grabbing the wrench with his other hand, and in the few seconds that they circled round noticed two things: there was something peculiar about Brodie's face, something he had never seen there before: it was pleasure: and through the window, three Land-Rovers in front of the pub. The drivers had heard the shot and were running towards the hut. Which gave him almost no time at all, so he swung with the wrench, missed, and got the knife across his face. Brodie stepped back. MacNair came on, and got him behind the ear. Brodie stabbed blindly, then his fingers slackened on the knife and he went down, not completely out but no longer a threat. The knife was deep in MacNair's shoulder. He tried to tug it out, but it was stuck fast. He looked round for the letter, but couldn't see it. As he ran from the hut he felt the wounds open and the blood begin to flow.

XXI

It was dark now in the courtyard, but one of the down-stairs windows was lit, and Thorganby could just make out the shapes of three men entering the inn. They spoke, but the voices were too low to catch. In a normal country three was not enough for a firing squad.

The door opened, and Miss Grant stood before him. She pointed him along the corridor to a white door at the end.

'Look here, Miss Grant, this is absurd . . .' Thorganby had thought out what he would say when he had some-one to say it to, but now it came to the point the words tumbled out in confusion. 'What on earth is going on?'

Miss Grant said nothing and continued to point to the white door. Thorganby, losing patience, brushed past her. He braced himself to meet his unknown captors, turned the door handle, and found himself in the lavatory. Janet Grant had always been a practical woman.

Brodie dragged himself off the floor of the hut and lurched to the door. His scar throbbed and his head was roaring, his vision kept coming and going, but by a ferocious effort of will he focused and held it long enough to see that MacNair was already out on the bridge. Somehow he held himself upright, hissing through his teeth with pain and rage. The drivers who had run from the pub crowded round, but he brushed them aside and ducked back into the hut. The Cortex from the charges under the bridge ran back to a detonator by the door, which was linked by two wires to a steel box set on a workbench under the window. MacNair had just connected the wires when Duguid had arrived. Shouting to the drivers to get back from the door, Brodie ran to the box and ripped off the lid. Underneath was a small T-shaped handle. Twist or push?

When Thorganby emerged Janet Grant was standing at

the top of the stairs. She started down the steep flight, and he followed, no longer inclined for conversation. At the foot she said, without turning her head, '*An Ceannard* will see you now.' He was shown into the inn's sitting-room.

A fire of peat and logs was struggling in the hearth, sending a thin cloud of smoke into the room as the wind and rain beat down the chimney. The room was lit by a pair of silver candlesticks on a table set with three places. A sofa faced the fire and on the sofa with his back to Thorganby a man sat reading the *Oban Times*. Miss Grant left the room, and he rose. It was Cameron.

At that moment Lord Thorganby's world fell apart. The windows blew inwards, the candles went out, a picture dropped off the wall: both men were flung to the floor by the explosion. They lay together in the dark as fragments of the bridge began to bombard the pub.

XXII

Statement by Scottish Office, 3 p.m. Sunday

The Secretary of State is confined to his room with a feverish cold and has cancelled all engagements for to-day and to-morrow. Lord Thorganby is staying privately with friends in Scotland.

'But how do you propose to find him if no one is allowed to know that he is missing?'

Harvey recognised in the voice that edge of scorn for the feebleness of politicians which he had heard so often in his career.

'A very thorough search is being made, Lady Thorganby. We may hear something from his kidnappers, if as we fear, he has been kidnapped. You must understand that it may be more difficult to arrange for your husband's safe return once there is publicity.'

The voice at the other end became shrill.

'I understand nothing of the sort. If you think David will allow himself to be traded like some fifth-rate spy, you are very much mistaken.'

Harvey could imagine her sitting through the day in the drawing-room at Eaton Place, listening to the ever more hair-raising reports from Scotland, waiting for the telephone call that did not come. Now in her alarm she was lashing out at the only target in sight.

'Well, Lady Thorganby, you must do as you think best . . .'

'That is precisely what I propose to do. Nothing is ever gained by hole-and-corner tactics. I now intend to telephone the Editor of *The Times*.'

XXIII

Brodie stood outside the pub and vibrated hate at the uniformed figure in front of him. The bloody nerve of it. They had put him on a charge.

A disgraceful piece of undiscipline, Cameron had called it, not what one expected from a man who had served in the Black Watch. First Scullard and now the Bridge— put him under open arrest pending an inquiry, Cameron had said.

'. . . I'm disappointed in you, Brodie. I had you recruited because I knew your history and I thought you deserved a second chance. Well, you've had that chance and you've thrown it away. It is essential—and I'm speaking here not only to you but to everyone in this room—it is essential that this army achieve its object with the absolute minimum of violence and destruction . . .'

The flaming, frigging nerve of it, sherricking him in front of those others. Cameron was a headcase. Oh yes, with Cameron the head was definitely away. And now they were all in the boozer getting bevied while he, Brodie, stood in the rain waiting for orders from this curly-haired goon—the face he had wanted to chib more than any other in his life. Warburton bloody Mackenzie.

'Why did you do it, Brodie? He couldn't get away, they'd have stopped him at the roadblock.'

'Mind yer ain bliddy business.'

'I never did teach you any manners, did I?'

'Ah'm no in the army noo an' Ah don't gie a monkey's ——'

A girl screamed in the darkness. Four men in glistening capes carried her into the light and on carefully through the pub door. The bones were sticking out of her hand. A second group followed, headed by a man in civilian clothes; their complexions varied from pure white to pale green. Warburton-Mackenzie was reminded of the faces of the aluminium executives when he told them he was an officer of the SLA.

'Captain . . .'

'Mr Mackie! Sorry, sir, I didn't recognise you . . .'

'There's a boy still out there, we can't free his legs . . . And we think there was another, running towards us when it happened. No sign of him at all . . .'

'Can you still get across?'

'Just—if you keep to the railing. But watch your step, the tide's running fast.'

Warburton-Mackenzie fired orders in all directions: search party, stretcher detail, blankets, ropes, torches, crowbars, outer post to withdraw this side of the gap. Mackie wiped his face with a handkerchief and began to look steadier. 'Is Duguid here?' he asked.

'I'm afraid he's been hurt.'

'Hurt? Where is he?'

Warburton-Mackenzie nodded at the pub. 'They've taken him up.'

'Did he mention a letter?'

'Aye, he had a letter,' Brodie said. 'MacNair took it.'

XXIV

'You're being intelligent,' said Cameron, looking up. He was using a claw from the lobster as a weight for the papers by his plate. Thorganby could see across the table that these were mainly maps with typewritten reports pinned to them.

Thorganby was not feeling in the least intelligent. The shock of learning that Cameron was the chief of his kidnappers had worn off, but he could find nothing coherent to say. The situation was preposterous beyond words.

'I mean of course,' said Cameron, 'that if you asked a lot of questions about the SLA and out of politeness I answered them, we wouldn't be able to let you go.'

The man talked like a cheap thriller. Even as a child Thorganby hated charades and dressing-up. 'I don't care a damn about that,' he said. 'You won't get any good out of this caper.' The smoke billowed into the room and the candles guttered in the draught. A cardboard box had been torn into sections and tacked over the window. 'I just don't know what you think you're up to, Cameron. If it hadn't been for the violence you've created, Harvey would have given way by now and the SNP would be on top of the world.'

'Ah yes. The SNP.' Cameron stopped as Miss Grant appeared, bearing a saddle of lamb and dressed now in a black cocktail dress made in Rome a quarter of a century before. She cleared away the lobsters with the air of one assisting at a historical occasion. After she had gone Cameron got up to carve.

'Do you know Africa?' he asked.

'Not well.' Thorganby disliked riddles too.

'There are twenty-odd countries in Africa now—flags, corrupt Presidents, unsafe airlines, the lot. But only two nations. Algeria and South Africa. The rest are lines on the map, but those two will last. Why? Because thousands of people were killed, chased out of their homes, lives turned upside-down in the making of them. Blood and tears. An old recipe, but we can't make Scotland without it.'

Thorganby sat silent as Cameron put a plateful of lamb in front of him. He had carved the slices exactly right, thin and even.

'You're a laird,' Cameron went on. 'Most of you have gone soft, and you're more English than Scot. But you know more about Scotland than Henderson ever will. An Act of Parliament, regular cheques from London, a Prince every now and then—that's what Henderson dreams of. A Scotland fit for attorneys and accountants and middle-class trade unionists. Neither you nor I could breathe in it for a day.'

Thorganby grunted. This was too close to his own thoughts. Cameron had abandoned for the moment the offhand crudeness which was his stock-in-trade.

'I can't show you our people,' he went on. 'But you'd be surprised. In fact you'd like them. No labels, no windbags, no nonsense about Left or Right. Sukey's your goddaughter, isn't she? She could run a country any day. So could I for that matter, so could a dozen of us. We've been waiting, showing a bit more of our strength each week, but now we've started.'

'Started what?'

But the door opened again. This time it was a vivid pink mousse, quivering on a superb Worcester plate of blue and gold.

'It's the one you like,' said Miss Grant to Cameron. 'There's this too. *Seonaid* brought it from HQ.'

She gave Cameron a folded note. He read it, tossed it across the table to Thorganby and laughed.

Report from 1136, The Times. Lady Thorganby rang Editor 18.45. Paper will lead with story of disappearance query abduction.

'One of the advantages, you see, of our brain drain,' Cameron said. 'It gives us a first-rate intelligence service.' He thought for a moment. 'Now we shall have to speed things along.' He swallowed a spoonful of mousse, and got up. 'I must go, there's a lot to do. I enjoyed our dinner.' And then, from the doorway: 'We won't harm you, but I hope you'll forgive us if we make you a little ridiculous. It's in a good cause.'

As he turned to go Sukey and Mackie appeared in the doorway. Sukey stood looking at her feet, but Mackie advanced into the room with a broad smile. He was wet through and bleeding slightly from a graze on his cheek.

'Looks as if I've missed a good meal,' he said.

Cameron laughed and said to Thorganby, 'Allow me to present my Political Adviser.'

Later, upstairs, Thorganby found his bed made and turned back, a pair of woolly pyjamas folded on the pillow and a jug of hot water on the washstand. There was even a toothbrush.

XXV

'Hallo, Hart. Thought I'd copped it, didn't you? Well here's another surprise, I've got your man . . .'

Or perhaps.

'Stuff it. You're a two-timing English bastard and I wish to God I'd never set eyes on you . . .'

No. Undignified. How about,

'Four months I spent in that flaming castle, so stop whining. Another five hundred and I'll tell you . . .'

Yes, good. Cheeky. Breach of contract, though, strictly speaking. Never liked to do that. Did they give me a contract? Hard to remember. Sleep on it.

No, never go to sleep. Never, never go to sleep when your guts are leaking and you can't move and you're up to your neck in concrete and water. Thoroughly bad idea. Just flex your fingers and twiddle your toes and keep your eyes on those hills.

I made a nice job of this bridge.

You did indeed, of Brodie too, though it's a pity you couldn't finish it. Let's think of ways to finish off Chibber Brodie, like plugging his ears with plastic or cutting his throat with his own bloody knife, or truss him up first and watch him sweat, slice him slowly like a side of bacon . . . I could keep this up all night. Night? It's light. There, behind the hills. You've made it, oh thank God I've made it. They'll see me now. Help is on the way.

Help is on the way from the man in blue pyjamas. How about that, and yes here comes the law, over here, boys, help . . .

XXVI

It was just dawn when the two men had pulled Thorganby roughly from his bed and carried him feet first down the stairs. At the back door they stood him up, put Wellington boots on his feet and a raincoat over his pyjamas. He was a slow waker, and even the fine drizzle on his face as they hustled him across the courtyard did not fully rouse him. But the smell of the butcher's van jerked him to his senses. Sukey stood at an upstairs window. 'I can't watch,' she said. 'It's just too cruel.' She turned away and sat on the bed.

Mackie stayed at the window, silent.

It was a short journey this time. After half a minute the van did a sharp about-turn and jerked to a halt. They opened the back doors without turning off the engine, lifted him out and drove away.

Thorganby stood in the road and shivered. They had taken away the raincoat. The light had spread behind the hills in the east, and he saw that he was on the bridge. In front of him half a dozen boys in anoraks were crouched with rifles behind a barricade of bedsteads, sofas and beer crates. One of them beckoned to him and pointed over the top. Thorganby walked forward. The rain was thicker, the pyjamas several sizes too big.

Beyond the rebel barricade the surface of the road split, then sagged sharply to a jumble of shattered concrete and twisted rods lapped by the waters of the loch, then rose again to an opposing barricade of sandbags, behind which the turrets of two armoured cars were visible. Clutching what was left of the railing, Thorganby started cautiously down. On the other side two police waved white handkerchiefs and at a signal from the rebels came down to help him across. As he clambered weakly up and over the sandbags an officer jumped off one of the armoured cars and called for blankets. A crowd of people closed in, gabbling cheerfully.

'You're very punctual, sir,' said the young man who reached him first.

Never in his political life had Lord Thorganby seen so many microphones and cameras.

THE WHEEL TURNS

I

'. . . and of course he couldn't swim,' Rennie said. 'The SLA got several shots at him before the armoured cars opened up. He was hit in the leg, it's a miracle he got across at all.'

Blair looked unsympathetic. 'Where is he now?'

'The Army are bringing him down in a helicopter. He's in quite a state. They can't get much sense out of him, but he's got some sort of document. I've spoken to the officer on the spot and he's pretty sure the information is important.'

'A helicopter,' Blair said. 'Do you have any idea what it costs to fly one of those things from Ballachulish to Glasgow?'

Rennie rotated the skin on his forehead with the tips of his fingers. He had not slept for two days. 'I was wondering, sir . . . Well, if Brodie really has come through with something big, couldn't we be generous?'

II

Henderson had trudged through the city to Greyfriars Churchyard, coat collar turned up against the wet, hat jammed over his head so that he would not be recognised. It had suddenly seemed necessary to be alone. The SNP headquarters in Gladstone's Land was full of the jangling of telephones, discordant voices rising higher, a flood of questions, an avalanche of advice. Throughout that hectic Monday, as Scotland slipped out of control, he, the

Leader of the Party, had sat at his desk, powerless and overwhelmed by noise.

Up on the desolate slope of the churchyard he felt better. As a solitary child he had brought his problems to Greyfriars, and the habit had stuck. Everything in sight was grey and solid—shining slate roofs, the church, the surrounding wall, the rain itself, blowing against his face in warm autumn gusts from the Castle. This was his Edinburgh, his Scotland, and grimly he set himself to think about its future.

The time for evasion and fence-sitting had gone. Harvey and the SLA—bitter to have to choose between them. But he had to choose now, or throw away all chance of influencing the future. Either choice meant a split in his party; either meant a risk of backing the loser; either meant allying with an enemy.

Lights began to show in the houses between the churchyard as the dusk thickened. He could no longer read the names on the tombstones, and his shoes were soaked from walking on the turf. A newsboy shouted a headline in the street beyond the wall; Henderson did not want to hear. He felt again the sudden stab of exhilaration which had come to him five years before when he had been chosen to lead the SNP, but this time more powerful than before. He knew now which way to go.

When he got back to Gladstone's Land, Mrs Merrilies was in his room. It was her third visit since the news had come from the Loch Linnhe bridge. 'Better and better,' she boomed. 'They'll be rising in all the towns to-night, they say. Thorganby's slunk off and won't see anyone. The patriots are pouring down through Argyll. This is our moment, James—your moment, if you're man enough to seize it.'

'What do you propose?' He knew very well: she had been proposing it all day.

'Why, you and I must call the press together to-night and say that from now on we will fight shoulder to shoulder with the SLA until the last Englishman is flogged across the border and Scotland has come into its own again.'

She stood in the centre of the room, hair unkempt, giant legs apart, fists clenched, like the wardress of some fantastic prison. He could not imagine how he had put up with her for so long.

He spoke very precisely so that she would understand. 'As Leader of our Party I have full powers in a time of emergency. I am now about to telephone the Prime Minister in London. I shall tell him that I am ready, at whatever time he chooses, to call a press conference. At that press conference I shall denounce the SLA as violent adventurers. I shall support the forces of law and order. And in return . . .'

But Mrs Merrilies was not interested in the rest. Her frame shook with frustration. It was to have been her heroic moment, the climax of her career, the birth of a splendid new legend, and this puling whey-faced accountant had let her down.

She picked up the chair on which she had been sitting and with a massive almost athletic twist of her body hurled it at Henderson. As the chair struck the panelling above his head, Mrs Merrilies burst into tears.

III

It was always easier to fight on one's own ground. Harvey had made the Chiefs of Staff and their planners leave their map-room in the Ministry of Defence and crowd into his study in the upstairs flat at Number Ten. The pile of newspapers, eggshells on a tray, Joynson lounging against a door and the Prime Minister in his turquoise dressing-gown—all this should shake them out of their professional straightjacket. Suits were creased and chins stubbly: few of them had left that night.

'I'm grateful to you, gentlemen, for coming across so early in the morning.' A flash of blue as Harvey took his seat behind the desk; the actor in him showed at times of

193

crisis. 'As you know, the Cabinet is meeting at eleven to discuss the situation in Scotland. I was anxious to get the purely military aspects out of the way first. I believe the Cabinet will ratify whatever decisions we reach. Thank you for the position paper which you sent me a few hours ago. I found it as usual admirably clear, even if the conclusion was not encouraging.'

Conclusion:

The SLA has established itself in a sector of the Highlands lying west and south-west of Fort William. Their hold on Fort William itself is now firm. Their capacity for offensive action is increasing hourly as a result of

(a) a steady flow of recruits, from the Scottish battalions of the British Army, and from civilian life.

(b) large stocks of small arms, origin unknown.

(c) the sympathy of large parts of the population.

(d) skilful leadership by Colonel Cameron.

(e) the constraints imposed on the counteraction of British forces.

So long as these factors are in operation, the whole of the west and south-west of Scotland must be considered at risk within the next 48 hours.

'Have you anything to add to that, Rickie?' Harvey said.

Admiral of the Fleet Sir Richard Anstruther, Chief of the Defence Staff, had risen to his high position by consistent pessimism.

'They took Oban an hour ago. The same motorboats, slipped past the destroyer. Moving south now through Argyll. Could be in Glasgow to-night.'

'Anything else?' Harvey showed no shock.

The Chief of the General Staff was a more polished performer.

'There were attempts just before dawn by small bodies of men to take over the barracks at Inverness and Stirling Castle. Both attempts were frustrated. But I must add, Prime Minister, that the desertion rate is a very worrying feature. You know about the lamentable business with the Black Watch on Sunday. I would be much happier if only English units could be used in future.'

'So you say in the paper . . . Where's Lord Thorganby?'

The question was aimed at Joynson, who detached himself from the door. 'The train from Edinburgh doesn't get in till ten-thirty. He'll be at Cabinet.'

'You'd better go to King's Cross yourself, or the press will crush him. My compliments, and I suggest he keeps off television for to-day at least.' Harvey turned back to the Service Chiefs. 'Well then, what do you suggest?'

'Combined attack this afternoon on Fort William.' The Admiral was ready for the question. 'There's a parachute battalion standing by in Belfast. We've made a plan, it's in the appendix to the paper. Knock them where it'll hurt most.'

'You see, Prime Minister, they've now moved into what we call the Second Phase of Insurrection.' The CGS prided himself on his analytical powers. 'In the First Phase you operate from the mountains using secret headquarters; holding territory is not important, and you avoid towns. But in the Second Phase you seize a town, in this case Fort William, and use it as a base to dominate quickly as much territory as you can, at the same time mounting your maximum political effort. The Third Phase is of course the capture of the main cities. If we can smash Fort William by to-night we can force Cameron back into Phase One.'

'Smash Fort William.' Harvey repeated the words without emphasis. Big Ben struck ten, not quite synchronising with the more musical chimes from the Horse Guards. 'How many casualties?'

'They would fight hard, sir, and it's already a strong defensive position, barricades up in the town, and the airstrip out of action. But a few hours should do it.'

'A few hours . . . but not a few men.' Harvey got up and faced them. His shoulders were a little stooped now, and the thin hair receded noticeably from his forehead. His personal authority over them was once again at the test. He wanted not just to give orders, but to persuade them that he was right. Perhaps that was hoping too much.

'Once the SLA has its martyrs there'll be no stopping them. You can push them out of the towns back into the glens, but once you start killing them the Scots will be on their side, and there'll be years and years of it.'

'It seems to me, sir, from the riots and desertions and shortage of intelligence coming in that the Scots are with them already.'

'I don't think so.' Harvey was firm on his own ground now. 'The SLA have suddenly burst into the open, so all the trendy little men who decide what is news in this country are busy building them up as something glamorous and exciting. But this kind of glamour wears off very quickly—unless we keep it alive by our own mistakes. Already I have had an excellent reaction from Henderson: we shall decide in Cabinet how to play that card. We must take a risk, and do as little on the military side as we dare.'

'What does that mean?' asked the Admiral. It was almost a protest.

'It means no attack on Fort William to-night. In fact no counter-attacks at all by any of the services. A general order not to fire unless fired on. Protect the approaches to Glasgow. Reconnoitre by sea and air. But no more interference with civilian traffic than is inevitable. Let the MacBrayne steamers carry on, and the Mallaig fishing fleet. No discrimination against the Scottish Division. Let the police handle disturbance in the cities till the last possible moment.'

The Admiral groped for words.

'That means doing nothing. It's a terrible risk. If he keeps off the main roads Cameron could be across the Clyde by nightfall. Plenty of little boats. God knows what'll happen in the cities to-night. Could get out of control quickly—not sure it isn't already . . .'

His words tailed off into incoherence. They were in

the heart and centre of politics now: here it was Harvey who wore the medal ribbons, and they knew he had earned them.

A small pale Private Secretary came in and whispered to Joynson.

'The Secretary of State for Defence on the phone. Wants to know why he hasn't been asked to this meeting.'

'How very remiss of us—I quite forgot, you should have reminded me. Please apologise and say I'll have a special word with him at Cabinet.' Harvey smiled round the room. It had been important to cope with the Chiefs himself without any colleagues present to question his political analysis.

'I'm off to meet Thorganby then,' said Joynson.

'I think we've just about finished, unless anyone has any questions.'

They had no questions. They would all have liked to argue, but there was no time. Crises were always like that; the man who had his mind clear first usually got his way.

As he showed them out Harvey said to the Admiral, 'By the way, Rickie, don't forget to fortify Derby.'

'Derby?'

'Bonnie Prince Charlie got as far as that.'

IV

Blair pulled the letter from its plastic folder. The envelope had already been clumsily opened and the sheets inside were smeared with dirt and blood. He read it carefully, then handed it to Rennie. The room had been cleared of hospital staff and two constables were on the door.

Rennie handed it back, grave-faced. 'We'll have to move fast,' he said.

'Yes,' replied Blair, his eyes shining with self-importance, 'we'll have to cut a few corners with this one.'

'Ah'll be a'reet then,' Brodie said. He was stretched on

a trolley, one leg swathed in emergency dressings.

Blair turned to him with a look of contempt. 'You're under arrest,' he said.

Brodie sat bolt upright, rocking the trolley, and shouted, 'No! Ye canny dae tha'! MacNair promised . . .'

'MacNair's dead,' Rennie said. 'He was found this morning under the bridge with your knife in him.'

V

It was not going well. Harvey had the politician's habit of watching faces while he was speaking. This morning there was no doubt that his Cabinet colleagues were badly flustered. He had opened the meeting with a statement to calm their nerves, playing down the desertions and the falling apart of the Highlands, playing up the statement condemning the SLA which Henderson would make that afternoon. He had been adroit, even-voiced, deliberately long-winded. He had done his best, and knew that his best was good. But it wasn't working.

Across the table sat Thorganby, silent and flushed. He looked as if he were nursing a high temperature. The others were fidgeting, scribbling, pouring glasses of water. Faces Harvey had seen dozens of times round the same table, faces he had promoted and established over eight years of office; faces which owed everything to him, including trust in his judgment.

'Outside this room,' he said, 'people are liable to panic. Press, backbenchers, even the Services—they're beginning to argue for extreme policies . . . total suppression or total abandonment. All the more reason why we should hold steadily to our own policy. We can't do business with the SLA, they have no political foundation. Ours is the only policy which has the faintest chance of producing a peaceful and orderly Scotland.'

When Harvey stopped most of them looked at Lord Thorganby, and Lord Thorganby looked at the table. With a flash of professional insight Harvey saw that he was fighting a wave of nausea, physically unable to speak. That was the kind of accident which made history, and escaped the historian. The silence seemed longer than it was; Ryder Bennett, Chancellor of the Exchequer, broke it. He more than anyone else present was Harvey's man. He ran a hand through his curly red-grey hair.

'That's all very well, Patrick.' It was the custom in Cabinet for them to address Harvey as 'Prime Minister'. 'It's been your policy, and it's natural you should want to stick to it. But the fact is that Henderson's washed up, and the proof of that's everywhere to see this morning.' He pulled the *Daily Mirror* from his red box. The front page carried a map with a blunt black arrow nudging Glasgow and a headline in two-inch type:

ENOUGH IS ENOUGH!

'We've got to face it now,' he went on. 'Either we put in everything and smash Cameron, or we pull out and let him take over. Anything in between won't work. If we delay, either choice becomes more difficult. It's incredible, and I never thought I'd say it, but here it is. I suggest we pull every English soldier back to the border at once, and let the Scots stew in their own mess.'

This time there was no silence. The cat had been belled, and other colleagues chimed in to agree. Croom, the Home Secretary, usually good for a bluster; the Lord Chancellor, who had been a hawk throughout; the Chief Whip, who read the latest Gallup poll aloud as if it were a passage from the Old Testament; and last the Defence Secretary, very angry: 'Since I understand from hearsay that the Prime Minister has already met the Chiefs of Staff and ruled out effective military action, I have no choice but to support immediate evacuation.' It had after all been a mistake not to ask him to the meeting.

It was essential that Thorganby should speak now. Here was the man who had roused the Party against appeasement, who had all through supported a tough policy, who had just been viciously humiliated by the Scots. He had too much influence still in the constituencies to be ignored. If he would say his usual strong piece in favour of the Union, then Harvey could come again down the middle with his policy bridging the two extremes. That was the way Cabinets were won.

'You must be feeling in need of a good sleep, David,' Harvey said, 'but I know we should all very much value your advice on this difficult morning.'

Lord Thorganby gripped the table and the sweat stood out on his forehead. He seemed to have shrunk in size since he had last sat in Cabinet.

'I think they will win,' he said.

'Win?' But Harvey knew already it was coming out wrong.

'It's no good carrying on, Bennett's quite right.' Thorganby's voice gathered confidence. 'This army of theirs, Cameron and the young people he's got there, I've seen them—they're not the same. It doesn't matter how they treated me. They've got something special, and very strong—I can't explain it . . .' He searched for words, then finished more loudly: 'All I can say is, they're like something out of the past.'

Those present recognised that in Lord Thorganby's vocabulary there was no higher compliment.

'So what do you recommend?' Ryder Bennett was keen to push to a conclusion.

'An immediate understanding with Cameron. Give him a free hand—he'll take it anyway.'

Some of them looked at Harvey, the more sensitive looked somewhere else; all knew he was beaten. Thorganby swallowed a white pill from his waistcoat. Joynson came into the room and spoke softly in Harvey's ear. All he said was that Sir Alan Blair, Glasgow Chief Constable, was on the line; but Harvey knew that Joynson would never have interrupted unless it was important enough to affect the course of the meeting in progress.

'I'm sorry—an urgent call I must take,' he said, getting up.

'Surely we should decide now . . .' said Ryder Bennett. He knew his man.

'No, no, I'll be back in two minutes.'

It was five minutes, and when he came back Harvey had recovered his authority.

'There has been a new and most serious development. It affects the whole security of the nation, if the report which I have just received is correct. It would not be right to discuss it here until certain facts have been confirmed or disproved. I shall want to consult the King and the Foreign and Defence Secretaries. I suggest we resume discussion at the same time to-morrow morning.'

'I wonder if that is wise. There are surely decisions which must be taken to-day . . .' But even Ryder Bennett was in retreat.

'I think we can manage as we are for the moment. I shall make a purely factual statement in the House this afternoon, and refuse to add to it. The Chiefs of Staff already have their orders. We can thrash the rest out to-morrow.'

After they had gone Harvey sat down and scribbled fast, then handed the result to Joynson.

'These are the things which need checking. I want definite confirmation or denial within four hours. Get both intelligence outfits on to it at once. And tell the TV I may want a broadcast this evening.'

'A broadcast?'

Harvey leant back in his chair, and for the first time that morning, laughed.

'Do you know why I deserve to be Prime Minister? It's because when the moment comes it's Patrick Harvey who gets the luck.'

VI

'Must you go as far as that?' said the King.

'I'm afraid so, sir. Under the same Crown of course, the same as before.'

'I know the history—but surely, if you're right about your broadcast to-night . . .'

'I hope that'll stop the SLA in their tracks, maybe more. But we've got to get a real settlement straight away. Nerves this side of the border won't stand much more, you've seen the papers to-day. And Henderson needs more than he got at Hexham for the settlement to stick.'

'Does the Cabinet agree?'

'I'll put it to them to-morrow. I thought I should have a word with you first.'

There was a pause.

'Very well . . . and good luck.'

Harvey put down the telephone and released the scrambler button. It had been a risk doing it on the telephone, but Kings were rarely in the right place when wanted and there had not been time to go to Windsor.

VII

'*Good evening. I want to talk to you to-night about Scotland . . .*'

'Turn it off, love. Fancy putting on one of them political things at teatime. Bad enough after the news, if you ask me.'

'Hold on. May be something special this time. Those bleeding Scots . . .'

'*I have to tell you that a large part of the Western Highlands of Scotland is now in the hands of the organisa-*

202

tion which calls itself the Scottish Liberation Army. They have made further advances to-day, and our own forces are regrouping round Glasgow . . .'

'He's going to chuck in the sponge,' said the Chief of Defence Staff, his voice louder than usual by one pink gin. The television room in the United Services Club was crowded.

'It is a sad and strange thought to all of us that this week, for the first time in more than two hundred years, the soil of our own island is a theatre of war. The job of the Government, of your Government, must be simply this: to bring the fighting to an end, and to do it in a way which will be just and final . . .'

'Dear God, it's an H-bomb on Fort William.' Jack Kemble was in Downing Street with the Outside Broadcast Unit.

'We have no desire to dictate to the Scots, no right to impose on them a future which they dislike. In the last few months we have shown again and again good will and good faith in trying to find an answer to the problem of Scotland. We have more than once come close to agreement with the elected leaders of the Scottish National Party, but each time the prize has been snatched away from us by senseless acts of violence . . .'

'Middling Central Office prose, but he's got something up his sleeve.' Ryder Bennett had slipped away from a meeting on final repayment of the sterling debt to watch the set in his office at the Treasury.

'In the last few days we have looked at our whole policy afresh without prejudice or rancour. We have asked ourselves in the Cabinet the question which must have occurred to many of you: is the Scottish Liberation Army the true

voice of Scotland?'

Lord Thorganby stirred on his pillows, and his wife shook the thermometer. 'Still far too high,' she said, 'and all that nonsense won't help.' She turned off the set; he was too tired to care.

'Because if I were convinced that the SLA could justly claim to speak for Scotland I would not hesitate for a minute. The keys of Edinburgh Castle, and with them the whole power over that kingdom, would be handed over to their commander to-night. I am determined that we shall not stay in Scotland one day longer than we are wanted . . .'

At Windsor the logs crackled in the wide grate; the King stirred uneasily in his armchair. The advance script promised by Harvey had not yet arrived, and he disliked suspense.

'From this inquiry which we have made, two facts stand out clear. First, the SLA contains many young men and women who are wholly inspired by their love for Scotland. We respect their courage and admire their enthusiasm . . .'

'He's going to give way,' said the minister hopefully to the other detainees in the lounge of the Station Hotel at Fort William. He had been held under guard for two days now. Neither food nor warmth were up to the standards of the Manse.

'But second—and here perhaps is the most tragic aspect of this whole affair—the leaders of that army have a very different purpose . . .'

Led by Cameron, a shout of derisive laughter went up in the Operations Room at Ardnish Castle. But Mackie and

Sukey sat silent.

'It is my duty to-night to give you some news even more serious than you have yet heard. I have in my hand a letter written a short while ago by Monsieur Serge Bucholz, the Communist Minister of the Interior in the French Coalition Government. It is addressed to Mr John Mackie, the Scottish Nationalist Member of Parliament for Glasgow Central, and one of the most influential of the SLA leaders. The full text of the letter will be released to-night. It shows beyond doubt that the SLA is dependent for arms and money on the French Communist Party under a plan aimed at installing a Communist dictatorship in Scotland . . .'

'Old gags are best,' said Kemble. 'Royalties to the Joe McCarthy Foundation.'

'Wait,' said Joynson.

'This letter was first read to me this morning. The text itself and the circumstances in which it reached me strongly suggested that it was genuine. Nevertheless I at once gave instructions for careful checking. A few minutes ago I received a telephone call from the Prime Minister of France. He told me that to his great regret the information in the letter had been proved to be correct. He has this evening asked for the resignation of Monsieur Bucholz . . .'

Below the window his men were hustling a group of indignant women from the Bowling Alley to temporary detention in the Skating Rink. Watching the set in the bar of the Cairngorm Palace at Aviemore, Captain Warburton-Mackenzie realised that he had made the first big mistake of his short and impeccable life.

'Let me emphasise that most members of the SLA had no knowledge of this plan. The arms concerned were

205

of the standard types now used in NATO, with mark of origin removed. Those who knew that the arms came from France were led to believe that they were supplied by the Breton Nationalist Front, a political group in Brittany which has for several years had friendly contacts with the Scottish Nationalists. Those who knew the facts are few in number, but they are the men who control the whole enterprise. There is no doubt that they are guilty of deceiving and betraying those whom they have led into battle . . .'

Mrs Merrilies listening on the car radio as she drove through Glencoe towards the rebels, had the presence of mind to swerve to the side of the road before she began to cry.

'I end this evening with a message to the people of Scotland. To any of you who are members of the SLA I offer an amnesty. Report with your arms to the nearest local police station or army post within twenty-four hours and you have nothing to fear. After the expiry of that time limit you will face a charge of treason. To the rest of you I say, out of all this confusion and violence can come the just and final answer for Scotland which you all want. Time is short. To-morrow morning I am flying to Edinburgh to see the leading members of all political parties in Scotland. We have failed before; but I believe that under God's guidance and with your help this time we can succeed.'

'Haven't had God in a ministerial broadcast for some time,' said Kemble. 'But he'll be needed.'

'Confidence trick, but it might save Glasgow,' said the Chief of Defence Staff, gruff with admiration.

'I'm going straight across to Number Ten,' said Ryder Bennett to his Private Secretary. Then, as the man looked surprised: 'Didn't you hear the cock crow?'

Tears still on her face, Mrs Merrilies turned the car round and began to drive back to Edinburgh.

Duguid switched off the set, and the silence in Ardnish Castle was total. Cameron broke it with a whisper; he was standing close in front of Mackie, trembling, on the edge of violence.

'Is it true?'

Mackie stood his ground, pale but firm. 'Look, Cameron, calm down. Harvey's exaggerating—there was no plan for a takeover. Bucholz was willing to help, that's all. And you couldn't have done it without him, right?'

'So you lied to us. For two years you've been lying to us all.'

'I knew you weren't ready, the people weren't ready . . .'

'You bet you're sweet life they're not.' With this anguished shout the fight seemed to go out of Cameron, and he turned wearily to Sukey. 'Were you in on this?'

'Yes, I knew.'

Cameron took a deep breath, looked from one to the other, then at Sukey's stomach. When he spoke his voice was level and controlled. 'In that case I advise you both to get out of here before you're lynched.'

VIII

After the broadcast Duguid drove into Mallaig. He parked by the Stornoway ferry and with a bodyguard of three, facing outwards, rifles held high, started on a tour of rebel dispositions. There had been trouble in Mallaig. The fishermen were not too keen on revolutionary politics or taking orders from boys with guns: a fight had just been averted by the SLA guaranteeing to buy their produce at double the market price.

It was a fine evening. The sun had dropped behind the cliffs of Eigg and the houses around the harbour were bathed in a flattering pink. The air carried the usual harbour smells, fish and salt water and diesel oil, and another, less easily defined: trouble. Duguid stopped by the office of the Herring Board. Normally this was the busiest time of day, boats double-parking along the quays, fish crates swinging ashore on the derricks, waiting sea-gulls and the shouts of the fishermen . . . To-night it was just sea-gulls.

He searched the windows and the empty street, and the top of his scalp began to tingle.

If Duguid had gone into the office of the Herring Board he would have found the whole SLA garrison bound and gagged. As it was he turned into the Marine Hotel and the fishermen got him there.

IX

Henderson was waiting for them on the tarmac of Edinburgh airport. He was up the steps and into the aircraft before the stewardess had given Harvey and his entourage their coats. After him, more slowly because they were tubby men, came the Chairman of the Scottish Labour Party and the President of the Scottish Conservative and Unionist Association. 'I think it might be better if we go into the city after all,' said Henderson.

The plan had been that they should all meet in the Commandant's room at the airport, out of range of demonstrations.

A biting wind, but the crowds were out as the Prime Minister's car drove down Princes Street in a thicket of police outriders. Prosperous, sober, a good many women, several thousand waiting people. No placards, no shouts, just a scattered clap when they got out at the Caledonian Hotel. A man dodged through the police cordon, and there was a moment of panic as he got within close range of Harvey.

'Good luck, sir,' he said.

'A city with a hangover,' said Henderson when they were through the swing doors.

It was as near to an epigram as he would ever get.

The talks were constantly interrupted by messages—telegrams from London, police messages, military signal forms, bulletins topped with the stylised thistle of SNP headquarters, phone calls hastily recorded on the hotel's notepaper. By lunchtime there was a pile each side of the table, mixed up with the ashtrays and carafes of water.

SLA deserters now estimated 400.

Mallaig occupied by RN 0900 to-day at radio request of Harbour Master. SLA prisoners 23, casualties 3. Capt. Warburton-Mackenzie and 4 bn. (Black Watch) deserters surrendered Aviemore Centre, have volunteered full information on rebel dispositions.

Your wife rang. Her mother has shingles. Will you call back at 1.30?

Oban retaken. Fort William now quiet. No damage to aluminium complex, snipers being cleared from pulp mill. Ballachulish Hotel requisitioned for interrogation SLA deserters.

Mrs Merrilies telephoned to say she was entirely at Mr Henderson's disposal.

Bucholz arrived Moscow by Aeroflot jet. Refused to speak to press.

Government casualties 4 killed 23 wounded. Estimated SLA and civilian casualties follows. Ardnish Castle evacuated. Cameron now withdrawing to area Glenfinnan.

Lunch was served in the conference room, cold salmon and the best British Transport hock.

Harvey ticked off 'Common Defence' on the checklist in front of him. The next one was tricky: 'All-party coalition in Scotland pending elections under new constitution.'

'I think it might be helpful,' he said, 'if I started by letting you know the views of the King . . .'

Tea, soggy toast, bright cakes, and the skyline through the windows beginning to blur in the dusk. The room was by now stale with smoke. It had gone so well that Harvey felt he could put the question which really interested him. It concerned Henderson alone.

'After all that has happened are you quite sure this is what you want?'

Another crowd at the airport, this time of journalists, but Harvey would say nothing. Just enough light on the tarmac to read the latest message. He showed it to Henderson.

SLA casualties 26 killed, 98 wounded, 273 prisoners. Total deserters estimated 600.

'Twenty-six killed,' said Henderson. 'If that went on . . .'
'It won't.' Harvey gave it as a promise. 'We'll finish it to-morrow.'

X

Mackie and Sukey stood alone on the beach, watching the Atlantic rollers break on the perfect sand. They had run as far as they could. From the castle at Loch Ailort they had driven through the night to the farthest limit of SLA territory, the lighthouse at Ardnamurchan Point. The SLA Section there had greeted them with delight; they had missed the broadcast and willingly routed out a wireless operator who on Mackie's instructions put out a coded signal on the trawler waveband. After breakfast Mackie and Sukey walked north along the coast until they reached the bay, and there they had waited all day, huddled for shelter in the seaweed-covered rocks. Six hours later, as the light was failing, the Poseidon tracker ship had appeared on the horizon and sent in a boat, which now bucked towards them through the surf. Already they could hear the shouts of the Russian sailors as they guided it in.

Mackie held her close and kissed her on the lips. They

had talked a great deal; there was nothing more to say. Hugging her tighter, he pulled her head to his shoulder and mussed her hair.

Please, no emotion, thought Sukey. He could be very mawkish. Later, she knew, she would miss him like an amputated limb but now she felt embarrassingly placid. She wanted to be alone.

But he got it right; a pat on her stomach, then he turned away quickly and walked into the surf and did not look back. She waited for a last wave but there was none; in five minutes he had been swallowed by the gathering dark. As she watched him go, the old tune drifted into mind: 'Carry the lad that's born to be King . . .'

Tout finit par des chansons.

She giggled, then tossed back her hair and laughed out loud. Kicking off her shoes, she started to run across the beach.

The amnesty was over, it was too late to surrender. They would catch her in the end, but even that would have its compensations. In all the centuries of feuds and eccentricity there was one grand gesture which had never been made: no Dunmayne had been born in prison.

XI

Cameron knew he was in trouble as soon as he heard the mortars. They weren't his, and they were too damn close.

He was standing on the crest of the hill above Glenfinnan, perhaps on the exact spot where the Gentle Lochiel, with doubt in his heart, had begun his descent with six hundred men to join the army of Charles Edward Stuart. Historical parallels apart, it was the best place to be. For eighteen hours the remnant of the SLA had been operating in two units and on two fronts, resisting the government advances from Fort William and Mallaig. The danger had been that the British would cut the road between and seal the escape routes; so during the night they had made contact and regrouped at this point, a good defensive position with easy escape into Knoidart. Cameron's plan was to make such a withdrawal; Knoidart was a trackless wilderness, the guerrilla's dream; they could hold out there for months. But now it was light and he was still above Glenfinnan, waiting for the forward posts to withdraw off the road and up the hill, and intending a last display of firepower to discourage pursuit.

It was hard to tell what was happening below. A thick mist still covered the valley. At the head of Loch Shiel only the statue of the Highlander on top of the '45 Monument was visible, rising from the mist like a ghost. Since dawn there had been sporadic bursts of firing, interspersed with the thump of grenades. No messages had come up the hill and the radio was dead.

And now the mortars: several, suddenly, firing at once: a rapid series of thuds, concerted and efficient: certainly not the SLA.

Cameron glanced at his troops. They were sprawled on the ground around him, mostly young, a few girls, perhaps two hundred altogether, sluggish with fatigue and cold. Some were brewing tea and others were still asleep beside the scratches in the earth which passed for trenches. A boy with a guitar was singing 'We shall Overcome'. The one thing they didn't lack was equipment: the hilltop was strewn with advanced infantry weapons, boxes and belts of ammunition, gas-masks, compasses, map-cases, emergency rations, first-aid kits and radios. The problem was how to use it, or even carry it.

Since first light he had been busy among them, encouraging, organising, instructing—daddy at the children's party. He himself was alert and spruce, in conventional Army combat kit with only the insignia changed. The chain of disasters which had hit the SLA since Tuesday had made no dent in his manner; he was now cheerfully talking to his lieutenants in terms of a long-term subversive campaign. And though they saw the look at the back of his eyes none of them voiced the suspicion that he was mad, because there seemed to be no choice: it was the hills with Cameron or a prison cell.

'Stand to!'

They all jerked awake. The youth stopped in mid-chorus, his hand poised above the strings. But before they could react to Cameron's command they were listening to a different sound, the pulsing whistle of approaching mortar bombs. One or two jumped up, most dived into the ground. Cameron didn't move. The bombs burst on the side of the hill a hundred yards below.

Smoke.

Now Cameron knew what had happened, and before the smokescreen could spread a line of troops emerged from the mist, and a second line, moving steadily up the grassy slope.

The rebels fired into the smoke with everything they had. After a lot of shouting Cameron got the platoon leaders together and rattled out orders against the racket—immediate withdrawal of main body to the north, 3 platoon to act as rearguard and delay pursuit, reassemble Loch Arkaig at 1800, take small arms only, 4 grenades each man, 100 rounds of ammunition and as much food as they could carry . . . The platoon leaders ran off. The helicopters came fast and low from the east and were over the camp before anyone knew. When he saw the first canister Cameron yelled 'Masks!' at the top of his voice. 'Masks! Masks! Put your bloody masks on!' But nobody heard and the canisters fell among them belching coloured smoke, blue and yellow and red, and they were shouting in panic then choking and weeping and falling because it wasn't smoke it was tear gas. A few got their masks on. Most just sat down and clawed at their faces. Some tried firing upwards, but their aim was wild and the helicopters kept veering away so the down-draught wouldn't disperse the gas. Some broke out and charged down the hill at the soldiers, firing from the hip and shouting historic battle cries. But the helicopters came after them, dropping more canisters in front, and they lurched and fell, tumbling down the precipitous slope in a tangle of weapons, haversacks and blanket rolls, staggering to their feet, groping for their weapons, falling again. The soldiers kept walking up, like impervious robots in their masks and helmets. They hadn't fired a shot. The whole hilltop was now obscured as the coloured gasclouds merged with the smokescreen and a voice was booming through the fog: 'LAY DOWN YOUR ARMS AND STAY WHERE YOU ARE. THE AMNESTY HAS BEEN EXTENDED FOR FORTY-EIGHT HOURS. I REPEAT . . .' Three more helicopters were coming over the hills, troop-carriers, with ropes dangling from their holds and clusters of red berets at their open doors . . .

Cameron put on his mask and ran.

I

Two months later, on the last morning of the year, Janet Grant put the chains on her van and drove from Clovulin to Strontian, at the head of Loch Sunart. After two calls in the village and a fortifying dram with the ex-commander of Morvern Section, an asthmatic ornithologist who had never quite got the gas from his lungs, she drove north into the hills, forcing the van in bottom gear up the steep track to the lead mines.

In terms of hospitable terrain, the moon compares very favourably with the hills above Strontian. Not a tree, not a bush can get a hold here; even in summer the sheep have a struggle to find a meal among the piles of shale and jagged outcrops of rock. In winter nobody goes there at all. The tracks of Miss Grant's van were the first to break the snow which had fallen a week before. When she felt the sump digging in, she stopped, backed a short way, turned and parked. The snow was not deep, but frozen hard and swept by a murderous wind. The world was black and white and grey; rock and ice and sky; the only source of colour was Janet Grant, in bottle green ski-pants, embroidered windjammer and red balaclava.

She left the car and climbed towards the old lead workings. Every few yards she stopped for breath, then started upwards again, head tucked down into the gale, arms working in a mad semaphore as she fought to keep her balance. For twenty minutes she climbed, until she reached the horizontal shafts near the crest of the ridge. With a last effort she stumbled towards a small black hole in the snow, ducked inside, and sank to her knees with a cry of self-congratulation.

It was almost dark in the shaft. A few yards in from the entrance a fire smoked weakly, surrounded by cooking implements. A kitbag and a sub-machine-gun rested against one wall, and beside them a pile of blankets lay on a flat bed of stones.

The blankets stirred, then rose slowly, revealing a pair of bloodshot eyes. Janet Grant remembered those eyes for the rest of her life: they had the total lack of expression of an animal waiting for death.

'It's time,' she said.

He recovered quickly. Later he began to sing in the bath, and at that she was overcome by a sense of waste. The tears tumbled from her nose and cheeks, hissing on the iron as she pressed it into the crumpled uniform.

II

It was over. Through the day they had coaxed and complimented her, building up her courage, making light of whatever was coming. And it had come, pain, fright, exhaustion, fearful pain again.

Sukey's consciousness ebbed and flowed with the anaesthetic, but she could sense that they were still bustling about the foot of the bed, down there where the fight had been. Her old nanny, efficient through tears, and the midwife from Inverness, and Doctor MacFadzean, trailing memories from the past, chickenpox and tonsils and her foot caught in the stirrup when the pony had dragged her over the rock up on the hill.

The fumes rose once more into her brain, and she clutched the hand which lay in her own. The hardness of the rings jerked her awake again. She had forgotten for the moment that her mother had come back. Doctor MacFadzean cleared his throat.

'It's a fine wee boy.'

They had asked the doctor to stay for dinner, but Lady

Dunmayne spoke to her husband as if they were alone.

'Before I go back we must talk about the girl's future.'

'You're not staying then?' Lord Dunmayne wondered if he managed to keep the relief out of his voice. His wife's unheralded return after eight years had appealed to his sense of fitness, but not to anything else.

'Why should I stay, now the girl's all right?' She had acquired a hard rich voice to go with the blue hair and the manhandled face. 'You didn't think I was going to bed down with you again in all these damps and draughts?' Old Doctor MacFadzean, warm with claret, giggled over his pheasant.

'She's got a boy, all she wants now is a husband. Plenty of sex, good family and a sight more sense than you had when you married me.'

Dunmayne found himself getting angry, and he too forgot the doctor.

'That's total nonsense. She didn't just fall into bed with this Mackie like some little deb full of champagne. She loved him, and I dare say he loved her, and they were both drugged with this lunatic revolution. It's no good supposing she'll slip back . . .'

His wife poured herself some more wine and did not pass the decanter on to the doctor.

'You're a fool, Ian Dunmayne, and the lousiest thing about you is you've no self-confidence. You've sat here all these years, you let me get away, and then you let the girl go too. Well let me tell you, she's got a lot of me in her and that's what's caused the trouble up to now. But she's got more of you than those long legs and damned deceptive good looks.'

She lit a cigarette from the nearest candle. Lord Dunmayne particularly disliked smoking between courses.

'She's tired now,' his wife went on, 'so things show through. For one thing she loves this house, every freezing hideous cranny of it, and that great sodden mountain opposite. Lying up there she thinks about her childhood, and, God save us, about you. Why you should get a second chance with her, I don't know . . .'

Dunmayne realised that his wife was about to cry.

Nanny was asleep in the bed at the end of the room, but her snoring had stopped. Even through the closed window Sukey could hear the soft noise of water. The two arms of the burn joined at the foot of the garden, and their competitive music was the sound of her childhood. She dozed. Suddenly she was jerked wide awake by a different noise. Nanny heard it too, and grappled with the casement to let in the full impact. The sky was not wholly dark; even at midnight a tinge of grey marked its western edge. The old woman shut the window again and the church bells softened.

'A Happy New Year to you both,' she said.

III

When the telephone rang Lady Thorganby's response was mechanical. 'Yes, he's comfortable and sleeping quietly . . . No, nothing new. How very kind of you to ring. Thank you so much.'

She had sent the night nurse away; the girl was due for a break and had wanted to go to the New Year's Eve dance in Chelsea Town Hall. She could easily have got a substitute, but the thought of yet another woman in the house bubbling with trivial sympathy was too much for her. She had always hated New Year's Eve, and it was better to spend it alone.

Alone, that is, except for the regular and heavy breathing of her husband in the big bed at the end of the room. She went upstairs again to the armchair near her dressing-table by the window. The street lamp outside in Eaton Place glowed warmly through the chintz curtains. She turned out the light by which she had been reading, and sat for a time in the semi-darkness.

She noticed the quiet as if it were new. In early years

the house had been full of their children: happy squeals on Christmas morning, sudden tears at a broken toy or the end of holidays, endless noise and rush. Then the parties which she and David had given, this room piled high with coats, men and women separately and then again together arguing, laughing, tossing this way and that the small talk of power. Then, later again, her own charitable committees, calmer elderly talk and the tinkle of coffee spoons against Worcester. A splendid spread of worthwhile noise over forty years—through her grumbles she had enjoyed it all. Now the quiet was coming.

And he? Was she imagining, or was his breathing getting harder? She went over to the bed. His flushed outdoor face looked unnatural on the elegant pillow with the flowered border, guarded on either side by an army of medicines and pills. Nothing to do unless he complains of pain, the doctor had said. He had a strong constitution, he had added, and gone away muttering about the strain of pneumonia on the heart.

Tories were of many sorts, she thought. Some wanted money, others power. Some, like Harvey, despised the left and longed with all their heart to do things better. Others, like herself, just enjoyed the bustle of it all. But David was different again. Earlier there had been others like him, in politics without any particular aptitude or purpose, just because it was a natural fundamental thing to do. Had he enjoyed the forty years of noise which she had created for him? She would never be sure.

His breathing had settled again, and she went back to her chair. They had nothing much more to say to each other, but it would not be right if she were out of the room when he regained consciousness. For some time she had not glanced at the little French carriage clock on the dressing-table, and its note took her by surprise. Twelve —and then the sweep of bells across London, filtering softly into the room through curtains and tightly shut window. Half against her own will, she opened the sash a few inches. The peals of the Abbey—coronations, state visits, coaches, crowds and Household Cavalry—they were familiar enough, but mingled now with other bells less known. It was a still, cold night and the noise carried well.

A few snowflakes drifted through the light of the street lamp. She was closing the window when she noticed a figure leaning against the lamp post. An unknown young man with fair hair, coatless despite the cold, white tie and tails now awry, just such a tall good-looking young man as she had married and bred for others to marry. He was happy, self-absorbed in a haze of champagne; the noise of his song came raucously upwards:

'Lest old acquaintance be forgot . . .'

With a bang Lady Thorganby shut the window.

IV

'The forecast said showers,' said the King.

'Edinburgh sleet,' said the Lord Chamberlain. 'There's none worse.'

From the second-floor window they looked out on to the wide stretch of gravel in front of the Palace of Holyrood House. Stands had been built on three sides for the Independence Ceremony, making a square with the front of the Palace itself and its jutting turrets. Immediately below them was a dais with a red carpet and gilt chairs under a canopy. In the middle of the square was a flagstaff, so tall that the Union Jack at its mast was almost level with them. As they watched, a file of Guardsmen, bearskins and grey greatcoats, took up position in front of the empty stands. Order arms, at ease, easy. The wind whipped the surface of the puddles on the gravel, and the Union Jack flew taut.

'I doubt if we'll survive,' said the King, turning away as the window blurred with sleet. 'Has the Prime Minister arrived yet?'

'Which one?' The Lord Chamberlain tried a joke, but found himself rebuked by prominent blue unamused eyes.

'Mr Henderson does not become Prime Minister of Scotland until he kisses hands to-night. I was referring to Mr Harvey.'

'Not yet, sir.'

The North British Hotel was largely under diplomatic occupation.

'Don't be so absurd,' said the Ambassador's wife. 'You'll be two hours on the stand. Put on that woollie at once.'

'But the buttons of the uniform won't meet.'

'Then you must wear a suit.'

'It is a matter of patriotism,' said the Ambassador. 'If I wear a suit to-day I shall be mistaken for one of my Communist colleagues.'

'If you don't, you'll be mistaken for a corpse, and perhaps no mistake either.'

Sadly the Ambassador clambered out of his uniform. He had been polishing the buttons since breakfast.

'All I want to know,' said Lady Blair, 'is whether to-day counts as a garden party.' She fastened a huge sapphire on her front.

'A garden party is one thing, an Independence Day is another,' said the Chief Constable, looking at his watch.

'So you mean, there'll still be a royal garden party this summer, as well as the ball to-night?'

'I mean no such thing.' Blair broke off. 'The Lord take us, woman, we're going to be late, it's the birth of Scotland we're assisting at, and all you can do is blether about parties.'

'You're a stupid man, Alan—up in the clouds as usual. Don't you realise I may have to get a new dress?'

The stands were full now, and it was almost time for the King to take his place on the dais. Harvey hurried into the room where he was waiting.

'I apologise for being late, sir. David Thorganby died two hours ago.'

'I'm sorry.'

For a few seconds the two men thought back over the years, hectic events, quiet routines, years which they had shared with the dead man. But there was never more than a few seconds to think back.

'They will open the doors on to the dais in one minute,' Harvey said.

It was coming to an end. Henderson had made his speech, dull but not too long, the massed pipes of the Scottish Division had marched and countermarched, the Moderator of the Church of Scotland had resonantly prayed. The icy greyness of the day, the flurries of snow on the Salisbury Crags to their left, the massive hulk of the Palace, even the familiar smell of the brewery drifting over the proceedings—there was something fitting in all of these.

Now for the climax, the changing of the flags. The line of schoolchildren drawn up in front of the stands began to flutter with paper, for the words of the new anthem were still unfamiliar. A long-drawn command, ending in a bark, and from one corner of the square a single officer marched, one arm swinging, the other carrying a bundle of blue and white trussed with a cord. A small colour party under a sergeant was already at attention under the flagstaff. The officer reached them and halted; the Guards presented arms; a roll of drums, then a single tap, and the colour party started to lower the Union Jack.

Slowly, without jerks, in total silence, the big flag sank towards the ground.

As the Union Jack was being gathered together at the foot of the pole, another officer began to march towards the centre from the opposite side of the square, bonnet and kilt, and something of a swagger in the very precision of his movement.

The BBC cameraman looked at his programme, which ran to twenty pages. 'Who's this then?'

'Must be the guy who runs up the flag,' said Kemble. 'Hence the fancy dress.'

'No, the first officer does that, the one who brought the flag out. Do you think they've cocked it up?'

'No, they never do . . .'

But then it became clear that they had. For when the second officer reached the group under the flagstaff, there was a moment of confusion. Words were spoken which no one in the stands could hear, then suddenly the two officers were struggling together for possession of the Scottish flag. A murmur of consternation swept through the crowd.

'Quick, on to them, close as you can,' shouted Kemble to the cameraman.

Then for the first time in nineteen years as a newsman, he gasped at what he saw. His commentary rattled out at double pace:

'My God—it's Cameron—Cameron, the commander of the SLA, on the run now for two months since his force was routed at Glenfinnan . . . That's the first officer knocked to the ground, Cameron's got the flag, he's trying to fasten it to the rope, the colour party are paralysed. Harvey and Henderson are both signalling, they've recognised him all right, the King too, what a fantastic and dramatic turn of events . . .'

The first officer picked himself up from the gravel, his head clear. He gave an order, and the colour party began to converge on the flagstaff. Cameron turned away from the flag and faced the royal dais. He began to shout, words tossed into the wind, sound and fury. The colour party closed in. Cameron turned to them. appealing. But the sergeant and two men rushed him, grabbing his arms. Cameron wrenched free, bent to draw the dirk from his stocking. A woman in the crowd screamed. The steel flashed in the air, an actor's gesture, then he doubled up, pressing the dirk between his ribs with both hands, and pitched forward, a uniform without a man, slumped beneath an empty flagstaff.

For a few seconds nobody moved, then several orders rang out. Two corporals ran on to the square with a stretcher, and Cameron was lifted on to it. A moment's hesitation, then the first officer covered the stretcher with the discarded Union Jack.

By the time the stretcher reached the exit from the square, the cross of Saint Andrew was climbing the flagstaff and the pipes were playing 'Scotland the Brave'. The snow began to fall in earnest, on the stretcher, the King, the whirring cameras, on the two Prime Ministers, on Lord Provost and Lady Provost, on Ambassadors and High Commissioners and on all the hats of the ladies of Edinburgh.